D1614797

014497687 8

THE DEAD HAND

Also by Judith Cutler

The Harriet & Matthew Rowsley mysteries

THE WAGES OF SIN *
LEGACY OF DEATH *
DEATH'S LONG SHADOW *
A HOUSE DIVIDED *

The Lina Townend series

DRAWING THE LINE
SILVER GUILT *
RING OF GUILT *
GUILTY PLEASURES *
GUILT TRIP *
GUILT EDGED *
GUILTY AS SIN *

The Fran Harman series

LIFE SENTENCE
COLD PURSUIT
STILL WATERS
BURYING THE PAST *
DOUBLE FAULT *
GREEN AND PLEASANT LAND *

The Jodie Welsh series

DEATH IN ELYSIUM *

* *available from Severn House*

THE DEAD HAND

Judith Cutler

**SEVERN
HOUSE**

First world edition published in Great Britain and the USA in 2023
by Severn House, an imprint of Canongate Books Ltd,
14 High Street, Edinburgh EH1 1TE.

severnhouse.com

British Library Cataloguing-in-Publication Data
A CIP catalogue record for this title is available from the British Library.

ISBN-13: 978-1-4483-1132-3 (cased)
ISBN-13: 978-1-4483-1133-0 (e-book)

All Severn House titles are printed on acid-free paper.

MIX
Paper from
responsible sources
FSC   FSC® C013056
www.fsc.org

Typeset by Palimpsest Book Production Ltd.,
Falkirk, Stirlingshire, Scotland.
Printed and bound in Great Britain by
TJ Books, Padstow, Cornwall.

Praise for the Harriet & Matthew Rowsley Victorian mysteries

"Fans of other married sleuths, such as ANNE PERRY's Charlotte and Thomas Pitt, may want to check this out"
Publishers Weekly on *A House Divided*

"With twists and turns aplenty, Cutler's variation on the classic locked-house mystery combines the requisite cast of colorful characters – in particular, the amiable sleuths – with a vivid depiction of upstairs-downstairs life in the Victorian era"
Booklist on *A House Divided*

"Offbeat cozy of manners"
Kirkus Reviews on *A House Divided*

"Thrilling, engaging and enjoyable from beginning to end"
Mystery People on *A House Divided*

"A gripping locked-room mystery with a suitably twisty plot, Cutler's latest also offers an intriguing look at social customs and gender roles during the Victorian period"
Booklist on *Death's Long Shadow*

"A lively, enjoyable book . . . Recommended for fans of *Downton Abbey*"
Library Journal on *The Wages of Sin*

"A captivating series launch . . . Readers will look forward to seeing more of this enterprising duo"
Publishers Weekly on *The Wages of Sin*

"A Victorian twist on the ever popular upstairs-downstairs storyline"
Kirkus Reviews on *The Wages of Sin*

About the author

Judith Cutler has been shortlisted for the CWA Dagger and the Barry Award. Her prize-winning short stories appear regularly in anthologies and leading crime fiction magazines. She is married to fellow crime-writer Edward Marston.

www.judithcutler.com

For Peter Yeoman
Thank you for making the past come alive

ACKNOWLEDGEMENTS

I could not have written this without David A. Hinton's scholarly papers collected in *The Alfred Jewel* (Ashmolean, 2013). Once this little volume had given me the initial idea, huge encouragement and support came from the volunteer guides at the National Trust property, Chedworth Villa, Gloucestershire. Huge thanks to Tina Pietron, my endlessly patient and supportive editor. Thank you for your kind patience.

ONE

June 1861
The Thorncroft Estate in Shropshire

'The wheat's in the ear already, Mr Rowsley,' Farmer Twiss said, pushing his hat back and wiping his brow as he leaned against a convenient gate overlooking the Roman excavations in the Thorncroft House grounds. Estate workers digging foundations for his lordship's new model village had come across the Roman site by chance last year. Now the place swarmed with labourers and with scholars, the latter staying in Thorncroft House. 'After all the cold and rain last year, it fair takes a weight off my mind, it does.' He gave his gap-toothed smile. 'And it's nice to feel the sun warm on your back, isn't it? Mind you, I was afraid of late frosts back at the start of the month.'

Dismounting from Esau more stiffly than I liked, I leaned beside him. 'Yes, it's been strange weather for June, hasn't it? Warm days followed by really cold nights. We've been glad of a fire in the evenings. How's Mrs Twiss after her fall the other day?'

'A bit sore still. But those nurses of his lordship's patched her up nicely, so she's not complaining. She's back in the brewhouse already: with all those extra men from the ruins, we'll be needing plenty of ale for the haymaking, and she likes to get beforehand in such things.'

'Of course she does,' I grinned. 'Just as you do. I bet every scythe and every sickle is already honed.'

'And locked away, gaffer. You know what your missus says – "just in case".' He frowned. 'I hear there's a deal of argufying, gaffer, over yonder.'

I had already heard from Sir Francis Palmer, the archaeologist leading the investigation, that there was trouble. The problem was that most of the men were navvies, trained only in digging. They were impatient with archaeologists' meticulous methods and with a lot of other things besides, it seemed. 'Yes. You hear right. Joe Sprue has already threatened to dismiss two men for brawling.'

'Quite right. And Marty Baines tells me he's banned a couple from the Royal Oak. Only kept their job because when they're sober, they can work hard, he says,' Twiss said. 'Boozers apart, there's no point in leaving temptation lying around, is there? Though Doctor Ellis says poor young Lord Croft is a mite better these days . . . not so' – he hesitated, biting his lip – 'not so wild in his ways, you might say.'

'No, indeed.' I was always touched by the villagers' continued devotion to his lordship, who had been confined, insane, to a secure wing in Thorncroft House for many months now. Personally, I doubted if the poor young man would ever again enjoy full sanity and with it complete liberty. In fact, the Family's lawyer was unceasing in his search for his lordship's heir, so he could learn the responsibilities of his future life. Meanwhile, a board of trustees was responsible for the management of all the Croft family estates, maintaining standards here, improving things there. There was not one of us, I believed, who was not working as hard for the estate as they would have done if the young man had been a martinet, watching our every move. My wife was both housekeeper and lady of the House, her ladyship having died earlier in the year. She never seemed to care about the responsibilities but was all too often embarrassed to assume the privileges. 'Let us hope and pray his mind is one day restored,' I said sincerely, however much I feared it was impossible.

He doffed his hat. 'Amen to that.' As if embarrassed by his diversion into emotion, he replaced his hat and coughed. 'If we're short-handed in the fields, can we call on the men working on the new village? I know those cottages are important, especially when you think those poor folk are living in little better than hovels, but we need everyone to pull together.'

'Of course. And maybe the history experts will help, too. Some of them will never have handled anything like a scythe before, so you may have to give them a lesson!'

He pulled a face. 'Can be murderous sharp, a scythe. Or a

sickle. Best get them gleaning or tedding or raking, gaffer, if there's any doubt. And as for the rowdy crew working for them, they can do the binding and stacking. That'll larn them.'

'It would!' They'd be doing women's work. 'I wonder how much longer we'll be needing these hand-tools. I've been at Atchingham for the day to see a new mechanized hay-tedder.'

He grimaced. 'You land agents and your modern notions! You're as bad as Prince Albert, begging your pardon. All these inventions and discoveries!'

'Things change whether we like it or not, don't they?' But there was no point in arguing further. 'Now, tell Mrs Twiss that if she needs extra maids in the brewhouse, Mrs Arden has just taken on a couple more girls she says she can send over if necessary: they'll need teaching, and Mrs Twiss'll have to keep an eye on them. Mrs Briggs—'

'She's the one who might take over the housekeeping from your missus?'

'Yes. She'll be leading the team from the House feeding and watering all the men in the fields, though my wife will always be at hand. But if you need her girls—'

'Thanks for the offer, gaffer. Shouldn't be needful, though. Our two wenches are old enough to be useful now.' He regarded me from under his thick brows. 'This schooling idea of yours for every child, boy or girl – what are you doing, gaffer? I make no bones about it – it's going against nature. Boys, I can understand, but not girls.'

'But girls need to read and write – even if it's only shopping lists!' I said with a laugh.

Twiss was not amused. 'And what if these reading and writing women want reading and writing jobs – where will we all be then? No dairy maids, no kitchen maids? They can't all be like your missus, though at least being a housekeeper is proper woman's work,' he conceded. 'I hoped for better from you, gaffer.'

'The decision to build a school here in the village wasn't just mine, you know, or even my wife's – it was all the trustees'. Let's see how it goes, shall we, when we've appointed teachers and everyone gets used to the idea? Meanwhile,' I said, looking at my watch, 'I really should be getting home: we have a house swarming with scholars and I should not expect Harriet to look after them all on her own. Now, please don't forget my message to Mrs Twiss.'

'Hang on, gaffer – what's going on down yonder? A mill, by the looks of it! Best we go and step in, if you don't mind my saying.'

I led Esau through the gate Twiss held open, but did not remount him; it struck me that two men on foot would be more likely to catch the miscreants in the act than one of us hurtling down on an already tired horse and the other struggling gallantly to keep up. In any case, as I silently pointed out to Twiss, someone else was already taking control.

TWO

Even before Lady Croft's death, many of her parish and village duties had fallen on me, in addition to my work as housekeeper. This afternoon, I had been visiting two sick old women, taking them calves' foot jelly and port wine, and passing on the contents of our baby box to another new mother. Robin, the pony drawing the trap, knew he was returning to his stable and I was content to let him go at his own pace through lanes he knew well. But then our calm was destroyed.

Some of the labourers on the site had gathered in a circle around two men. Some were trying to prise the fighters apart, but most seemed to be yelling encouragement. A couple of archaeologists were making polite requests for order, to very little effect. I called Robin to a halt and, summoning a lad on the edge of the ring to hold him for me, jumped out of the trap.

'Ned Marples!' I shouted as soon as I could see who was involved. 'And you, too, Harry Tyler.' The effect was flatteringly immediate. Now some of the other men could pull them apart and make sure they stayed that way. 'What *do* you think you're doing? What would your mothers say? And what will your wives say when they see the state of those shirts! All that blood! Heavens, you're not children. You're adult men, doing paid work.'

Mr Sprue, the foreman in charge of the labourers on both the new village and the Roman site, stepped forward, tugging his forelock. 'Sorry you should have to see this, Mrs Rowsley, ma'am. Young hotheads. I can't have them working here any longer, and that's God's truth. Seemingly, it was all about— Oh, drat the idiot! Trying to attack Sir Francis now!'

But Francis had Ned by the bloody shirt and was waving his finger within an inch of his nose.

I called, 'Ned! Harry! Here. Now. That's better.'

I stared at the two miscreants. In an instant, they were young men no longer, but children caught scrumping.

'Mr Sprue is right,' I said flatly. 'You both deserve the sack. Don't you?' The hung heads suggesting they knew I was right, I continued, 'But if you're dismissed, that throws you and your families on to the parish. Because no one else around here would take on two idiots quicker with their fists than their brains. Am I right, Mr Sprue?'

Mr Sprue nodded. 'None in their right mind, not here nor round about.'

'What am I to do with you? You can't continue here on the Roman site. But you can continue to work for his lordship. Ned, you will present yourself at the model village site at seven tomorrow. You will do whatever Mr Sprue tells you to do exactly as he tells you to do it. Is that clear? If I hear of one word of grumbling, it'll be the parish for you.' As for Tyler, I needed – yes, I needed Mr Twiss, who had mysteriously appeared on the scene with Matthew. Nodding at the farmer, I continued, 'Harry – I'm lending you to Mr Twiss. There's a huge pile of manure that's built up at the back of his farmyard.' Mr Twiss grinned. 'Normally, he'd leave it till the autumn, but I see no reason why you shouldn't clear it. Starting at seven tomorrow. And there is to be no word of complaint, no moaning to your mates in the Royal Oak.'

'Marty's banned them both,' Mr Sprue said.

'Excellent. One other thing. You won't get paid. No. But your wives will. Jemima and Polly. They will come up to the House every Friday at nine o'clock to collect your wages, and if I see any sign on their faces of a black eye or a split lip, I shall summon Constable Pritchard to haul you off to the lock-up. Is that clear? Good.'

Sprue said, 'I'd like them gone now, ma'am, if it's all the same.'

'Of course. Harry, get yourself cleaned up a bit – I don't want you scaring Polly half to death – and go straight home. Ned, go and cool your head in that stream. Mr Sprue, will you send him off in about ten minutes? I'm not having them continue this stupid business in the village.'

Harry sloped off; Ned was pushed face down in the stream and fished out with an equal lack of ceremony.

I looked enquiringly at Mr Sprue. 'Do you think that will work?'

He snorted. 'Should both have been booted out and set to walk to Shrewsbury to find work, if you ask me. But then, with both their missuses in the family way . . . yes, this is better than them being thrown on the parish.' He shook his head sadly. 'Are you happy with this, gaffer?' he asked, turning to Matthew.

He side-stepped the question, with a tiny wink at me. 'My wife's known them for years: it's the perfect solution, I'd say.'

'Absolutely,' Francis added, shaking hands first with Matthew, then with Mr Twiss and finally with me. 'If you were a man, Harriet, I would suggest we all celebrated with a glass of Mrs Arden's wonderful ale; there's some left after lunch.'

'I beg your pardon?' I couldn't keep my eyebrows down. Francis and I had been friends ever since I had been a young maid at another great house and he the son of a visiting family. We had come across each other by chance, separately withdrawing to an attic to conceal our tears. I had been unjustly accused of breaking something; he was facing the prospect of going back to a hated school. It was a moment of revelation for us both – that people from such different backgrounds could have feelings and need sympathy. And then he lied for me: he said it was he who had broken the vase.

'Very well, my dear – we will *all* celebrate with a glass of Bea's ale, though I fear after all this time it will be warm and flat.'

Back in the stable yard, Matthew didn't wait for me to descend from the trap myself, nor did he hold out a decorous hand. Hands around my waist, he lifted me off my feet, swinging me round and round.

'Put me down!' I said, hoping he wouldn't. 'We must pretend that we are staid and respectable people. Put me down before anyone sees we are not!'

One more twirl and he obeyed. Dan, the stable lad, was amazingly straight-faced as he led Esau away. Robin patiently awaited his turn.

'What's troubling you, my love? The trouble at the

excavations apart. You looked as if you'd lost a shilling and
found a rusty button.' He discovered a sugar lump for Robin.

Dan reappeared before I could answer. 'How did you find
Mrs Gornal, ma'am?' he asked.

'Not well, I'm afraid. Not well at all. I found Mr Pounceman
praying with her when I arrived.'

The young man pulled a face. Our rector was not popular
in the village – though recently, possibly because of a bereave-
ment, he had made a real effort to behave as I thought a man
of the cloth should. Once being interested, it seemed, in only
the richer members of his congregation, now he was far more
attentive to the poor, showing not just condescension but
genuine kindness.

'I think he brought her a lot of comfort, Dan.'

'Not as much as those soups and jellies you took, begging
your pardon, ma'am.'

'We have Mrs Arden to thank for those, remember; I was
just the person taking them.'

Robin suggested he needed more attention. Dan obliged.
'But you're going out with me in an hour, you idle old bu –
beggar,' he said. 'To the station.'

'If he's still awake!' I called after him. I turned to Matthew.
'Professor Head discovered he'd forgotten certain necessities
and had to go into Wellington. He said his late wife always
used to pack for him.'

'Indeed. I'm surprised he didn't have a valet. I wonder,' he
mused, 'what it must be like to have your tie tied—'

'Not to mention having someone deal with your studs for
you!'

'Are you implying I'm an idle old bu – beggar, too?'

'Matthew! Such language!'

Hand in hand, we made our way across the yard to the House.
'How did you enjoy your ride?'

'It was good to be on Esau again. But I've rediscovered parts
of my body I never use on the train or in the trap.' He pretended
to stagger.

'And yet you want me to learn to ride!' I laughed. 'Driving
a trap is one thing; sitting on a lumpy, bumpy animal is quite
another. Look at the effect it's had on you!'

He quickly recovered his dignity as we went in through the servants' entrance. There was a good deal of organized activity we dared not interrupt.

As we climbed the back stairs, I asked, 'How was the rest of your day? What did you think of the mechanical tedder?'

'It has a future, no doubt about that. But,' he sighed, 'as for it catching on widely . . . Heavens, if decent men like Twiss dislike progress in the form of girls going to school, what on earth will they make of machines like that one – and other new inventions? They're designed to make life easier, but I see them changing the pattern of farmers' lives for ever. Not to mention the lives of their labourers.'

'I'd trust Mr Twiss with my life, but he's never going to take to anything new. Not like Bea – she would put you on a spit and roast you in front of a fire if you tried to take away her closed stove.'

'Would I even dream of it?' He waited until he had closed the door of our bedchamber before asking, 'Have you had a chance to talk to Mrs Briggs again, now she's had a chance to settle in?'

Removing the hat I favoured over bonnets, which reminded me uncomfortably of the blinkers over Robin's eyes, I reflected on the time I had spent today with the woman who might become deputy housekeeper; she was one of two to whom we were giving a month's trial. The choice had been very limited; many of the women we interviewed preferred a place nearer a town, and others were disappointed that the lack of visitors meant there would be very few guest tips. 'She's settled into a good routine, and she's not cutting any corners – not that I can see. She seems cheerful around the staff – perhaps she's inclined to drive them rather than lead, but I'm hopeful they'll get used to each other's ways. I'm not at all sure, though, that she's happy. We explained, didn't we, that we were an unconventional household in many ways, but she seems to be alternately bemused by and aghast at our ways. You observed her face, poor woman, when she saw the maids' pretty caps. And I suspect she doesn't think much of that list of advice I gave her.'

He gave a snort of ironic laughter. 'Advice? You mean instructions!'

I grimaced. 'Very well. I do. But some things are important here that would be regarded as trivial in other establishments. Let us be positive: she's only thirty-eight. I am sure she will quickly pick things up and wonder by the end of her month why she ever worked in any other way.'

'How are you getting on with her? It must be hard for you to let go of things you've taken such pride in, and – yes – hard for her if she thinks you're always peering over her shoulder.'

'It would have been better if we could have gone away for a few days and let her find her feet, perhaps – but with a houseful of these assorted historians and archaeologists, we could hardly do that.' I sighed. 'I always wanted to promote one of the young women I've worked with and be able to sit back and put my feet up and let her get on with it.' I sighed. 'But having two of the most promising girls die – dear God, what a waste of young lives! – and then one marrying and becoming pregnant rather reduces the options available, doesn't it? Meanwhile, Mrs Briggs is doing her best. At least in the evenings she doesn't have me peering over her shoulder, since she eats in the servants' hall and the Room with Dick Thatcher. I did wonder if Bea and I should do the same again.'

'Surely not. It's easier for her to get to know her colleagues without you. As for you and Bea, you both earned that privilege, and earned it the hard way.' He kissed me. 'Come, my love; you know that you have so many responsibilities that you worry about not carrying out any of them well. You need someone to take over the day-to-day running of the House. You can't do all the menial stuff and still be a good hostess to our guests.'

'I have two more to be hostess to. The bibliographer that Francis heard was good . . .' I snapped my fingers.

'Professor Marchbanks?'

'Thank you. Yes, Professor Marchbanks. He's arrived, with an assistant – his wife. But she's not brought her lady's maid. The measles . . .'

'Someone like young Primrose could oblige?'

'She'd be ideal if we had enough maids. Mrs Briggs rightly says they all have quite enough to do without one leaving the team to serve a guest full-time. At least, praise be, they brought none of his nine children.'

'Nine! We have our own real-life Mr Quiverful!'

'He's not as poor as Mr Trollope's creation, I fancy. And since he has a post at the university, he's not in need of a sine-cure. He's tall but hunched. He was polite enough, but . . . Let's wait and see.'

'His wife?' He started to unhook my dress.

'Interesting. She arrived in a veritably Puritan bonnet so I could see nothing of her face and could hardly hear her speak.' I glanced at my watch. 'Now, my love, while I look out tonight's gown, you just have time to get in your nice new-fangled shower – I promise not to tell Mr Twiss! – and rid yourself of the smell of dear old Esau.' I waved a hand under my nose.

'At the risk of sounding like Twiss, it still feels strange to stand amidst the water, not to lie in it.'

'Strange it may be, but it's quicker. Imagine all those servants wasting hours toiling upstairs with clean water for the hip-bath and then having the fag of emptying it. Quick – off you go!' I gave him a gentle push.

THREE

Freshly showered – it took so little time! – and wearing the smoking jacket we suggested our guests might, in the absence of valets, prefer to wear for dinner, I fastened Harriet into her dress.

'Do you think this is too grand?' She pirouetted.

How might I give her a compliment she would not turn? I said seriously, 'As the trustee chosen to run this huge house and to act as hostess to those staying as guests, you have to dress the part. Think about this afternoon: you looked as authoritative as you sounded when you dealt with those stupid hotheads. I was so proud of you,' I said, 'and annoyed Sprue thought he should check if I approved of what you did.'

I knew she would fend off my praise. 'But I couldn't have done it without the fortuitous arrival of Mr Twiss.'

'Couldn't you? Of course you could.' I led her to the mirror. 'You're afraid of looking grand? Just remember that we are the hosts; all those scholars and archaeologists will be expecting an elegant woman to head the table. And that, my love, is you. Look – the cut of the dress, the quiet but excellent jewellery that her ladyship wanted you to wear, the tiniest, neatest of caps.' Cupping her face, I looked her straight in the eye. 'I am so grateful you consented to become my wife.'

'And I that you asked me.'

Neither of us could have said more at that moment.

At last, I offered her my arm, and we descended the main staircase together to receive the guests as we gathered on the sun-warmed terrace before dinner.

Naturally, our promotion to hosts for the duration of his lordship's illness or until the arrival on the scene of his heir was not to everyone's taste – in social terms, we were, after all, neither fish nor fowl. Some people accused us publicly of masquerading as quality. One of my grandfathers was an earl, had I ever wished to make a point, but Harriet, a workhouse orphan as she dryly described herself, sometimes suffered badly from others' snobbery. Tonight, however, as we greeted our guests, she had the support of one of her oldest friends, Sir Francis Palmer. Loving her as a sister, he was not the man to let anyone slight her unavenged. This evening, he was chatting to two history undergraduates, would-be archaeologists who had volunteered to work on his excavations. Both young men were still very shy, it seemed, flushing scarlet whenever Harriet greeted them. One glass of sherry soon found its way down the drinker's trousers. With discreet aplomb, Luke, the senior footman, mopped and refilled the glass almost in one movement.

Two more guests, both trustees living in the village, arrived in rapid succession – Ellis Page, the doctor, and the Reverend Theophilus Pounceman, the rector. Ellis fell into easy conversation with the two young men, while Pounceman joined Francis, with whom he enjoyed little more than an armed truce. The evening air was soon loud with the sound of male voices, including now two older archaeologists, also house guests. Wells, his hair burnished into an unlikely copper by the sun, still preferred to be called an antiquarian; Professor Head, who came in late after his trip, enjoyed the more recent term.

Harriet never gave the impression of being ill at ease in such a situation; she feared the unadulterated society of leisured ladies far more. But she would probably welcome the arrival of Bea Arden, the cook, who, like Harriet, had served the Family for years. Our dear friend was a fellow trustee. Although she had once been reluctant to move out of what she saw as her station in life, these days Bea was happy to join us at the dining table when she knew her team were ready to serve the meal. How much longer Bea would remain in her post was a matter for conjecture: both Ellis Page and Marty Baines, the innkeeper and another trustee, sought her hand in marriage.

At long last, Thatcher announced Professor and Mrs Marchbanks. Hunched the professor might be, but despite his height, he reminded me disconcertingly of a hedgehog, his hair so spiky it could have been used as a brush. As for his character, I soon had no doubts at all: within seconds, finger jabbing the air, he was addressing Pounceman and Francis; from their expressions, the words 'holding forth' might have been more accurate. Mrs Marchbanks was taller than her spouse but appeared to shrink herself deliberately when she stood silently beside him. Her hair, which might once have been the amazing red of Elizabeth Siddal's, was now fading into grey and largely covered by a beaded cap that inescapably reminded me of chainmail. Abandoned by her husband as he dug further into his colleagues' company, she looked about her with something like terror. And – could that be anger? Surely not. Harriet and Thatcher exchanged another glance; he glided away. No doubt he would be modifying the seating plan so that the poor woman could sit between two particularly congenial guests. Meanwhile, Harriet had taken Mrs Marchbanks' arm under her own and was entrusting her to Dr Page and the older historians. The blushing young men must learn to sink or swim. I had better make sure it was the latter. Our conversation staggered along until Thatcher might appear to summon us to dinner.

But when he did come, it was not to announce our meal.

He was discretion itself, indicating he needed a private word with me. 'Nurse Webb is worried about his lordship, sir. It seems that Hargreaves is having trouble controlling him.'

'Oh dear.' I knew a euphemism when I heard one. 'His lordship is having one of his attacks, is he? Thank goodness Doctor Page is here. Did he bring his medical bag with him?'

'As always, sir. Even when he's hoping to be spending the evening in someone particular's company,' he said with a decidedly unprofessional twinkle in his eye. 'Shall I see that it's conveyed up to the Family wing?'

'Please. I'll speak to Doctor Page myself.'

The young man bowed and was gone.

Ellis must have seen the exchange. Already, he was excusing himself from Mrs Marchbanks – who would take pity on her now? – and making his way to me. With a sad grimace, he pointed upwards.

'I'm afraid so. Luke will slip down to ask Bea to hold back dinner as long as she can. Or,' I added, with a twinkle in my eye, 'to save some for you to eat in the kitchen?'

'That would ruin Harriet's table plans, would it not? I'll be as quick as I can. If there is a real crisis – and there must be trouble indeed if young Hargreaves can't deal with it! – I'll send down a message.' And he was gone.

Hargreaves, once his valet and now his devoted nurse, endured much at Lord Croft's hands. The violence was mostly verbal, but occasionally, usually when the poor, sick young man had a childlike desire to do something impossible, it sometimes descended into a physical rage. Whatever the problem, it must be serious for him or the capable Nurse Webb, trained by Miss Nightingale herself, to ask for extra help.

But I must turn from these sad reflections and put our guests, Mrs Marchbanks in particular, at ease.

FOUR

I was about to rescue Mrs Marchbanks from her humiliating isolation when I saw that Matthew had got there first. Any relief I might have felt was dispelled when I was accosted by the professor himself.

'This library,' he began with a social smile that revealed remarkably good teeth but failed to reach his eyes. 'What makes you think it's worth looking at?'

'His late lordship believed there were items of interest,' I said carefully. 'I am merely implementing his wishes and those of my fellow trustees.'

He laughed dismissively, as if he had caught out one of his undergraduates in a slip. 'Palmer said something about you taking responsibility for it. So tell me, why am I here?' He smiled again. Was this charm? It felt more like mockery. I had never before had reason to doubt Francis' judgement but I was beginning to now.

'If, Professor, it was Sir Francis who told you about my role, then you know we have what we believe are treasures. Ideally, not just the obvious gems but the whole library should be catalogued, as should a great deal of family and other documents already unearthed by a former employee here.'

He threw his head back and laughed with angry disbelief. Then he glared, the furrowing of his brow pulling his scalp so that his hair looked like a hedgehog's spikes. 'Good God, woman, you've brought me here just to catalogue someone's laundry lists!'

That was not what Francis would have told him. I countered, 'Some scholars find even such lowly items of interest, or so I have heard. I suppose it depends on whose bedlinen and smalls the lists refer to. I should imagine if they were Shakespeare's, the scholar discovering them would be hailed as a hero of the civilized world.'

'Possibly. But I have heard no evidence that the Bard was ever here.'

'Would King Charles be of interest? We know he came to Shropshire and hid in one of our Salopian trees. Heavens, our village inn is called the Royal Oak. Though, perhaps, history does not record if his laundry was washed at Boscobel House – or perhaps it does, and it only needs someone to investigate?' I had started to enjoy myself at last. 'In all seriousness, a visiting scholar recently identified an important portrait of Queen Elizabeth lying around in the attic here: it is now on loan to the National Gallery. Who knows what lies in the family archives? What scandal? Before he fell ill, his lordship had certainly sown some wild oats. What if he had actually married one of the girls involved? 'If the task is not to your taste – and, indeed, cataloguing the books alone will be a labour worthy of Hercules – perhaps you will be able to recommend someone. For instance, one of your students might wish to undertake such research – for an agreed fee, of course.'

'*Fee*, madam?' he exclaimed so loudly that heads turned towards us. '*Fee*? The undergraduates at Oxford are *gentlemen*. Such a word as *fee* would never soil their minds, let alone their lips.'

I declined to look or feel chastened – or perhaps insulted. 'Very well, then, Professor, let us confine the search for the moment to locating priceless books that should be housed for safety's sake in a great library or museum. The British Library, perhaps?'

He bridled. 'I am initiating a room in the Bodleian for volumes of domestic significance.'

'Really?' What could he mean by that?

'Are *you* aware of any volumes that might be of interest?' The implication was that Robin the pony was more likely to have expertise.

I smiled in a way that would have made any of the staff wary of crossing me further. But I said, without any apparent rancour, 'Yes. I have dusted some of them myself.' I had. I had been the only maid allowed to touch them. Occasionally, his late lordship had let me hold, even let me open, one. Even now, I could recall my first glimpse of a Book of Hours, the jewel-like colours of which gleamed as fresh as if they had been applied that day. 'There are some true wonders,' I said.

'Perhaps to an *amateur* eye.'

The timely arrival of Thatcher meant I did not have to respond to him. 'Ah, pray, excuse me.' I turned to Thatcher, stepping to one side with him.

'The doctor says there's nothing too serious; he suggests we offer one more glass of sherry apiece down here. By the time the guests have emptied them, he'll be able to join you for supper. I have informed Mrs Arden.' He bowed and nodded to Luke to make another round with the decanters.

Mercifully, the professor had turned away to another group, but I was immediately joined by our antiquarian guest, the Reverend Dr Benjamin Wells. He was in his late fifties or early sixties, with a beard so vivid it looked as though his lower face was on fire. The rest of him was less spectacular. His chestnut hair had retreated from his head, leaving an overlarge tonsure, and his shoulders, like the professor's, were beginning to stoop. Of his character, I knew nothing except what little Francis had told me. Bands he might still wear, but his clerical duties had not precluded him from spending much of his time investigating the past. Francis confessed that he had been in two minds about inviting him. Apparently, he was a particularly fine scholar, as his books attested, but he had amassed from somewhere a large personal collection of historical artefacts. No one would take anything away from this site, Francis assured me. I trusted him; I knew from his preliminary excavations that he was meticulous about recording each and every find. But I too would be cautious.

'Good evening, Doctor Wells. Have you had a useful day?'

'Indeed. The trenches have yielded some statuary, possibly votive. The artefacts are still caked with earth, so I haven't yet been able to examine them properly.' He gave an eager smile revealing regrettable teeth and emitting halitosis. 'Cleaning them is such a delicate task, of course, requiring gentle but precise work. Just such as I imagine only a lady might do.' He stared pointedly at my hands.

I suppose I should have been grateful to be considered a lady. But before I could decline his implicit offer, Francis appeared beside us.

'Good God, Wells, I hope you're not suggesting that Harriet

does the archaeological washing-up! She runs this whole establishment, man, and does goodness knows what else besides. But perhaps Doctor Page or Mr Pounceman might know some village women who would be delighted to do such work. I see Page is still absent – some problem in the Family wing, Harriet? – but let us ask Pounceman. Yes, he'll know which women need to earn some money.'

The expression on Dr Wells's face suggested that payment had not been uppermost in his mind. As he turned to ease the antiquarian away, Francis winked. Our dear friend had the strongest of social consciences and was resolute in promoting Mr Carlyle's opinion that a fair day's work merited a fair day's pay. Mr Carlyle had mentioned only male workers. To the horror of many of our acquaintances – some of them women, alas – Francis included female ones, too.

At least I could see none of our guests, not even Mrs Marchbanks, standing in shy silence. Bea Arden had joined us, looking quite at ease in the company of those whom she had fed so well. There was no doubt that one or two at the table would have been astonished that the elegant woman they were addressing was not 'a lady'. Meanwhile, the volume of noise now suggested that at least one more glass of sherry had found its way into each guest. I would be very relieved to see Ellis return. As if on cue, he appeared, giving Bea a slightly anxious glance as she chatted to Dr Wells. But he smiled across at me. Clearly, all was well upstairs.

I returned the smile, edging from the antiquarian towards him.

Ellis said quietly, 'It seems his lordship, thwarted in his desire to take a swim in the lake, lashed out at poor Hargreaves. What a saint he is! The things he has to put up with! Anyway, this time he ducked, with the result that his lordship smashed his knuckles on a door. Some blood, a lot of bruises. Nurse Webb had already tried to dress the injuries, but when the poor deluded young man became difficult, she sent for me.'

What Ellis did to calm him in every similar crisis I did not know, but he clearly shared the pity we all felt at the ruin of the once-promising life.

*   *   *

Although at dinner I should have had the most important guest at my side, Matthew and I had decided I would be flanked by the young students. Thatcher feared they might bore me to death; I countered by pointing out that he had been a tongue-tied youth once – he was now nearing his twenty-sixth birthday, still very young for such a responsible post – and that I had put up with him. What a lovely easy relationship we shared, despite the difference in our ages. Dear me, my next birthday would be my forty-fourth!

The students, however, treated me as if I was their grandmama – one deaf and slow in understanding, too. It seemed they were both wet bobs, not dry bobs; both rowed for their college and neither had any enthusiasm for any land-based sport. So I could not draw them out on my favourite topic with young gentlemen – cricket. Instead, their voices identical and completing each other's sentences, they told me all about their lectures and their tutors, the books they read – I suspect they assumed that I did not read much myself – and at last their ambitions to excavate the past. Mr Hurley, the one with smooth brown hair and an optimistic beard, had already tried his hand on a Hadrian's Wall site; Mr Burford, the one with fly-away blond hair and mutton chop whiskers that were sparse at best, was related to an army man called Lane-Fox, he said proudly. It was a name that meant nothing to me, so he had to explain that although Lane-Fox was now a lieutenant general, he spent most of his time digging up the past. Mr Burford was awfully proud of his second cousin who had inspired him to follow in his footsteps – 'But not the military ones, obviously.'

Both agreed that Francis was absolutely top-hole, and it was an honour to work with him – a fact I would relay when I was next in his company.

Some of our guests, not least Mrs Marchbanks, whose cap beads truly quivered with shock, were clearly disconcerted to learn that in the House the gentlemen should not expect to spend an hour or so smoking and drinking without feminine company. Tea and coffee would naturally be served in the yellow drawing room, and anyone wishing to drink port was welcome to drink that there, too. Any smokers must withdraw to the terrace.

Dr Wells raised his hands in shock. 'But some topics – a discussion of the nude statuary we could find, for instance – might be distasteful, shocking even, to the gentle sex!'

'Then perhaps those topics are best avoided,' Bea said with the firm but polite tone she had always used when her late ladyship had suggested a wildly unsuitable menu. Allowing her amusement to show, she added, 'Though you may find it harder to shock us than you think. As for enjoying your cigars, the trustees are bound by law to ensure that until his lordship or the heir is able to take responsibility for the House, it is protected in every way – and since a chance match burned down that house in Staffordshire in February, we have been told that smokers must enjoy their pleasure outside. It is out of our hands.' She spread hers, a female Pontius Pilate. She carefully omitted to point out that she was a trustee herself and involved in making the decision. 'So do not blame us and we will not blame you if you excuse yourself to blow a cloud – or, of course, to take advantage of the new facilities.' Just to remind anyone expecting their waste to be removed by the maids, chamber pots only appeared in the bedchamber when guests were ready to retire. We had smart new water closets: let them be used.

Our guests drifted in twos or threes from the dining room. Several men were dawdling. Dr Wells was vehemently making some point. Marchbanks stood arms akimbo. One of the historians, whose name briefly escaped me, was shaking his head implacably. The other – Professor Fielding? – was clearly trying to get a word in edgeways, possibly a disagreeable one. The boys gaped as if watching a prize fight.

Professor Head, the archaeologist, made a point of waiting for me just outside the dining room. 'Forgive me my late arrival before supper, Mrs Rowsley.'

'Don't worry – I know from experience how slowly Robin prefers to travel. The pony,' I added as he frowned. 'Was your trip successful?'

'Thank you, yes – but listen to that!' It was almost as if he was grateful for the argument, as furious as it was loud, that grew behind us.

'Should we . . .?' I was turning back – to act as peacemaker, perhaps.

Raising his eyebrows with quite an attractive irony, he said, 'We academics always have such peaceful discussions, do we not? We never get irate, never raise our voices.' Tucking my arm firmly under his, he set me in motion.

I resisted. 'They seem to be arguing about a life-or-death issue.'

'The hottest debates, Mrs Rowsley, are usually over the most trivial matters – trivial to laypeople, but of absolutely vital importance to the participants. Professor Anonymous has a theory Doctor Someone disagrees with. Probably both are mistaken. Soon they will forget their bitter enmity and unite against Sir Anyone Else. My dear late wife wished she could knock disputants' heads together, as if they were bickering schoolboys. She would, by the way, have been much taken with the idea of keeping the sexes together after dinner – she used to hate the vapid conversations she was expected to conduct. And I am intrigued to hear that on some evenings at Thorncroft guests read plays together. I hope I will be privileged to join in. You run this establishment very well, if I may say so.'

'Thank you.' I did not agree, but perhaps he was right. I made conversation. 'In fact, the trustees have suggested that since I have so many other duties, I should step back from the day-to-day details; now we have a new housekeeper who is working very hard. Have you met her yet? A tall, handsome woman.'

'Yes, I've met her once or twice since my arrival; she's been very polite and pleasant. I was hard put to find the right person to run my own modest establishment now I am on my own. Sometimes the applicant you locate through the servants' registry office is ruthlessly efficient and scares you to death; another might be charming and gentle and completely unable to run a household . . . Now, what play will we be reading?'

FIVE

The new House custom had developed as a way of ensuring that when there was a preponderance of male visitors, Harriet and Bea – who after all spent a lot of time together each day – were not left twiddling their thumbs waiting for other company. The huge benefit was that we had found delightful ways of passing the time: apart from relaxed and pleasurable conversation, we had half read, half acted our way through much of Shakespeare. Bea, who had once been shy in company, found herself excelling in whatever role she took.

Was this unusual arrangement why Mrs Marchbanks looked so distressed, fretting at her fan, her head drooping so that her chainmail hung across her face? Bea and Ellis were seated near her, apparently making every effort to include her in their conversation. Others had not yet appeared at all. Harriet, coming in slightly late herself and laughing at something Professor Head was saying, spoke briefly to Luke who was distributing whatever refreshment was required, Thatcher being now off duty. Soon he was breathing in my ear. 'Mrs Rowsley tells me there is an argument in the dining room, sir. Shall I . . .?'

'Thank you. I wondered where everyone was. Let's see who's missing. That historian whose name I can never recall. Professor Marchbanks. Doctor Wells. Mr Hurley – or is it Mr Burford?'

'As like as two peas, aren't they, sir, except I fancy Mr Hurley is the one with brown hair.'

'Of course. Ah! Sir Francis is trying to catch my eye.' I raised my eyebrows in reply to the slight movement of his head. We made separate and, I hope, unobtrusive exits.

What did we expect to find? One of the academics speared with a dessert fork? In the event, the dining room was empty but for footmen clearing the table.

'There were some guests in here,' Thomas said. 'Four or five. They shot off outside, but I don't think they were actually smoking, just continuing their argument. I didn't think it was our place to interfere, Mr Rowsley. But I could pop out and offer them refreshments if you wish.'

'With your eyes and ears open,' Francis said with a smile and something of a wink. He had a well-deserved reputation for generous tips at the end of each stay. As the young man bowed and headed briskly on his way, he added, 'It's a fine evening, Matthew; do you fancy a stroll in the direction of the excavations? No – that would leave too much for Harriet to do. She's like a juggler, isn't she? Clergyman here, professor there – whoops, there's an unhappy wife!' He mimed vigorously. 'She has to keep them all happy.'

'I agree; I don't think we should both go,' I said flatly. 'Equally, I'm not sure either of us should go alone. *Just in case!*' we chorused together, that being Harriet's motto. As one, we turned back towards the drawing room.

'Has she got over that nasty business with your cousin and his wife?' he asked in the quiet of an empty corridor. 'Not that she's broken any family confidences, Matthew – you must know that. But I gather she was not well treated. Truly, the devil makes work for idle tongues as well as idle hands.'

'Indeed he does, if the ladies she encountered there are anything to go by.' I shook my head in chagrin at what the house party had exposed her to. 'I doubt if she would say this, but I will: I should never have taken her there. But she handles – *juggles!* – everything so well here, I thought she would enjoy herself. A superb art collection, a fine library, cricket – what could go wrong? Well, we found out, didn't we?' I added ruefully. 'Francis, this Marchbanks: what do you make of him?'

He laughed. 'At Oxford, he truly has an excellent reputation. He has worked in the library at Chatsworth, so he is used to handling and evaluating priceless material. But as for the man himself and the way he treats his wife, I reserve judgement.'

'You already have doubts – admit it!'

'Mea culpa.' He beat his breast dramatically. As we paused outside the drawing room, he added, sotto voce, 'Ah, he has deigned to return and support her. I saw him in conversation with Harriet earlier, by the way. I fancy he was trying to patronize her.'

'Did she let him?'

'I think that experience at your cousin's might have stiffened her spine. She parried every blow and landed a couple of her own. Ah! There is young Hurley. Heavens, undergraduates get younger every year, do they not? Or does that observation show my age?'

'If it does, it shows mine, too. But this pair seem more like puppies than young men ready to take their place in the world. And young Burley, too – I beg your pardon: young Burford.'

'I suspect Hurley and Burley might be all too appropriate,' he murmured. 'But we shall see.'

When he finally joined us, Wells ostentatiously withdrew to the furthest corner of the room, folding his arms tightly across his chest and tapping his foot. Professor Marchbanks, however, made a bee-line for his wife, towering over her in a way that was as intimidating as it was rude, given that at last Ellis and Bea had persuaded her to join in their conversation. Her belated smile disappeared immediately. Would she stand as she was apparently expected to? No, Bea laid a gentle hand on her sleeve and continued what seemed to be an amusing anecdote. The professor had perforce to sit down somewhere else or risk making a scene.

There was a spare seat beside him. I moved swiftly to take it, ready to draw our guest's fire. Meanwhile, Ellis escorted both ladies over to Francis – they would be safe with him – and Professor Fielding, who greeted Mrs Marchbanks with a charming smile and seemed as kind as Francis. Ellis caught my eye, mouthing that he must leave the gathering as he needed to take one more look at his patient.

In fact, though I was braced for awkwardness at the very least, Marchbanks proved a good conversationalist, to all appearances interested in our plans for the model village about which I found it very easy to wax with passion. Then he made an unkind reference to the Great Unwashed, one I countered by pointing out that it was hard to maintain personal hygiene when the wells dried up – hence our insistence that all the cottages would have a pump to supply running water and a privy.

'And do I gather that you run a free hospital for these labourers of yours?'

I was beginning to like him less. 'Where else would they be treated? And how could they pay? Lady Croft was unwell for some time before her death; her son's insanity means he has to be confined. You have seen the size of the building, Marchbanks – why not put one huge and otherwise unused wing to good use?'

'Confined? Lord Croft is not free in his own home?' He sounded outraged.

'If he were, he would be a danger to himself and others. I can think of no other establishment where the cook locks away her knives when they are not in use. In any case,' I added, 'you have both already seen that the contents are as precious as the fabric itself is important. We take care of them not just for his lordship but also for future generations.'

'Your wife and Mrs – that cook of yours – were talking about trustees,' Marchbanks said.

'*Mrs Arden* is as devoted to the family as my wife is,' I said, 'both having worked here long before I became his lordship's agent. The young man wanted to bring about reform; my predecessor was more interested in feathering his nest than in carrying out his employer's wishes. So I am proud to work alongside them so that everything will be in place when the heir is found.'

He looked around. For a fleeting moment, he seemed to be appraising rather than appreciating what he saw. 'And the trustees?'

'A diverse group of hand-picked men and women.'

'Women! And are any of this diverse group experts in house and estate management?'

'In the theory and the practice,' I said firmly, if disingenuously. 'The chairman is the family lawyer, whom you will meet shortly, I hope – perhaps next week. Naturally, he wishes to see how his lordship's projects are being handled. Project, I should say. The new village. No one knew anything about the Roman remains till the men digging the foundations for the village uncovered them. As you will have gathered, Sir Francis and my wife are old friends, so it was natural he should be asked to investigate them.'

He waved a hand in both acknowledgement and dismissal of the information. 'And the library? Your wife seems to think there are some interesting books there, but I'm sure you can tell me more.'

'On the contrary. She knows far more than I do. Her mentor was his lordship's father, a man of taste and great knowledge.'

'A dilettante? Rowsley, you have no idea how many great men believe that the geese in their libraries are, in fact, swans.' He sighed extravagantly. 'Well, my work may be done sooner than I expected. But my wife and I will start betimes, and thus I fear I must bid you and the company goodnight.'

I smiled. 'Your wife works with you?'

He bridled. '*For*, not *with*. She writes to my dictation and then packs the volumes I take away. Don't worry – she no longer needs my supervision.'

'You do understand that nothing can be removed from here without the express permission of the trustees, and the lawyer in particular? Moreover—'

'If that is what the trustees want . . .' His tone implied they were either fools or knaves. 'Meanwhile, we start work early – at half past nine sharp.'

Early? Farmer Twiss would declare that they had already missed the best part of the day. 'I will warn my wife. She will—'

He nodded. 'Ah, yes – breakfast arrangements, of course.' He raised his voice, clearly intending to be heard by the entire room. 'Now, I understand there is a chapel here. I am sure one of our distinguished fellow guests will be more than delighted to lead us in evening prayer.' He rose, looking around expectantly.

Also on my feet, I raised a warning hand. 'The chapel is long overdue for refurbishment. Naturally, we would all like to see it restored, but since everyone is happy to worship at our parish church, it is not as urgent as the other two projects, as our rector will explain. I assume you have met Mr Pounceman – no? Allow me to introduce you before he calls for his carriage.' I led him across the room.

It was unlikely that Mr Pounceman or I would ever consider the other a friend, but our relationship had mellowed considerably, much, probably, to the villagers' relief: in a small community, it was vital that everyone with the ability to help others would work together in hard times.

Having introduced them, saying all that was proper, I backed away, wondering if I should bring Wells into their conclave. But he was just bowing his way out of the room. Should I call him back? I looked across at Harriet, who shook her head very slightly, touching her brow and mouthing, 'A headache.'

By now the professor and Pounceman were coming my way.

'I fear I must leave you, Rowsley,' the rector said, shaking my hand. 'Old Mrs Gornal is on her deathbed, and I promised to look in on the way home. I have already thanked your kind wife and Mrs Arden for their generous gifts – the soup, the calves' foot jellies, even some port wine – but now I need to give her my contribution, my prayers. However, I would like to ask a favour. Professor Marchbanks tells me he would like to see your chapel. When it is convenient, I would love to accompany him. It is so long since I saw it.'

The professor bowed in acknowledgement, no more, and he turned away before Pounceman had left the room. Within moments, he and his wife were following him, he with a jutting jaw, she with downcast eyes, their words to Harriet perfunctory. Francis, smiling quizzically, caught my eye and gave an almost Gallic shrug. Kissing Harriet's hand, he too quit the room, soon to be followed by everyone else except Bea, with whom we strolled gently through the entrance hall to find, as we expected, Ellis's horse already waiting and Ellis standing beside it. Reassured after a quick enquiry about his lordship, Harriet and I melted away.

SIX

'You didn't think to inform the professor that I must be present in the room while he was examining the books! Oh, Matthew! You pest!' I could say very little more as he was unhooking my corset. At last, I could breathe properly again. I turned to face him. 'I can't imagine he will greet the news with anything approaching pleasure.'

'I did try twice, but he simply overrode me, so I gave up. It was that or snub him hard. In any case, now you have the pleasure of telling him yourself,' he said, straight-faced.

'And I am equally sure you would like to be a fly on the wall when I do.' I plumped down on the bed. 'What if he is so enraged that he storms off back to Oxford?'

'We heave a sigh of relief and find another expert. Actually, Francis can do penance and find one. "Excellent reputation"? Well, we shall see. But I could drift past the library at an appropriate time. No, that would look as if you couldn't handle the situation yourself.'

'The fact that he has brought his wife complicates things too, doesn't it? She works *for* him?'

'Absolutely not *with* him. Not all couples enjoy a partnership like ours.' He kissed me.

I returned the compliment.

We remembered that he was still wearing his dress shirt, complete with studs. 'Up you get!' As I started on the first stud, I asked, 'Does he expect the trustees to pay her separately or will he dole out her pin money from his fee? To be fair to Francis, I think he was as disconcerted by her arrival as I was. Stop fidgeting. One last one. There! Could you make anything of her?'

He sat down on the dressing-table stool. 'I could see a lot of things – as you probably did. Anxiety at being in a new situation. Shyness. Anger.' He paused. 'Did you see her face when the professor came into the drawing room and stood over

her? Bea was certainly worried about her. And Ellis, too. Do
you think they'll make a match of it, by the way?'

I considered. 'I don't know. Two decent, honest people who
care a great deal for each other. And yet . . . Do they feel this
for each other? Or this?'

The professor gazed askance around the breakfast room,
deserted but for me and Tom, the most junior footman.

'Good morning,' I said with my hostess's smile. 'I'm afraid
the gentlemen working on the site left over an hour ago. My
husband also sends his apologies: there is a dispute between
two of his lordship's tenants which he wishes to nip in the bud.
Now, what would you like for breakfast?' He peered towards
the covered dishes on the sideboard. 'Almost empty, I'm afraid.
But Mrs Arden's team will prepare whatever you want. Mrs
Marchbanks, what may I offer you? Do you prefer tea or coffee
– her ladyship's taste in both was impeccable and we still buy
her favourites for guests,' I added, to forestall, I hoped, any
suspicion we might be living beyond our station.

Their orders conveyed via Tom, I hesitated. Should I stay
and watch them eat? Stay and pretend to eat myself? Engage
them in conversation at a time when many people preferred
silence? I would compromise, ask about the comfort of their
room, the quality of their sleep and, the only thing I was really
interested in – what time they wanted the library unlocked.

'Very well, I will be there at half past nine.'

'Indeed, Mrs Rowsley, we don't need to inconvenience you
in person. You must have so many domestic tasks to perform.'

I did not like his choice of verb. I would have preferred 'to
oversee'. I merely nodded. 'As my husband probably told you,
no one, no matter how distinguished, is allowed to be in the
library unattended.' It was a milder word than unsupervised,
but the professor was surely astute enough to understand what
I meant. Rather than allow a dispute to grow, I continued, 'The
staff's tasks for the day have already been allocated, so I will
see you at half past nine. Ah, here is Tom again. He will look
after you.'

For years, my habit had been to spend the first hour or so of
the day in the Room, as the housekeeper's lair was universally

called. My feet almost took me there now. But if I appeared, it could give the impression that I did not trust Mrs Briggs to do her work properly. So, telling Tom where I was going, I made my way straight to the library; there I made one or two preparations. I was sitting at his late lordship's desk when an out-of-breath Thatcher appeared.

'Ma'am, there's been an accident upstairs. In the long gallery! One of the pictures dropped off the wall as Milly was dusting it! Such a to-do she's making.'

'Is she hurt?' I asked, locking up and heading up the stairs.

'More shocked than anything, I think. But the picture's not looking too good.'

Nor was it. The frame had cracked from top to bottom – though I suspected that George, our estate carpenter could effect one of his miraculous repairs. The portrait, of a particularly ugly woman, had a bad tear.

'And it's a Lely,' Thatcher breathed. His sepulchral tone did nothing to stem Milly's loud sobs.

Putting my arm around her, I passed her a handkerchief.

'His late lordship always used to say that the pictures with what he called doubtful provenance had been hung here. And it does say it's School of Lely, not actually by Lely himself. Now, Dick, could you send another maid up here to look after Milly. After that, get a message to George – no, first would you convey my apologies to Professor and Mrs Marchbanks and open up the muniment room?'

With an anxious look at the maid, he sped off – without ever running.

'And now, Milly. Are you hurt? There? Dear me, that's a nasty lump,' I said, pushing back her hair. 'We'll get Nurse Webb to take a look at that.'

'Oh, no, ma'am. That picture! I'm so sorry!'

'Just tell me what happened. Gently, now.'

Milly sobbed out her tale of woe. In short, as usual she had been wielding her feather duster when suddenly the picture dropped off the wall. She'd tried to catch it but all she'd managed to do was make it smack her head. The sooner she had treatment from Nurse Webb the better.

But then I saw the cord from which the picture had hung.

'It's not your fault, Milly; look at this.' I held up the two ends. 'Do you see what I see?' She needed to see what I saw. Just in case. 'It's completely worn through, isn't it?'

She revived enough to look. 'Oh, ma'am, I didn't do that! Couldn't have. Look, seems someone cut it, but not all the way through. And then when I dusted it – only ever so lightly, like you taught us – there it is, torn apart, all frayed. Whoosh. And down it comes.'

'Well done. You're absolutely right. Ah! Here's Primrose. She'll go with you to the Family wing to get that lump treated. Tell Mrs Briggs you must be on really light duties, if, that is, Nurse Webb says you're fit to work at all.' I turned to the slightly older girl. 'Make sure you tell Mrs Briggs that, too. And if Milly needs to rest, come straight to see me in the library.' That would undercut Mrs Briggs' authority, I realized as I picked up the picture and followed the girls. But ultimately the responsibility for the welfare of the staff lay with me.

As, of course, did the library. I walked just as Thatcher had done. Fast. Via our bedchamber where I locked the damaged picture. Just in case.

There was no sign of anyone in the library corridor. The muniment room? Just as empty. So where would our honoured guests be?

Thatcher materialized, his face the curious blank it went when he was furious. Without meeting my eye, he bowed and flung open not just one but both the library doors. He clearly wanted me to make an entrance. He bowed deeply and closed them behind me.

And whom did I find in the cherished space?

My greeting was civil at best. Any anger, however, might bubble over when I discovered how they came to be there. I moved towards the desk, on which I had earlier spread my papers.

The professor moved to the door, holding it open. 'Thank you,' he said. When I did not respond, he added with a sideways jerk of his head, 'Well?'

I had never been dismissed from this room like that. Ever. Especially by a man wearing a butler's apron and protective

sleevelets over his jacket. 'I am so sorry if you were inconvenienced by my absence.'

'Not at all. I complained to the argumentative young man
who says he's the butler and demanded to speak to the housekeeper. What an efficient woman she is! So calm and helpful. She
might have demurred yesterday afternoon but this morning
she fetched the key and opened up forthwith.'

Mrs Marchbanks, also wearing an apron and sleevelets,
murmured something I did not catch because her husband's
glance silenced her.

'Professor Marchbanks, Mrs Marchbanks, please let me
explain—'

'Good God, woman, I don't need explanations! This is a
library. I am a bibliographer. Be so good as to leave me to work
in peace.' He stepped towards me much as he had approached
his wife last night. 'I don't need a mere servant to tell me
anything.'

'I think you are under a misapprehension, Professor. I am
indeed a mere servant – but one who is the person legally in
charge of this room and everything in it. You may wish to verify
that by reading this copy of her late ladyship's will.' I pushed
it towards him.

Eyes bulging, he skimmed over it.

'And here is another document, drafted by the Family's
lawyer, which also explains my presence.'

Mrs Marchbanks took it, staring as if it were a slice of bread
in her hand. Expressionless, she passed it to her husband. Dear
me. Could it really be the case that the woman could not read?
I must be mistaken. She was there to take notes from her
husband's dictation. Perhaps she simply needed spectacles.

I tried to lighten the atmosphere. He was a scholar; I must
let him get on with the task for which he was being paid. 'Please
understand that I am not here to interfere in any way with what
you are doing. On the contrary, I am going to spend my time
reading, which is something of a treat.' I held up *The Woman
in White* and sat down in a way that brooked no argument. As
for reading it, however, I might have turned pages, but my eyes
were mostly on other, older books.

*   *   *

'Surely that is unnecessary!' the professor expostulated as I locked the library door behind them and ushered them into the muniment room. 'And not permitting us to take refreshment within the library! This all smacks of paranoia.'

'You had several books laid out on the tables. Would they have benefited from a baptism of tea? Of coffee?' I smiled. 'Come, Professor, would you expect your children deliberately to flout your wishes? Of course not. Lord Croft was not my father, but as soon as he discovered I could read, a friendship grew up between us and flourished. I can tell from your face you think such a thing is unlikely, but I truly believed he loved me as a daughter; I certainly loved him as a father.' I was holding his hand as he died. I straightened my shoulders, hoping they would not notice that my eyes had filled. 'Tell me, have you found anything interesting yet?'

I suspect that his language was deliberately obscure, involving what sounded like Latin words, to put me in what he presumed ought to be my place. But I asked a few questions before concluding, 'There is so much to take in, Professor, that I shall be glad to see your notes when you have put them in order. Now, we take lunch at half past twelve; it will be a very small group of us since the archaeologists and historians prefer to eat on site. Would you and Mrs Marchbanks care to join them there? It's not a long walk and there's already a great deal to see . . .' And I would certainly prefer to have their company diluted.

He agreed for them both. I dispatched a passing tweeny with a message for Bea and the duty lunchtime footmen, and we returned to the library. This time I did not even pretend to read Mr Collins' exciting book: in my head, I was rehearsing a conversation with Mrs Briggs. Somehow I had to strike a balance between praising her initiative and condemning her for over-reaching herself.

My colleagues had already loaded trestle tables with a hearty cold luncheon; it was understood that the labourers might take any leftovers back home to their families. The men were subdued rather than sulky, I thought, but I made a point of speaking to those I knew, asking after their families and speaking of the new village, to which many of them would soon move. One point at issue was pigs: they knew we were happy for them to keep poultry, but there was a rumour saying porkers were forbidden. I reassured them: we knew how important the meat and indeed the fat the overweight beasts produced were to all the families during the winter. I pressed home a pet topic of my own: fruit trees. Dr Page insisted that apples in particular were beneficial to many aspects of health, especially during the winter. From time to time, he mentioned the paper he was writing, to be printed in a learned journal – but progress on it was slow.

I glanced around. All seemed to be well. Explaining to Francis that I had an urgent matter to attend to at the house, I slipped away. At the very least, Mrs Briggs should not publicly have overruled Thatcher, especially in front of others. I had to speak to her about that, no matter what else I wanted to say – or rather, to ask.

Servants' dinner should be over by now, with Thatcher and Mrs Briggs retiring to the Room to eat their pudding, as it was still called, even though these days the guests completed their meals with dessert. It was unlikely to be a happy encounter if the professor's account was accurate. In fact, Thatcher was nowhere to be seen; it was only the smell of cigarette smoke wafting through the window that suggested where he might be. Would he eavesdrop? In his place, I might be tempted to.

'Please sit down, Mrs Briggs,' I said, taking Thatcher's chair myself. 'But first of all, might I trouble you for a cup of that tea? Thank you.'

'I'm so glad you're here, ma'am,' she said, taking her seat and clasping her hands on her lap. 'I've been ever so worried. It's about young Jenks.'

It took me a moment to realize she meant Milly.

'That nasty accident? She—'

'Accident it may be. But that was a valuable picture, ma'am, and I won't lie to you: I think you should make her pay for the damage. Stop it out of her wages, ma'am.'

'Is that what happened at your last place?'

'Of course! There was a lot of china at the Hall, too – very little got broken, I can assure you. And I can see you have a

lot of fine stuff here – I'd hate to see it getting damaged
at all.'

I smiled. Possibly in farewell to the wind that was
being taken from my sails. 'We all would. The trouble is it
would take the mistress of the House or a full meeting of the
trustees to make a change like that. So things will probably
have to stay as they are. As for poor Milly, she had a terrible
bang on the head. I'd call that punishment enough if punishment were needed. Now, this morning while I was seeing to
Milly, something unfortunate happened—'

'Oh, you heard about the kerfuffle with Thatcher? Locking
Professor and Mrs Marchbanks out of the library, indeed! When
they assured me that you had told him to let them in! The very
thought!'

Was that what they had told her? I shook my head in genuine
disbelief.

'However did a man like that come to call himself a butler
in a big house like this? He was no-ing and can't-ing and
mustn't-ing – quite forgot he was a servant and meant to serve.
Such distinguished visitors, too.'

'Did he explain to you and the guests why he felt himself
unable to do as they asked?'

'He said something about rules and treasures, but I told him
there were valuable pictures hanging all over the walls, and
all the statues and pots and things, and no one turned a hair
about them. So why all this bother about a few books? And
when he refused point-blank to get the key, I fetched it myself.
Ask him. He's out there sulking.' She jerked a thumb toward
the window. 'In other places I've worked, he would have a
formal warning, and if he didn't mend his ways, the next Quarter
Day he would be out on his ear. I know many a man who'd
make a better butler than him, and that's God's truth.'

I kept my voice gentle. 'He's been here many years.'

'I got to be thirty-five before I became a housekeeper.' Clearly,
I had touched a nerve. 'How can some spotty youth have that
sort of experience? Poor lad, he's right out of his depth, isn't
he? Maybe with an experienced man to teach him . . . Now,
there's a Mr Duffield, down Banbury way, who's looking for a
move. Or Mr Brewer – he's just left Coughton. They've worked

with the best families, I can assure you, and can deal with a houseful of guests without turning a hair.'

'I suppose the guests in those houses would be expected to take valets and maids and so on,' I mused.

'Indeed. And both those gentlemen would be well able to manage them all.'

'They'd find life here very dull after such good times. And no fat tips, of course. As I explained, as long as his lordship is ill, we have no society guests. The gentlemen here – and Mrs Marchbanks – are here to work, are they not?' I got to my feet. 'Mrs Briggs, if they told you that Mr Thatcher had locked them out, they were misleading you. Lying, to be frank. I explained to them why they could not go in. Mr Thatcher's decision to keep them out was right. He was acting on the trustees' instructions, you see.'

'Trustees! Grand folk who live in London, I daresay. You know the saying, Mrs Rowsley – what the eye doesn't see the heart doesn't grieve over. Anyway, since I was in the wrong—'

'You were *put* in the wrong, Mrs Briggs!'

We exchanged a smile.

'I'll make up with young Thatcher,' she continued. 'And I'm sure we'll rub along nicely.'

'I hope so, Mrs Briggs. He's the rock on which the manservants and indeed the whole household depend,' I added in a somewhat louder voice, in the hope that one listener at least might hear good of himself. 'In future, if ever you're in doubt about any sort of rule or regulation, please just ask me.'

'Oh, I don't like to disturb you, ma'am.'

'I had rather be disturbed twenty times than have one wrong decision made as a result of some guest's lies.' I stood, ready to leave. 'By the way, how is young Milly now? I didn't see her in the servants' hall. She did have a very nasty bang on the head, you know.'

'She had a bit of a bruise, I could see that. But all that rubbish she and her friend were talking about her lying down in a darkened room – well, I said the long gallery had blinds, didn't it, and she could carry on with what she was supposed to be doing, only to be more careful. And off she went.'

'And then did she eat any dinner?' I asked idly.

'Said it made her feel sick. So I thought a bit of fresh air wouldn't harm her – she's gone down to that picnic to help there.'

I nodded coolly. 'I wonder who said she should be resting?'

She shrugged. 'You know what these young girls are like.'

'I do. Very well. I've known Milly since she was a baby.'

Thatcher blushed and stubbed out his cigarette as soon as I appeared.

'Who'd be a servant?' I asked with a grin. 'Heavens, what bad manners, what absolute rudeness we have to put up with from guests – and sometimes, it seems, from our colleagues.' Putting my hand briefly on his arm, I added, 'I'm sorry, Dick – it must have been very hard this morning.'

'They lied to her, Mrs Rowsley. And she believed them. But I wish she'd argued with me in private, not in public. She's been fitting in all right till today, to be fair. Apart from one or two odd things that set us all a bit on edge.'

'Whatever anyone says, we are a team, just as we have been since you took over from Samuel. And don't think I don't know that you spend hours up in the Family wing reading to him. He'd be proud to see how well you're doing in very strange circumstances.' I spread my hands. 'It isn't just this morning's incident, but the whole strange masterless household. No mistress for me to refer to – to defer to.'

He bit a hangnail. 'Never thought to leave here, Mrs Rowsley – but she said—' He jerked his head in the direction of the Room.

'There is no need for anyone here to worry about leaving, Dick. You have my word.' We shook hands on the promise.

'I am worried about something else, Mrs Rowsley. Milly. She was sent all the way down to the Roman ruins. On her own. And the poor child with a headache so bad she could hardly see.' He nodded grimly. 'So I sent her up to Nurse Webb – and Tom's gone instead.'

'I'm very grateful, Dick. Thank you. But I think you should tell Mrs Briggs that Milly got worse and that was why you acted, don't you? After all, the maids are her responsibility.'

And the last thing I wanted was an unlovely game of tit-for-tat below stairs.

Although I knew Bea would be at her busiest, I took in the kitchen on my way back upstairs.

'She's willing, I'll say that for her,' she said. 'And she's prepared to roll her sleeves up and muck in. Very keen on sweeping, she is.' She grinned. 'A real new broom sweeping clean, in fact. In many ways, I'd say she was ideal. But then this library business, and she comes bustling up here to the key safe as if she owned the place. Anyway, I'm glad you spoke to Dick,' she added quietly. 'It takes a lot to make a patient lad like that flare up, but I'll tell you, you could have cut the atmosphere with a knife during servants' dinner. Now, go and keep an eye on that dratted professor – remember, I'm your eyes and ears round here.'

SEVEN

'There are times,' Harriet sighed as we withdrew to our bedchamber to change for dinner, 'when all I want to do is go back to our own house and shut the door on the outside world.'

'And in particular on Mrs Briggs or Professor Marchbanks?'

'Both. Dick's sure Marchbanks deliberately misled her and she naturally took his word – a gentleman's word, granted – instead of a colleague's. She's over-keen; that's the problem, perhaps. But I do wish she'd spoken to me first.'

'Will you let her see out her month's probation? To see if she improves?'

'In all fairness, we must. But to be equally fair, Mrs Rose should have a month's trial, too. Perhaps she will be more suited.'

'If not, that brings us back to the impossibility of your doing everything, including supervising the library. Could you let me be your deputy? There are times when I could work at your desk just as well as in my own office.'

'I would be very grateful.' She frowned. 'We have another problem, too.' She darted into the dressing room and returned with something wrapped in a sheet.

'But that – that's from the long gallery, isn't it? My love, you don't want that to hang in here, do you? Heavens, think of the fuss and palaver if poor Samuel ever got to hear of it! And she is so very ugly,' I added truthfully.

'She has also been injured in a fall. Look.' She pointed to a tear in the canvas. 'And why did she fall?' She turned over the frame. The thick cord was still attached to the frame's eyelets but was hanging loose.

I picked up the two loose ends. 'Very badly worn. And then with the extra pressure – oh, dear.'

'Oh, dear, indeed. Yes, I'd say it's been cut. The whole thing landed on poor little Milly's head when she was dusting it.

She's spending the night under Nurse Webb's eye, by the way. Who might have done this, Matthew, and why? Goodness, no one would want to steal it.'

'What shall we do?'

'My love, I was hoping you might tell me. I seem to have run out of ideas.' She looked utterly weary, almost defeated. 'George has inspected as many of the other pictures as he can reach in the long gallery, but he's seen nothing to worry him. Tomorrow he will work his way around the House. And I have asked Primrose – what a competent girl she is: such a find! – to pass the word round the other housemaids that they must be vigilant and report anything unusual directly to me.'

'Good. If anyone wanted to harm a picture, why such an undistinguished one and why in such a rarely visited part of the House?' I mused.

She smiled. 'It was so far from all the other House activity that his late lordship tried to teach his lordship cricket up there. It did not end well. But I can't answer your question. And I worry about the other pictures in the house. And the damage to people or property if they fell. Imagine that Van Dyck over the stairs taking a tumble . . .'

'Hung by chains, not cord, of course. Harder to interfere with. And more obvious – you'd need proper tools which would be harder to carry around than a pair of scissors on a chatelaine or in an etui.'

She tipped her head sideways, as always reminding me of an intelligent sparrow spotting a crumb. 'Is there a male equivalent, I wonder?'

'We have pockets, my love. All the same, it might be hard to explain the presence of a pair of pliers in your trousers. Look, Constable Pritchard and I are playing cricket together on Saturday. I'll talk to him then. Meanwhile, I think it's time we got dressed, don't you?'

She nodded with very little enthusiasm. Yes, she really wanted to go home. Our house was only a few hundred yards away, but it might as well have been the other side of the country for all the time we were able to enjoy in it.

*   *   *

Arriving on the terrace to greet our guests again, we found
Thatcher, stony-faced, on duty on the terrace. Harriet touched him
lightly on the arm and stepped towards Dr Wells. I turned to
Thatcher. 'You know you have our support whatever others may
say?' I shook his hand.

'Thank you, sir. I'd hate to think of the cricket team playing
without me.' His smile was suddenly boyish. 'But Mrs Rowsley
might want to take my place!'

'She might indeed. I know you'll want a better place one
day, Dick, and we won't stand in your way – you know that
– but very few men could have taken over from Samuel as
well as you have. And you know how grateful we are. Ah,
Professor!' I applied a smile as swiftly as Dick replaced his
with his professional impassivity.

As the men, minus last night's village guests, gathered in
loud conversation, it dawned on me that there was no sign of
Mrs Marchbanks. The obvious person to ask where she might
be was her husband, of course, but what I had seen the previous
evening had convinced me that despite – or perhaps because of
– the numerous progeny, all was not well in the marriage. So
since no one needed my conversation, I went back inside to
buttonhole a maid. The first I saw was Primrose.

'I've not heard she's ill or anything, sir. Do you want me to
. . . I don't know . . . offer my services to help her dress?'

'That's an excellent idea. Thank you.'

'Thank *you*, sir.' She might not have looked at the coin I'd
slipped her, but I wager she could tell it was a half-crown piece
simply by its weight. Yet her smile was very cool. Very cool
indeed.

Neither maid nor Mrs Marchbanks appeared; surely it
could not take so long to dress one woman? Thatcher himself
agreed to lead the servants in a quick search. The talk continued
unabated. Harriet caught my eye and pointed upwards, where
the earlier light puffy clouds were coalescing into rain clouds.
I mouthed the word 'Problem', and she was with me as soon
as she could release herself from Professor Fielding's vigorous
conversation.

'I didn't like to ask Marchbanks,' I admitted.

'Quite so. Give me five minutes. If we've not located her then, you'll have to speak to him.' And she was gone.

Thatcher materialized beside me. 'It seems there has been an accident, sir. Young Tom has found Mrs Marchbanks. He was just casting one last look at the dining room to make sure everything was in order and he found her unconscious on the floor. I've sent for Doctor Page, and Nurse Webb is with her.'

'Dear me! I'll warn the professor this instant!'

Thatcher tugged his ear, a sure sign he was worried. 'The thing is, Mr Rowsley, it may not be an accident. There is a distinct smell of alcohol about her person. Perhaps a slight delay – until she has been conveyed to the Family wing?'

'I'll tell him she's slightly indisposed.' Would he fly immediately to her side? Somehow I did not think so. 'By then things might be clearer.'

'And cleared up, if you get my drift.' He vanished.

It was apparent that Professor Marchbanks regarded my approach as an interruption to an important discussion with Wells, sighing audibly when I asked if I might speak in private.

'Dear me! Is that all? Women's troubles, no doubt. Again.' He tutted in exasperation. 'Tell her that when dinner is served, I expect her to take her place at the table. Now, where was I?' He turned back to find, to his further irritation, that Wells was now conversing with young Hurley.

We eventually dined without her, the places having been hastily spaced to disguise the gap. Dinner over, Bea and Harriet excused themselves, ostensibly to sit with the sick woman. The rain that had been threatening settled into a miserable drizzle. Any arguments would have to take place indoors.

EIGHT

Matthew and I had been granted the use of a former bedchamber as a small drawing room for our use when we had to be on extended duty in the House. It was there that Bea and I adjourned to drink tea. Mrs Marchbanks was still being examined by Ellis Page, who promised, with a smile, to report to us when he could.

'Fancy being drunk enough to fall down insensible like that!' Bea said.

We shook our heads as one.

'And such a quiet-looking woman, too. But they say still waters run deep, don't they?' she added.

'I'm sure you're right; there's more to her than meets the eye. But can you imagine having to live with a bully like the professor? It was he who made Mrs Briggs overrule Dick Thatcher. He's actually had several tries at bullying me.'

'Heavens above, I wish I'd seen it!'

'I quite enjoyed facing him down, to be honest. But it must be harder to stand up to someone you're married to. Especially if he – how can I put it? He might be a gentleman, but you feel he's this far from being violent.' I made a minuscule gap between my finger and thumb.

'Yes, you're right. I was truly afraid he'd hit her yesterday evening, and he didn't exactly seem full of concern this evening, eating his dinner as casually as if she'd not been carried off to Nurse Webb. Now, what's all this about the pictures falling down? With George to look after them?'

'Ah, it's not quite as simple as that . . .'

Her eyes widened as I explained. 'Deliberate damage! Who on earth would do that? And why? And when? Heavens, it's as if someone wants an innocent maid to be hurt!'

'Or our attention to be drawn away from something else . . . Like the Marchbankses getting into the library without me this morning.'

'Would either of them have risked such a thing? Or bribed a maid or footman to do it?'

'Yet it must be someone with a legitimate excuse to be out and about the House, mustn't it?'

Before she could answer, there was a tap at the door: Ellis.

'Shall I ring for fresh tea?' I asked, as he sat down.

'I've just shared a pot with Nurse Webb, thank you.'

'And how's your patient?'

'She is apparently restored to health. Between ourselves,' he continued conspiratorially, 'we're both puzzled by her apparent lapse into unconsciousness.' He ran his hands through his hair. 'You see, although her dress smelt of alcohol, her breath certainly didn't.'

'Really? Did she simply faint?'

'I don't know. I couldn't detect any signs of a disorder that might have caused her to.' His eyes gleamed. 'Even a mistress of tactical unconsciousness like you, Harriet, didn't manage to fake appropriate symptoms, did you?'

'Ah!' Bea exclaimed. 'That time when Mr Pounceman was about to inveigh against – was it just that poor maid his lordship got pregnant or women in general? You were very convincing, Harriet!'

I pulled a face. 'If these wretched fashionable new corsets get any tighter, I'm not sure I shall need to feign anything,' I observed dourly. 'Very well, what happens to our guest now?'

'She is still lying down in Nurse Webb's care. Still fully dressed, may I add, and still insisting on wearing her cap. An unusual woman, I feel. Very . . . intense? Nine living children and more miscarried or stillborn. Two dying in infancy.'

'Oh, the poor soul!' I exclaimed. 'What a dreadful burden to bear.'

'And what a husband to inflict more on her,' Bea said tartly.

'How did you find out? I've hardly heard her speak.'

'She let drop some of the information when Bea and I talked to her yesterday evening.'

'Nothing about the miscarriages, though,' Bea said, shaking her head in sympathy. 'Or the dead children.'

'I suspect the answer to any and all of her illnesses – she

spoke more to Nurse Webb, in strict confidence – would be a year's sojourn in a spa in Switzerland.'

'While her husband is safely still busy in England,' Bea concluded for him.

Whatever the cause of her illness, Mrs Marchbanks was back in the library the following morning. Although Matthew had offered to take my place, we both felt that a woman should be present should she be taken ill again. She and her husband worked well, I had to admit, listing sheep and goats of the book world. Once again, I feigned interest in my book. At eleven o'clock, we adjourned to the muniment room.

As Luke poured our coffee, Primrose appeared at the door, clearly agitated.

I joined her in the corridor, closing the door behind me.

'Seems another picture is likely to fall down, ma'am, George says to tell you. Found it while he was checking, he did. On the blue landing. Yes, ma'am,' she said, as my eyebrows shot up. 'Seeing as it's so close to the Family wing, George did wonder if his lordship might have . . . But Nurse Webb says he's not got out for a month or more. The men at the door say the same, ma'am. And George wants to know what he should do – mending it apart, that is.'

'Thank George very much. Yes, he should replace the cord.'

'Please, ma'am, maybe with wire or a chain?'

'That's a good idea. And ask him to use the strongest stuff he can to replace any other damaged cords.'

'And to keep the old ones and show you, ma'am?'

'Absolutely. Before you dash off, Primrose, I know Milly is back at work – you will tell me if . . . if she tries to do too much?'

'Or if anyone tells her to?' she said, with a knowing look.

'Thank you, Primrose.'

She knew she had gone too far. 'Sorry, ma'am.' A quick curtsy and she was gone.

'It is really most inconvenient, Mrs Rowsley, to have to wait for you to finish conversations with menials before we can start our work.'

I allowed my eyes to drop to the half-drunk cup of coffee in his right hand and the biscuit in his left.

'Indeed it must be,' I agreed, shamelessly drinking my own coffee but – corset in mind – eschewing a biscuit. 'But it gives you an opportunity to reflect on your work so far and tell me what – if any – treasures you have found. You suspected his late lordship was optimistic in his appraisal of the library. Are your fears justified?'

To my amazement, he shook his head. 'Not entirely. There is dross – no doubt about that. But there is a fair collection of first editions – nothing of national worth, I fear, but worth keeping together for future generations. I have yet to inspect the volumes behind the grilles, of course.'

'Why do I not unlock one section now? I will tell my colleagues I don't wish to be interrupted so we may enjoy the sight of *Parlement of Foules* together.'

He remembered he should be cool and critical. 'There are several in the Bodleian.'

'Of course. So you know how exciting it is to hold a copy in your hand. Yes, his lordship insisted on gloves. They are in the desk drawer. And there is a bookrest on that shelf there.' I pointed.

He bore it from the muniment room into the library as if it were a chalice. I followed, making it clear to Luke that Thatcher and he must sort out any sort of problem without me.

'I'm surprised you don't lock us in,' Mrs Marchbanks said.

Was she being ironic? Or simply aware of the potential value of the book? Whichever it was, I was so astonished I almost dropped the grille key. The lock opened sweetly. But the books were so closely packed that the covers had stuck together. I dared not pull an individual volume lest I tear a spine. Had they always been like this? I rubbed my forehead in anxiety but then recalled that his lordship had had the book on the stand on his desk when he had shown it to me.

We stood in silence. At last, donning gloves myself and passing them to the others, I reached for a ruler from the desk and slid it, inch by inch, under the books – a whole row of them. Little by little, I could then ease it under a volume. No. Several rose together. But deftly Mrs Marchbanks slipped her hand under them, spreading her fingers to support all five. Then her husband reached over them, finally pushing gently to ease them on to her hand. At last, the precious pile lay on the desk. There was a gasp: I suspect none of us had breathed during the whole operation.

We inhaled the smell of old dust and older leather. Gingerly, I separated the books.

'There.' I laid the Chaucer on the bookrest.

The professor opened it reverently. 'Caxton. 1478.' In silence, he turned the precious pages. 'A holy grail of scholarship,' he breathed at last. 'Printed very much later than it was written, of course. Mrs Rowsley, this deserves—' He broke off, looking up as there was a faint sound. A book had fallen sideways into the vacant space on the shelf, quickly followed by two or three others – ancient volumes even I had never handled.

'Dear me!' If I was prone to genuine fainting fits, I would certainly have passed out now. Those treasures! I gasped. 'My God! If one had fallen to the floor!'

'But none did.' He smiled at me with something like charm. It was as if a hitherto disappointing student had suddenly produced an excellent answer and had gone up in his estimation.

'Clarissa, my love,' he said, over his shoulder, 'if you would be so kind . . . Thank you.' He turned back to me. 'These appear to be in no order whatsoever – graded only by size, perhaps!' He tutted, shaking his head.

'Indeed. And it shows why your expertise is so vital, Professor. The books have never been arranged in any sort of logical order. It was something his late lordship always meant to do one day – then his health failed, and he felt enjoying his treasures was more important than organizing them, which, as you can see, is going to be a monumental task.'

He smiled. 'Let us begin by packing this in the case of books we will take back to Oxford. I presume you have packing cases?'

'The House has enough tea-chests to transport the entire contents of this library and other rooms. But for the time being, remember, all we can do is prepare a list of books which should be on public display or available to scholars. Those you think are beyond price can be moved, if you advise it, to a safe until the trustees, and Mr Wilson in particular, agree to their leaving here. Shall I make a list or do you and Mrs Marchbanks prefer to keep your own records? They could certainly be far more informative, even if you had to go to the trouble of writing them in language accessible to non-experts.'

Mrs Marchbanks fainted. She lay like a dry Ophelia, carried away on a tide of history.

What should I do? Leaving her husband to deal with her, I gathered up the Chaucer and other volumes and locked them back in their places.

'To put the safety of books before the health of a human being! Before that of my own dear wife!' the professor exploded. 'Are you a sentient being, Mrs Rowsley? Have you never heard of the milk of human kindness?' He looked me up and down. Any recognition that I might be an intelligent person evaporated. 'A barren woman, of course. *The barren womb, the land never satisfied with water, and the fire that never says, "Enough."*'

Somehow I had to keep my temper. He, after all, was so busy losing his that he ignored the still prostrate heap beside whom I was now able to kneel unimpeded. Just as he had ignored her illness last night. 'Pass me my reticule, if you please, Professor – I have smelling salts in there. Thank you. Please call a servant and summon help.' I removed her spectacles and put them in her reticule, which he snatched from me.

'How dare—' He bristled, his legs wide apart and braced, so much like a hedgehog bracing itself for a fight that I nearly disgraced myself further by laughing. When I ignored him, he thrust the reticule at me and strode out.

Mrs Marchbanks' pulse was still as strong and regular as Ellis had reminded me mine had been when once I faked a swoon. Her colour was good. Even now, she was flinching from the smelling salts.

Mrs Briggs was first on the scene, wringing her hands in horror. Thinking they could be put to more practical use, I set her to chaff Mrs Marchbanks. I also retrieved my reticule from the floor, locking it in a desk drawer.

Mrs Marchbanks' revival was swift. It was watched by a

gathering of anxious tweenies, through whom the professor had to push.

Mrs Briggs suggested our patient needed to rest, and offered, with Primrose's help, to assist her to her bedchamber.

'A pattern card amongst women,' the professor observed, as he swept out of the room behind them.

Which one of them was not clear and I could not find it in me to ask.

NINE

I arrived to find a pale-looking Harriet at the al fresco luncheon near the remains and Francis in a full-blown argument with Dr Wells.

'On this site – on any of my sites – I do not permit spoil-heaps,' Francis was saying, pointing at a large pile of newly dug earth. 'Everything, I repeat everything, small or large, must be logged, and a record kept of where it was found.'

'What nonsense! We are excavating a Roman building, a very large one. Clearly a fort.'

'From the shape of it, it's a grand villa. Very grand.'

'Sir, I have worked in Rome itself, where I can assure you they do not indulge this nit-picking practice that you advocate. You, sir, are an amateur. You play around with your photographic apparatus. You waste people's time with agricultural riddles, as if they will reveal the next wall.'

For a moment, I stared: how on earth might word-games be involved? But then I saw what looked like some of Farmer Twiss's giant sieves.

'They may not reveal the next wall, but they might just help reveal the purpose of that wall.'

'Heavens, man, you'll be enacting Pyramus and Thisbe next. And I tell you this is – further to quote the play – Moonshine.'

'You do not think that finding a strigil helped identify the bathhouse?'

'It was clearly a bathhouse simply from its position in the ruins.'

'Only if it was a villa, not a fort.' Francis jabbed home the point with a furious finger.

Harriet chuckled quietly. 'Professor Fielding warned me about scholars' tiffs. Let's ask Dick to sound his gong. Oh.' She stared as the Marchbankses appeared.

Francis excused himself from further bickering to greet them.

The professor was as full of the morning's work as if he had discovered all by himself the Chaucer he especially rhapsodized about and indeed the other ancient volumes, so full I was not surprised when his wife drifted off, wandering amongst the ditches and banks of detritus, where she spoke briefly first to Head, then to Fielding. As he drifted away, politely doffing his hat, she explored in solitude, something probably missing in her everyday life, after all. Some men were kicking a football on an as yet unexplored corner of the site; other men simply lounged under the trees, where last night's drizzle hadn't penetrated. Joe Sprue sat a little apart, whittling a piece of wood.

Detaching us deftly from Marchbanks whom he foisted on Wells, Francis surveyed them benignly. 'They're entitled to a break. Some of the work is sheer hard labour, some is finicky and some demands both skill and strength. I wish some of my scholarly colleagues might indulge in something similar – surely, Harriet, you could organize an impromptu game of cricket.'

Her smile was perfunctory at best. Francis and I exchanged a worried glance. But she said with something like her usual positivity, 'If it is fine tomorrow, I'm sure I could. But it will be at your own risk. Hard things, cricket balls, and fragile things, Roman artefacts.'

'Indeed. Let us raise a glass to the weather! How fortunate that this is in a separate ice-bucket from the rest,' he declared, producing from under the deep linen tablecloth a bottle of Chablis. 'Oh, from his lordship's cellar, of course,' Francis admitted cheerfully. 'Thatcher's choice. If I did not love you so much, Harriet, I would try to poach him.'

'It would be pistols at dawn if you tried,' I declared, accepting a glass and toasting them both. Only one response was enthusiastic. 'And any judge in the land would spare me if he knew the reason for my challenge.' I caught his eye: which of us should try to discover what had so disturbed Harriet?

His response was to tuck her hand under his arm and lead her towards the ruins. I decided that mine was to attack from a different angle as it were, to speak to the man with whom she had spent the morning.

His beard aflame in the bright sun, Wells accosted me as I casually drifted towards him and Marchbanks. 'These trustees,

Rowsley. Professor Marchbanks says they wield an enormous amount of power. Surely you have ways of getting around their strange demands. *Sign for that. List this.* It reduces us, who handle priceless objects every day – yes, like that Chaucer Marchbanks tells me he has discovered – to the level of mere tradesmen, as if we were delivering your groceries!'

'Please understand that this applies to everyone – every quarter, I must submit the estate accounts to be approved by the Family's lawyer. Equally, Thatcher, my wife and Mrs Arden have regularly to present the household figures.'

His lip curled. 'But we, sir, are gentlemen, whose word is our bond.'

Marchbanks nodded. 'And we are held in thrall to those who know nothing of what we do!'

'May I correct you, gentlemen? You merely have to explain what you are doing to a group of intelligent men and women who individually have no powers, but as a group have voluntarily undertaken a great deal of work to protect the legacy of Lord Croft, his ailing son and the heir who is yet to be discovered. I think our Lord tells of good servants, who toil on behalf of a sometimes imperfect master.'

'I cannot understand why you do not open your chapel,' Marchbanks said pettishly, perhaps recognizing my intransigence. 'Or why your rector acquiesces in your decision.'

'I believe I explained on your first evening here, Professor. We are trustees—'

'*We!*' Marchbanks repeated in outrage.

Wells joined in. 'So *you* are one of them!'

'Indeed I am, and honoured to be one, too. We are obliged by law to husband other people's resources as if they were our own. We are to maintain the House and the estate, to invest in the new village, to pay all the employees.'

'Of which you are one. Your wife too, no doubt.'

At any moment, my rising temper would get the better of me. 'Indeed. She was appointed personally by her late ladyship and remains in post since she knows more about the House than anyone, including me and the butler.'

'The butler! That whippersnapper! Wells, he was the one I spoke of. Thank goodness your housekeeper has more sense.

She was very good with dear Clarissa this morning, too – tending her while that wife of yours locked up books.' Disdain dripped from his voice.

'Including one you yourself have just described as priceless. But now, gentlemen, the work I am paid to do calls me. Pray, excuse me.' I bowed and turned towards the House, pausing only to tell Thatcher where I was going.

With a grave smile, he relieved me of the glass I was still carrying. I stared at it stupidly as I thanked him.

To my surprise, I was interrupted before I even had time to open the ledger I needed to work on.

'My dear Pounceman!' I got up to shake his hand. Today I was glad of any ally, even an unlikely one. 'Is all well? Please sit down. May I offer you tea? Or something a little stronger?' I rang.

He sank on to a chair. 'Some brandy would not come amiss. Thank you.'

Luke nodded, immediately adjusting his usually cheery face to the apparent solemnity of the occasion. We sat in silence until he returned with decanters and glasses, one of which he passed to our guest. 'And you, sir?'

'No, thank you,' I said. The brandy smelt good but it would far from calm my bubbling anger. Luke bowed himself out. 'I collect you are not here to bring good news?'

He shook his head. 'It was a very hard deathbed. Very hard. Poor Mrs Gornal fought to the last. But her pain, Rowsley. Her pain. Doctor Page did his best. But she . . . To see a good, devout woman push away the sacrament she has always taken so gratefully, so respectfully . . .' He covered his face with his hands. 'Imagine, to live all your life in decent, quiet faith – and at the last moment to lose it!' He collapsed into silence.

To ease the tension between us – he seemed embarrassed to have revealed so much emotion – I suggested that we look at the chapel. The key had turned disconcertingly easily in the lock, and the doors had swung open with nothing of the Gothic creak the interior might have demanded. Here, all was dust and decay, with enormous cobwebs high on the vaulted ceiling. Pounceman looked around us, shaking his head.

'Shades of Mrs Edgeworth!' he said with a surprising mock-shudder. 'I'd forgotten how it had been allowed to go to rack and ruin. Don't I dimly remember paintings hanging on those walls?'

'I should imagine so. When I was doing a preliminary inspection for his lordship—'

'Even in the first flush of his inheritance, I fear he will not have been interested – come, Rowsley, it was you who initiated the inspection, was it not?' To my surprise, he was laughing.

'Guilty as charged! I found several paintings stacked against the pulpit. I knew they would be at risk from damp, and indeed mice, so I asked her late ladyship if they might be removed and stored where they were less at risk. She chose several to hang in the corridor outside – I'll point them out when we leave.'

'I hope and pray that when the new village has been built and all the other maintenance work done – you mentioned chimney repairs a few weeks ago? – there will be enough money to at least clean this space properly.' Bowing his head as he walked towards the altar, he mounted the pulpit steps and recited the twenty-third Psalm.

'The acoustics are excellent,' I said as he joined me again. 'One thing puzzles me, however. We keep the place locked, yet someone must have been here – see how clean the floor is.' I bent and ran a finger over the tiles, showing him the clean tip.

'However does Mrs Rowsley's team find time to sweep some-where no one goes? Whenever I am here, I see no one at rest, every last servant doing something. Even learning to read,' he added with a smile.

'Harriet is so grateful for your help; I think there's some competition between her pupils and yours to see who can become proficient most quickly,' I said. 'And it's clear that some of the young men feel more comfortable being taught by another male, especially one with such standing in the village. But it's true the servants have to work very hard when we have guests. Normally, we could bring in extra from the village, but with the hay harvest due . . . Of course, we trustees did agree, did we not, that until Mr Wilson scented another possible heir, not all the staff who left should be replaced.'

'Yes. Indeed, I voted for the motion. But I realize now that many families round here depend on their older children finding work that pays better than toiling in the fields. I was pleased to suggest to that fierce antiquarian – Wells? – several women who would love to undertake the work he wanted your wife to do. I also recommended an appropriate rate of pay.'

Truly, our rector had had the modern-day equivalent of a road-to-Damascus moment. But now he was focused on other things, not least the dirt and the dustsheets in front of him. Shaking his head, he said, 'I still believe we trustees made the right decision to leave the restoration here until the village people were rehoused.' He spread his hands. 'Undoing all this damage and making good the fabric will take years, will it not? And be so very expensive. All those niches should have statues. Was it Henry or Cromwell's influence that had them removed? I suppose we will never know – not unless Professor Marchbanks has time to unearth this part of the past.' He looked at me sideways. 'How does Mrs Rowsley deal with all his demands?'

'With her usual patience. As you know, we hope to appoint a deputy to help her with the day-to-day running of the House. One is on a month's trial now. A Mrs Briggs. Then, if we do not suit each other, a Mrs Rose.'

'Suit each other?' he repeated doubtfully.

'Indeed. If she does not find our ways accord with her ways, then she has as much right to walk away as we have to ask her to leave.' I broke off. Surely I could not hear movement? But as Pounceman gave no sign of having heard anything, I continued, 'Trust in a place like this is more important than anything else, I believe. We have trusted Thatcher for months, ever since poor Samuel was taken ill, and he has never let us down. But he and Mrs Briggs . . . do not always see eye to eye.'

'Thatcher is growing into a fine young man. I believe he spends a good deal of time with his predecessor, Mr Bowman.'

'As do you. I know he values your reading from the Bible and your prayers.'

'And I have come to value his simple honesty, Matthew.'

On impulse, I said, 'I know that this place needs to be recon-secrated, but I would still be grateful if you offered a prayer here.'

We knelt together, on the clean tiles. In the silence at the end of the Lord's Prayer, this time we both heard a noise.

'Mice, perhaps. Or rats,' he suggested with a shudder. 'Might I suggest we adjourn elsewhere?'

He heaved an audible sigh of relief as we stepped into the corridor.

I sensed – did not see, did not hear – something moving. I threw myself on top of him. And knew no . . .

TEN

After a few minutes in conversation with Professor Head, Mrs Marchbanks was dawdling back to her husband; any moment, they would wish to return to their work in the library. It was time for me to quit the warm sun and the frivolous company of Francis.

I bade him the casual farewell of one old friend to another, expecting the same in return. Instead, he chose to fall into step beside me.

'You may think you got away with it, but both Matthew and I know that someone or something has upset you. Seriously upset you.' He tucked my arm under his. 'And I would like to know who or what it is. Dear me, Head doesn't mean to join us, does he? Let us go via the woodland walk. That will confuse him. Oh, and here comes Wells, too!'

Professor Head bustled off back to the House, nodding not very cordially to Dr Wells as their paths crossed.

'You know what our experts will demand next? That you build splendid new lavatories outside to match the bathrooms indoors. They are such an improvement, are they not?'

We entered the shade of the woods.

'Has one of them been patronizing you again? Or worse? Harriet, what has Marchbanks been saying now?' He stopped and took my face between his hands. Suddenly, I was crying into his shoulder as I would never have done with Matthew.

'He threw my . . . my childlessness in my face.'

'Why should that worry you? Many of us are childless – there will be none springing from my loins, and no one judges me for that. Do they?' He shook me gently.

'But you're a gentleman, and I am a mere woman. He managed to turn my–my barrenness into an insult!'

I explained about his wife's swoon. 'Mrs Briggs sailed in like a ministering angel, you see, while I was gathering up books – and yes, I was locking them away.'

'Just in case!' he said, hugging me and pushing me gently upright. 'It was your absolute duty to protect them. Heavens, if one of the servants had trodden on one! Think of the fuss he'd have kicked up then.' He produced an immaculate linen handkerchief. 'When he proposed, Matthew knew full well that you could not bear his children. Has he for one moment ever repined? It is you he loves. You. Not your capacity for adding to the human race.'

'My head tells me that. Ninety-nine per cent of my heart tells me that. But being childless, being barren, is – it's like a biblical curse!'

'Yes, an Old Testament one. There were some particularly nasty people around then, weren't there? As for modern nine-teenth-century families, people can't distinguish between quality and quantity, can they? As far as I can see, poor Mrs M is little better than a brood mare to his ill-favoured stallion.'

'You have some decidedly disreputable opinions, Francis,' I said, unable not to laugh.

'I shall take that as a compliment. Now, the Marchbankses apart, is all well?'

'Apart from the person who is trying to kill a tweeny or two,' I said, with a grim laugh, as we resumed our walk. 'The cords suspending some of the pictures have been damaged. When young Milly dusted one yesterday, it fell on her head. A nasty blow. And George reports similar damage to other pictures.'

'Pictures? Why? Come, you must have a theory! In another world, my dear little sister, you would have been a police officer.'

'What, blue serge and all?'

'Ah, a decided minus to my theory. Very well. Home Secretary. One day, women will get the vote. And maybe they will become police officers. And lawyers.' He gripped his lapels as if he were in court interrogating a witness. 'Your theory, Mrs Rowsley, if you please!'

'His late lordship was never a soldier, but he was interested in what Roman writers had to say about warcraft. Someone called Vitruvius? And Julius Caesar. And I think he would ask me whether the damage was a distraction from something more important or a skirmish for its own sake.'

'And your answer would be?'

'I wish I knew. But there seems to be a campaign. I want to dismiss it as trivial, but I can't. And unless I get rid of all our guests – yes, you excepted – and dismiss Mrs Briggs, leaving just people I would trust with my life, I don't see it ending. Do you?'

'You fear someone will get more than a glancing blow?'

'The painting and its frame, of course, that hurt Milly were fairly small. Imagine what a Van Dyck might do. George is going around the House replacing cords with wire or with chains, but it will take him a long time. Thatcher is making regular inspections of rooms or corridors in regular use. I can't assist myself because I have to be closeted with the Marchbankses or they can't have access to the library. And you and Matthew apart, who else could inspect the pictures? You have your work cut out to keep your motley crew working as a team; Matthew has the estate to run. Even as we speak, he's wrestling with a tenant's financial problems.'

'This ministering angel – Mrs Briggs? Ah, what have I said? You didn't like her ministering role?'

'I didn't like the way she overruled Thatcher and Nurse Webb.' I explained. 'By doing that, she undercut my authority, too. In truth, I feel she would be better suited to a more conventional establishment.'

'It sounds as if, in your head, you are already writing a reference for her!'

'Perhaps I am. Indeed, I would far rather write one for her than for Dick. As you can imagine, there is little love lost between them. I saw at Matthew's cousin's home how things can go wrong when butler and housekeeper can't work together; it mustn't happen here.'

'So we are at an impasse – until a flying portrait smashes priceless porcelain or, even worse, someone's head?'

'Heaven forbid! I shall ban dusting pictures. No! I shall ask *Mrs Briggs* to ban dusting pictures until each one has been rehung. At dinner tonight, Matthew can ask everyone to keep well away from them. But you, Francis – what would you do?'

'I would do what I always do – pick your brains, Harriet!'

We strolled toward the House, still laughing.

But here was Thatcher, running to meet us. One glance at his white face silenced us. 'Mrs Rowsley – you're wanted in the Family wing. There's been an accident. Another picture cord cut. Doctor Page is on his way!'

Francis seized my hand and ran. Beyond that – how did I reach there? I had no idea. All I knew was that Matthew, head bandaged, eyes closed, hands clasped on his chest, lay flat on a bed. Mr Pounceman was on his knees beside him, praying aloud.

My ears roared. Yellow clouds swamped my eyes. And . . .

There was the sound of Ellis Page's laughter. The smell of ammonia. And – dear God, was this some miracle! – this was Matthew leaning over me.

'You're alive,' I managed.

'I'm alive. And so are you.'

We clasped hands.

'No, stay where you are. You didn't feign that swoon, Harriet, did you? So you should lie flat a little longer,' Ellis said, kneeling and taking my pulse. 'Then you and Matthew will return to your room for a calming rest and a nice cup of tea.'

'I thought you were dead.' I sobbed the words out. 'I thought he was dead, Ellis. Dead. With Mr Pounceman praying for him.'

'Indeed, I was.' Mr Pounceman seemed to be on his knees beside me now. 'I was thanking God for Matthew's swift actions, which saved my life, apart from a cut and a big bruise.' Automatically, perhaps, he touched it and flinched. 'And he was relatively unscathed himself. And he joined in those prayers.'

'With his eyes closed and his hands clasped upon his chest. Just like a knight on a medieval tomb,' Nurse Webb confirmed with the touch of asperity she always brought to a conversation about religion. 'May I suggest, Doctor Page, that you all adjourn to a more congenial spot than my emergency ward' – she shot me a gleam of a smile – 'just in case.'

Thatcher brought us tea in our rather crowded private sitting room himself, as if trusting no one else to act with suitable dignity. But emotion overcame him as he lowered the tray to the table. 'Matt – Mr Rowsley, sir: we all thought you were dead.'

Matthew rose a mite unsteadily and grasped both the young man's hands. 'In this room, Dick, we are happy to be Matthew and Harriet. Do you know, I feared we'd lost Harriet – she fainted clean away when she saw my bandage.'

'Mr Rowsley saved my life, Mr Thatcher.' That was the nearest Mr Pounceman could get to informality. But his voice too shook with emotion.

Ellis gave another snort of laughter. But I wondered if he was actually disguising uncomfortable feelings. 'We must all thank God that Matthew has such a thick skull. Thank you.' He took his tea from Dick's still-shaking hands, as did the other men.

On impulse, I stood, to hold Dick close for a moment – and why not? He and his colleagues – my colleagues – might not be my children but they were my family.

Soon he decorously withdrew. But he returned with Luke behind him before our conversation could settle into rational discussion.

'In honour of the occasion, sir, ma'am,' he declared, producing champagne.

ELEVEN

At last, all was as calm as an afternoon could be after an unexpected glass of champagne, Page permitting Pounceman and me just the tiniest amount.

Turning to me, Harriet said as evenly as if she had never fallen into that terrifying swoon, 'So far, you have all kindly spared me the details of this afternoon. Where were you? And who or what was it that hit you?'

'In the chapel corridor. Yes,' I responded to her questioning eyebrows, 'we had just been into the chapel to see how much work it would take to restore it.'

'I fear it would be a great deal – with commensurate expense. So much dirt. So much damage,' Pounceman said with the sort of regretful sigh that a man would make as he waved farewell to a pet project.

I clutched my head. 'We were aware of two strange things. The floor was clean.'

Harriet stared in disbelief. 'Clean? Swept or—?'

'Swept and then mopped, I would say,' I said. 'And a credit to the House team.'

'Indeed,' Pounceman agreed.

'But a House team not led by you, I would say, judging by the expression on your face.'

'Oh dear! Mrs Briggs! I told her we kept it locked. I told her that the masonry might be unsafe. I told her that the staff had quite enough to do to ensure the guests were well served.' She took a deep breath. 'You said there were two strange things.'

'The other might not be strange at all, Mrs Rowsley. We heard what we thought might be rodents. That's why we left – I am afraid that though we are supposed to love all God's creatures, I find it hard to find any affection for rats.' He shuddered convincingly. 'It occurs to me now it might have been human feet we heard, after all. Anyway, we left – Rowsley, I fear we did not lock up!'

64 Judith Cutler

I rang. 'We had other things on our minds at the time.' I broke off to speak to the duty footman, who undertook to make sure the chapel was completely empty before he locked it. 'Go with a colleague,' I added. 'Just in case.'

The lad grinned at Harriet and bowed his way out.

'You had other things on your mind,' Harriet prompted.

'Indeed. And, in fact, on my head. The Bellini *Madonna and Child*.'

'Heavens! That's supposed to be one of the finest paintings in the House!' Page gasped.

'Quite. Far more precious than the fubsy-faced Lely that struck poor Milly – more precious in every way,' I said. 'But I think the only damage to it is a little of my blood on the frame.'

'A good deal of your blood,' Pounceman corrected me. 'Which but for your quick thinking would have been mine.' He touched his head. 'Thank you. And thank God you were not more seriously harmed.'

Page's eyes narrowed briefly as he registered Pounceman's movement. His 'Amen' was perhaps more perfunctory than the others'. 'This has happened before?'

'Someone is damaging a lot of the cords supporting the masterpieces hanging on the House walls,' I said. 'We have no idea who. Or why.'

'Is it,' Harriet said, 'part of a larger campaign? Or is it something to divert us from something?' Realizing that Pounceman and even Page were gaping, she added dryly, 'That was what Francis and I were wondering. Francis and I were having a discussion at about the time you two were being struck down.'

'Palmer is a classics scholar?' Pounceman asked approvingly, as if he was now prepared to forgive him much.

'His late lordship was,' she said quietly.

'Ah! No wonder your questions are so very pertinent,' he said with the sort of kindness he probably praised Sunday school children. Surely he had known Harriet long enough to realize that she would resent being patronized, even, perhaps especially, unintentionally.

Page certainly did, and he jumped in. 'I suppose one way of working out the answer would be a further question: is there any connection between the paintings that were used as – well, as weapons?'

I shook my head. 'School of Lely and Bellini? I can't imagine so.'

'Both women,' Harriet murmured, adding more loudly, 'George will have prepared a list of the ones he had to rehang.' She rang. 'I'll send for it. Actually, for him, not just his list – he will have a good idea of what was used to cut the cords. I should have asked before but I have been tied up in the library, of course.' She clapped a hand over her mouth. 'Dear me, the Marchbankses! They're still locked out. At least, I hope so.'

'I'll go and see,' I said, standing up briskly but finding I needed to stand still for a moment.

'My dear Rowsley,' Page said, 'you may have a thick skull, but not so thick that a bang like that can be shrugged off. It may be a week before you are your usual energetic self. Harriet, too. She has had a bad shock to the system. A lesser woman would have taken to her bed.'

Instead, she too was on her feet, ringing the bell, reaching for paper from the tiny desk and writing. When Luke responded, she passed him a note. 'For Professor Marchbanks, wherever he may be. And could you ask George to come up, please? Thank you.' As the door closed, she sat down heavily, so pale I feared she would faint again.

Page reached for her wrist, saying meaningfully, 'Surely someone else can take command for a bit?'

I spread my hands. 'Who? Bea is the obvious answer, and she would do it very well indeed – but with a house full of guests?'

There was silence.

It was broken by a knock at the door. Luke with George who brought to the genteel little gathering the smells of glue, sawdust and varnish. The older man looked around, wiping his hands on his trousers and looking not unreasonably disconcerted. 'And, Luke, could you ask all of our colleagues to gather before supper tonight at half past six? Everyone, whatever they ought to be doing. Five minutes, no more. Thank you.' She turned to George with an apologetic smile. 'I'm so sorry. That was very urgent business. But this is, too.' She sat, folding her hands in her lap.

It seemed I was the one to question him. 'I wonder if you kept a list of all the pictures with damaged cords,' I began.

He wrinkled his nose. 'I got a list of all the rooms they were in, and I could point them out to you easy as winking. But some of those names, gaffer, they didn't make sense to me, so writing them down was a bit of a puzzle. As you can see,' he added apologetically as he handed over several sheets of paper.

He had done his best, no doubt about it. I could make some pretty good guesses. As far as I could see, however, there was little to connect them. Royalty and peasant alike had all risked a tumble. I passed the list to Harriet, who reached for her reading glasses.

'George, did you notice anything in common with the pictures?'

'Lots of them wenches. Ladies. But then most of the pictures seem to be of ladies, one way or another, don't they?'

She nodded, adding with a grin, 'Some wearing fancy clothes, some wearing very little at all! But I wonder if there's anything else. Their position on the wall, for instance.'

You could almost see George visualizing each room – he had an extraordinary gift for remembering details of where things were, or where they should be. He smiled slowly. 'They'd be low enough for a man to reach without steps or anything.' He demonstrated. 'He'd have to be an inch or two taller than me, maybe – but then, when God gave out long legs, I wasn't in the queue,' he cackled. 'You'd do it easy enough,' he told me.

Page got to his feet. 'Forgive me, but I promised I would look in on Mrs Berry. May I offer you a place in my gig, Rector? You've had a nasty shock. Though I know you've taken to striding around the village, *your* legs may not feel like walking home today.'

'That would be very kind. I will pray for both of you,' he said, smiling from Harriet to me. 'And wish you joy in your task of locating a tall villain – heavens, there's hardly a short man in the building at the moment. No, don't ring. Page and I can claim the privilege of old acquaintances and make our own way out.'

'And I hope you can both find your way back this evening for dinner,' Harriet said as first one man then the other kissed her hand and shook mine.

And so we were free to explore – slowly – with George.

We stood outside the impressive chapel doors, looking at the Bellini, now propped against the wall.

Harriet shuddered, clasping my hand. 'How did that not kill you?'

George took the question literally. 'See that slice there in the cord? And think about chopping down a tree. You make a V-shaped cut – and that's the way your tree will fall. I reckon it's the same with pictures. But they're not necessarily as predictable as trees. And I'd say, to be frank, you had luck on your side. Or maybe it was you trying to save the rector.'

'Or the prayers we'd just said inside the chapel,' I said, not entirely joking.

'Mr Pounceman mentioned sounds as you were inside,' Harriet said. 'Could that have been someone hiding somewhere? You might have been followed – or just seen going in, providing an opportunity to stage this.' She gestured.

'And they hid behind this lot,' George said, patting an above-life-size statue of a man in Roman draperies disdaining a woman kneeling with one breast exposed near his extremely large feet. 'Weaken the cord. Lurk. Pop out and tug the frame. Splat.' He drove a fist into the palm of the other hand. He said slowly, 'What worries me, gaffer, is if someone took a knife to some of the pictures in the bedchambers. Could fetch you a nasty blow if you were lying flat in your bed.' But even as he voiced his fears, he raised a strong index finger. 'No, all the damage has been in public areas, and how indeed would anyone get into a private room? "Excuse me, ma'am, I've come to make sure that great ugly painting kills you in your sleep."'

We laughed obligingly. 'And you think a knife does the damage.'

'All the cords I've seen have had just one cut.' He mimed a sort of sideways slice.

Harriet nodded. 'I don't think a pair of scissors would have worked, would they? In any case, those we carry in our chatelaines or etuis are designed not for strength but for accuracy, delicacy even. I don't suppose you've had time to check on those you've rehung, George?'

'Just in case?' He nodded sagely. 'Mind you, Mrs Rowsley, ma'am, there's not many that'd carry a pair of wire-cutters with them. Or pliers, to tackle the chains.'

She had to admit the logic of that.

'So all we can do,' I said, suspecting we were getting nowhere, 'is, as we planned: to warn everyone to avoid getting too close to the works of art, wherever they are and, indeed, whatever they are. Thank you for your time, George – and if you want, get a couple of sound lads to help you. It would be good to get this dealt with before the hay harvest.'

'Yes, indeed. And with luck, everyone will help in the fields and they'll all be too tired for such tomfoolery as this,' he said, touching his forelock and getting ready to leave.

'Reddle!'

George stopped in his tracks, turning to gape at Harriet. 'My goodness, you're right, ma'am! I'll get some from Harry Shepherd and get those lads you suggested, sir, to help me with it!' And off he strode.

I merely gaped. 'What on earth were you two talking about?' I probably sounded tetchy.

'You recall that policeman down in Herefordshire who put reddle on a corpse so if anyone tried to steal from the body they would be caught literally red-handed?'

'Of course! So George will smear reddle on the picture cords and anyone trying to interfere will—'

'*May* get it on their hands or even their clothes.'

'Excellent. I had the feeling we were never going to get any closer to an explanation. I suppose,' I conceded. 'We learned that the perpetrator wasn't you, unless you've learned to carry a stool concealed in your petticoats,' I laughed as she reached vainly towards the replacement wire on an anonymous Pieta.

She made sheep's eyes at me. 'You can search me if you like – but perhaps not in this corridor.'

'Nothing would give me greater satisfaction. But not in this corridor,' I said with an attempt at a lascivious leer. *And not with this thumping headache.*

She looked at me with narrowed eyes. 'You're not well, are you? Let's abandon our inspection for now, and find some lavender water. I wonder if that bandage is too tight – let's talk to Nurse Webb. And then you will take to your bed.'

'How can I? I'm sure Nurse Webb will have some of her magic drops to hand. And I will be as right as rain. I promise.'

'You will. Because you will be spending the evening resting. Francis can host an all-male event tonight. Oh, drat. That wretched woman . . . Let me think . . .' But while she thought, she propelled me inexorably towards the stairs leading to the Family wing.

'I'm not asking you, Mr Rowsley; I'm telling you. No riding or strenuous exercise.'

'But the cricket match!'

Nurse Webb silenced me with a glance. 'No burning the midnight oil, either. You will retire to bed now. I can offer you one choice: a bed here in the Family wing or your own bed in your own room.' Her lands lightly crossed on her apron; she might have spoken fiercely but her smile was as benign as if she was talking to a child.

'Thank you for your advice,' I began stiffly, ready to ignore it. Then it occurred to me that there were very few things in the world that I wanted more than to rest my aching head. 'I think I would prefer my own bedchamber.'

'It will probably be quieter: this is usually the hour when poor Mr Fellows starts crying.'

I was dismissed.

Harriet forbore to speak.

'Of course I shall sit with you,' she said, as she tucked me up in bed.

'But who will host and look after our guests? Even you, my love, can't be in two places at once. Three places . . . I don't know,' I said pettishly.

'If I had been injured and came out with all those questions, what would you say to me?'

I managed a laugh. 'That no one is irreplaceable. That . . . I don't know . . . What would I say?'

'You would tell me not to worry. That for once you must be sensible. And that perhaps – perhaps you should send for Montgomery Wilson.' She beamed. 'And I would nod and say, "What a good idea." Thank goodness you need worry no more, my love. Luke took my note down to the village and sent a telegraph; one has come back. Mr Wilson is coming by the first train tomorrow.'

TWELVE

I stood in our sitting room wringing my hands and trying not to weep. It was one thing to be positive and practical in front of Matthew, another to maintain the pretence with my old friend. 'I simply don't know what else to do, Bea.'

'Involving Mr Wilson is a good idea. He can face down any queries or complaints about us trustees. I reckon even Professor Marchbanks will quail under that stare of his.'

'I hope so. Meanwhile, there's Mrs Marchbanks and the question of chaperoning her, especially this evening. Whatever I suggest she does is going to be wrong or insulting. Will she join you with the gentlemen? I can't inflict her on you on your own. I can't tell her to retire to her room and read a book of sermons. What would you do?'

She put her hands on my shoulders. 'Nothing, I'd say. I will talk to everyone in the servants' hall so that you don't have to. In your place, I would go into dinner as usual – I'll send Milly up to help you change, unless you plan to go as you are? Yes, why not? – and tell everyone the news about Matthew and explain that although you would love to carry out your duties as hostess, you have a yet greater duty to care for your injured husband.'

'And can we trust that Marchbanks doesn't point out that we have professional nurses in the building?'

She snapped her fingers. 'You dab your eyes. I'm sure Francis will join in the conversation and shoo you away – you know his style – and he can deal with Mrs M. Or Ellis and I will if she tries one of those so-called fainting fits.'

We shared a laugh. 'Bea, it's been a long day for all of us, hasn't it?' I began.

'It has, indeed. So I shall tell the kitchen staff to send the food up promptly to prevent the guests from lingering. I might go and sit with Mrs Briggs for a bit after dinner while Ellis visits Matthew. I thought it would be interesting to see what she makes of all the goings-on. I suspect all this isn't what she expects in a well-regulated house.' She gave a conspiratorial wink. 'Perhaps she will hand in her notice to save you the trouble of asking her to leave.'

I pulled a face. 'We need her! As an extra pair of hands if nothing more.' But then I thought of the clean chapel floor. 'Or does she make work where there needn't be?'

'Worry about that tomorrow. At the moment, your place is with Matthew.' She hugged me and let herself out.

Francis appeared next, flourishing a bunch of garden flowers already in a vase. 'Cut and arranged by my own fair hand!'

'Thank you. I'll add you to the flower rota, shall I? Francis, this is what Bea suggests for this evening . . .' I gave a brief outline.

'What excellent ideas. And after dinner, surely one of the assembled academics and clergy can work out ways of entertaining Mrs M without offending her sensibilities.' His eyes twinkled. 'We could resume our Shakespearean readings: she might be Octavia or Calpurnia – one of those tedious virtuous women. Or Lady Macbeth . . . No! She is destined to be Cleopatra!'

'Wait till tomorrow when she can play opposite Mr Wilson,' I said, feeling guilty to be laughing while Matthew was ill. 'Meanwhile . . .' I gestured towards our bedchamber.

'Of course. Look after him well, little sister, and look after yourself, too – content in the knowledge that everything is in my hands.'

My announcement and plea that everyone else should avoid a similar fate to Matthew's by staying away from paintings that had yet to be rehung were greeted with first a stunned silence and then a barrage of questions.

I raised a hand. 'Tomorrow we will be joined by the Family's lawyer, Mr Wilson. I hope to be in a position to welcome him formally to our gathering, so I hope that you will understand if I invite you all to join us for luncheon here, not at the Roman site.'

Again there was a rumble of conversation.

Now Francis stood. 'My dear friend Matthew lies unconscious.

Please do not think to keep Harriet here a moment longer. Shoo, my dear, shoo.'

Luke and Dick opened the double-doors for me with a flourish and a smile apiece. And I could be back by Matthew's side.

'You're awake, my love! I thought I would find you asleep!'

'Nurse Webb came and woke me up. She says that rest is not the same as sleep, and some consider that it is better, with a head injury, to stay awake. So I lie here obeying her.' His smile was decidedly less strained. 'And I might obey her in something else. She recommends a little soup, if Bea made any today.'

'Don't sound so plaintive. You know she makes it every day.' I kissed his forehead, which was reassuringly cool. 'If I read aloud to you, would that be restful or soporific?'

'*Empedocles on Etna* would have me snoring in thirty seconds.'

'And the woman reading it . . . What about *The Woman in White*? The little of it I managed to read while I was observing the Marchbankses was exciting – no, it's not restful at all.'

There was a knock at the door. Dick entered, carrying a tray with legs, ideal for a meal in bed. 'Doctor Page, who has just arrived and promises to visit you later, agrees that you might indulge in a very light supper, sir.'

'So your medical advisors are as one,' I said. 'Perhaps there will be enough for me, too, Dick?'

His butler's bow was funereal but his eyes danced. 'Indeed, Doctor Page further observed that you must be fed, too. Young Tom is bringing up a folding table as we speak. I fear that Luke and I will be engaged with the guests but Tom will do his best to look after you both.'

'No, Harriet, you will not keep vigil while Matthew sleeps! The very idea! Bea has arranged for the bed in the dressing room to be made up for you. A trained nurse will watch in here all night. Not that I anticipate any worsening in Matthew's condition but – to use your words – just in case,' Ellis added with a kind smile. He continued in a much firmer tone, 'There is to be no argument. In fact, I advise you to take the very mild sleeping draught Nurse Holley has in her bag.'

The bag, which the young woman patted shyly, was enormous – larger than Ellis's own medical case. How on earth did she carry it? And what, apart from medicine, might it hold? 'It don't taste too bad, ma'am,' she said, her accent surely from Lancashire.

Despite her encouraging smile, I shook my head. 'No, thank you.'

Arms akimbo, Ellis sighed. 'If you don't sleep, who will run this establishment? All of it – because if I know you, you will try to take on Matthew's responsibilities as well as your own until I permit him to return to work. I know you are more accustomed these days to giving orders than taking them, but as your physician, I now tell you to look after yourself as you look after your staff. Do you understand?'

I nodded. The sleeping draught might find its way down the handsome new water closet across the corridor, but who would ever guess?

THIRTEEN

What was going on? Was Harriet in danger? I was too befuddled to understand. But I was out of bed before I knew it.

Nurse Holley was on her feet, I knew that – but what was she doing at the bedchamber door? The candlelight showed her pressing hard against it. I joined her.

'My knitting,' she whispered. 'One of the needles.'

What on earth did she want a knitting needle for? Then I realized. A boot between the door and the jamb: someone was determined to get in. Whoever it was was stronger than her – but not as heavy as me. I added my weight to the young nurse's, gesturing her to let me take over.

It took her but seconds to dash back to where she had been sitting and return, holding her knitting needle like a dagger to plunge into the booted foot. It would hurt even if it did not penetrate the leather.

There was a yelp.

The foot disappeared and at last we might shut the door. No key: we could not lock it. We had never thought of doing so. Although, for modesty's sake, there were bolts on dressing-room doors to prevent maids entering to find the occupant in a state of undress, this was a house that had relied for centuries on trust – and, as Francis reminded us from time to time, on dreadful punishments for people caught stealing.

Appearing from nowhere, Harriet seized a chair to jam under the handle. So far so good. Nurse Holley pointed: we were to move a chest of drawers to replace the chair. Panting, we stood looking at it and then at each other.

Nurse Holley was the first to speak. She had a very flat voice that suited the sudden bathos: 'At moments like this, I always find a nice cup of cocoa helps.' She left us staring open-mouthed at each other. Was Harriet laughing? Was she crying? I held her, not knowing if I was doing either or both myself. But the nurse was young and on her own, so like children, hand in hand, we joined her in the sitting room. With immense concentration, she was applying the bellows to the fire. Harriet and I lit candles. When the fire glowed to her satisfaction, she produced from her capacious bag a trivet, a small saucepan, milk in a screw-top jar, and two scraps of paper which turned out to conceal sugar and cocoa. As the milk warmed, she shook her head in apparent self-reproach. 'Only two mugs!'

Harriet rode to the rescue, of course. 'We always keep spare cups and saucers in this cupboard.' Her hair, gleaming in the soft light, fell forward as she bent. Despite her bravery and common sense, I wished Nurse Holley anywhere but here.

But soon we all sat together, Harriet and I now at last in our dressing gowns, in a bizarre parody of a picnic – for from that bag the nurse now produced biscuits. It was as if just fifteen minutes ago we had not apparently been fighting for . . . who knows what? Our lives? The thought seemed monstrous now.

'Now, Mr Rowsley, it's back to bed for you. And you too, Mrs R. Off you go.'

We waved goodnight to each other like obedient children.

Nurse Holley took her seat again, gathering up her knitting and tutting at a dropped stitch. And despite my resolve to stay awake to protect Harriet, I was soon asleep.

Not having suffered at all in the night's adventure, I insisted on not merely getting up but getting dressed. After all, I wanted to see if last night's would-be intruder had left behind any evidence in the corridor.

Everything looked as clean and tidy as ever. Mrs Briggs clearly kept the staff to Harriet's standards. Except – the feathers in feather dusters were surely not as soft and delicate as these? I captured two and then a third, returning to share my find with Harriet.

She wrinkled her nose but then passed me an envelope. 'Best to keep them, just in case.'

Laughing, I stowed them in my collar drawer.

To my horror, I was exhausted by my tiny excursion. Graciously, I conceded that I would eat breakfast in our room, as long as Harriet joined me – we needed some legitimate privacy, after all, I pointed out. She protested, feebly, that she ought to host the guests' breakfast. I played the winning card, that I was an invalid and needed to be indulged; she responded by sticking out her wifely tongue. How long was it since we had been alone and able to laugh together? But we had serious business to discuss: who was responsible for what happened last night? Before we could even theorize, we were interrupted by Ellis Page, who solemnly checked my pulse and vital signs.

'All normal,' he declared.

'You sound almost disappointed,' I joked, as he pressed around the bruise and cut on my head.

'I am actually impressed,' he said. 'After all, Nurse Holley tells me you all had a most interesting night.'

'We did, indeed,' Harriet said. 'She really has the coolest head – and was truly brave.'

'And made us all cocoa as if she had done no more than get rid of a moth around a candle,' I agreed. 'A remarkable young woman.'

'At least she will now be in bed catching up on her sleep. Whereas I deduce that you two believe you should return immediately to your normal duties as if nothing had happened.'

'I don't think we can, do you?' Harriet asked. 'Someone wishes to disturb what one might call the gentle tempo of our lives—'

'Let us call a spade a spade. A night-time intruder who did not want to take no for an answer. Nurse Holley tells me she had to stab this person in the foot. Yes? With a knitting needle? Even if she drew no blood, there must be someone with a bruised foot, possibly bad enough to cause a limp.'

Harriet nodded. 'I will be watching everyone – staff, guests, men and women. But I have no right to challenge—'

'Nor should you take such a risk, not if half of what Nurse Holley tells me is true. The only one who should do such a thing is Constable Pritchard – whom I advise you to consult immediately. I can't believe anyone tried to enter your room with good intent!'

And neither could we.

'Officially, you are very ill, Matthew. I will ask for his urgent help this morning.'

'So I should hope,' Page said. 'And do I deduce that you intend to take precautions to avoid the indignity of being assaulted by another picture?'

'George is taking care of the pictures. And Harriet has sent for reinforcements in the form of Montgomery Wilson.'

'So Bea told me. But won't he be even more at risk than you two? A man with a lot of power, after all.'

'Dear Lord, I'd never thought of that!' Harriet gasped. 'What do we do? There are always a couple of footmen on duty to patrol the House at night but they can't be everywhere. And I think we should tell them for their own safety to stay together.'

'What if we removed a couple of potential victims – you and Harriet? I'm sure you could be found a comfortable room in the Family wing. I know the guards are in place to keep his lordship in, but equally they would keep intruders out.'

However impassive she tried to keep it, Harriet's face spoke volumes. I understood completely. Our present accommodation was beyond the dreams of many, and we had been allowed to furnish it, using the furniture in the House, more or less to our taste – but it was not our home. And although the accommodation in the Family wing might be supremely 'comfortable', it was even less ours.

Harriet took a deep breath; for a moment, I thought she might accept. But then she said slowly, 'If we returned to our own house, just until George has found a key for our room – yes, everyone's room, actually – we could invite Mr Wilson to stay with us. He might, of course, really prefer his usual rooms since he likes to work in the smaller one. What do you think?'

'No one need know apart from you, Bea and Dick Thatcher,' I pointed out. 'We could just appear at mealtimes, carry out our duties and disappear at night, as we do already. If we have to work alone in the House, we can make sure a footman is always within earshot.'

'With those provisos, I would say Harriet's motion is carried, as Wilson would say, nem. con.,' Page said.

But, eyes filling, Harriet was speaking. 'To continue with your image, I must withdraw the motion. We have been here so long that at home the beds and bedding are unaired. The boiler is unused. It would take an age to light the range and boil a kettle. So there will be no hot water, night or morning. *We* could camp in such circumstances, but I could not ask anyone else to.'

My heart sank alongside hers.

Page nodded. 'In that case, Harriet, as your physician, I urge you to contact our good constable without further delay.'

There was an urgent knock on the door. 'Sir, ma'am – the doctor's needed urgently! In the village, doctor! Now, if you please. Your gig will be waiting at the front door.'

He left with no more than a wave of his hand.

We stared silently at each other; we knew almost everyone in the village, one way or another. A young mother? A child? One of the workers? I knew she was praying under her breath, as was I. At last, though, Harriet said, 'Whatever Ellis is doing, I think we should take his advice. We need Constable Pritchard now. And George to fit a bolt if he can't find a key.'

Preferring lying low to outright lying, I accepted half of Page's original suggestion and did my morning's tasks in one of the unused rooms in Nurse Webb's sanctum. Without interruptions, of course, I achieved far more than usual, but I was prey to all sorts of anxieties. Had Pritchard responded to what to anyone else would have been a summons? He was not the man to take such news lightly. Why had he not come up to see me? Heavens, I had turned overnight into a tetchy, demanding patient.

I turned my thoughts to Harriet. Had the Marchbankses behaved themselves or somehow inveigled themselves into the library? Had she managed to exclude them while she drove Robin to the little railway station in the grounds? How would Montgomery Wilson react to the different facets of the situation in which he now found himself?

A junior nurse bobbed her way into the room with a tray bearing fresh bandages and a short note from Harriet: the constable was giving evidence at Shrewsbury sessions and would not return till much later in the day. I gnashed my teeth.

As the nurse secured my new bandage, she froze. Bells rang throughout the wing. She hesitated. 'Are you all right, sir? Because that means there's an emergency and it's all hands to the wards.'

'Of course.'

She left with a swish of skirts. I could hear her footsteps accelerating down the corridor.

Who was the new patient? The one Page had dashed off to treat?

I tried to return to my work but failed. Leaving a note of explanation for Nurse Webb, I returned to the main body of the House.

'Sir!' Primrose bobbed a curtsy as I slowly descended the stairs. 'Please, sir, George says he's looking for keys, sir. And Mrs Rowsley has gone to the station to collect Mr Wilson, she says to tell you. She'll be back in five or ten minutes, I should say.'

'Thank you. Primrose, do you know who has been brought to the Family wing? An emergency, they say?'

She shook her head. 'But I'll find out directly, sir, and come and tell you.'

'Thank you. I'll be . . . I'll be in the main entrance hall.' Where I could sit and persuade myself that Page was wrong and I was quite well again.

But I didn't even have time to do that. By magic, two footmen appeared to throw open the doors. Our guest had arrived. I got to my feet.

'I had a most satisfactory journey, thank you, Rowsley.' Montgomery Wilson, the Family's lawyer and the chair of the trustees, shook my hand as I led him up the lovely semi-circular flight of steps to the front door. 'The train was punctual to the minute, and Mrs Rowsley and I had a most useful conversation as she drove me here.' We watched her urge Robin into action; it was only when it dawned on him that he was heading for his stable that he picked up speed. 'Are you sure you should be standing, Rowsley? With such a head injury?'

'Do you remember how we used to read plays aloud after dinner? And sometimes we would don an item of clothing to look more the part?'

'I do, indeed. Ah!' He smiled. But now someone else was joining us. 'Palmer! How good to see you again! I hope you will have time to show me all that you have been doing in your excavations.'

Francis waved earth-stained hands by way of a greeting. 'The pleasure is mutual, Wilson. I would be delighted to give you a conducted tour. And I think I should make it soon; the local men working for us are sure it will rain this evening, if not before.'

'Unless anything else supervenes, would directly after luncheon be a convenient time? Rest assured, I do not wish to interrupt anything urgent.'

'Excellent – and now if you will excuse me, my hands and these clothes are not fit for civilized society.'

We followed him indoors, stopping as usual for Wilson to cast wondering eyes at the domed ceiling. 'This never ceases to amaze me. Or to remind me how much responsibility we carry on our shoulders to keep the whole House safe for the next generation – and, indeed, the ones after that. I should be more specific – how much responsibility falls directly on your shoulders and on Mrs Rowsley's.' I doubted if he would ever easily use our given names: despite the gusto with which he had joined in our ad hoc play readings, he genuinely appeared to enjoy formality. I suspected that he used it to control the slapdash arrogance of some of his clients who would see a middle-class professional man as someone to patronize and, if possible, ignore. Yes, he could be irritatingly rigid – but in truth, he was bound by his profession to obey the minutiae of the law.

'Yes, on hers especially. As you will recall, we have tried to ease her situation in particular by appointing a deputy – no, more of a *replacement* housekeeper.'

His frown told me that Harriet had already confided in him. 'Mr Thatcher is clearly a reliable and responsible young man; I cannot imagine what drove this Mrs – Briggs? – Mrs Briggs to overrule him, and to do so in public.'

'Professor and Mrs Marchbanks are quite persuasive. She thought that a professor's request must trump the rules laid down by us trustees.'

'And, indeed, specified in his late lordship's instructions. Conversations must take place, Rowsley, must they not?'

FOURTEEN

Although Matthew was clearly far from unwell, he insisted he must join us, albeit at the last minute, for luncheon. Today this was being served in the dining room so that Mr Wilson might meet all the archaeologists and historians together without some of them wandering off. I circulated amongst them, watching carefully for limps or winces as they walked or stood. I saw none; the only injuries seemed to be blisters on hands or sore backs and knees.

To my surprise, Mr Wilson claimed that he had met Professor Head already. 'In Shrewsbury. We were in the same gentlemen's outfitters when that youth dropped the drawerful of collars,' he added.

'I fear you are mistaken, sir,' Professor Head responded, turning to Dr Wells.

Then another professor, arriving later than most, demanded my attention, something he did with undiluted ire.

Professor Marchbanks strode straight towards me. Perhaps his wife had been on the receiving end of some of his anger: she was nowhere to be seen. 'A whole morning wasted! Just because one uneducated woman decided that she had other more important duties. The frustration has given my dear wife one of her headaches and it is all because of you and your damned intransigence. Madam,' he added belatedly. 'The sooner you produce the trustee whose name you keep hiding behind the better, and I can tell him what I think of imposing on me rules designed to stop tweenies breaking vases with their feather dusters, not scholars at their work.'

'Mrs Rowsley is known for her efficiency and willingness to please, Professor, so permit me to introduce the very trustee whose presence you demanded. Professor Marchbanks, Mr Wilson.' Francis, materializing suddenly, was suave to the tips of his fingers.

I almost wondered if he had stage-managed the next incident

– the vigorous sounding of the luncheon gong, which reminded me ludicrously of the roll of drums at a fairground melodrama. The archaeologists responded instantly. Since this was not a formal meal, there were no place cards – and apart from myself, no women, of course. Someone would have to urge people to take the most convenient seats, so I slipped away from the likely combatants, much as I would have loved to hear their exchange, acting as a sheepdog. Then for once, ostensibly to care for him, I sat next to Matthew, whose new bandage was spotlit by the midday sun.

'I wish you had been sensible and stayed where you were.'

'There was an emergency. I made my escape.' He took my hand under cover of the tablecloth. 'Everyone is gratifyingly interested in me and my heroism, so I fear I must act the invalid a little longer. It's quite unnecessary, and I don't want to worry you for one second. In fact, I'm concerned about you: you're very pale.'

'My absence this morning interfered with the professor's work and the frustration has given Mrs Marchbanks a migraine,' I explained, adding dryly, 'with all of which he is currently regaling Mr Wilson.'

In fact, that seemed to be precisely the case. Mr Wilson sat nodding, all sympathy.

Matthew squeezed my hand. 'Mr Wilson is a skilled actor, is he not? Let us suspend judgement until he speaks at the end of luncheon. And though an invalid like me may not drink, there is no reason why you should not. Not for Dutch courage, but because Dick Thatcher will be very disappointed if you do not like the wine that he has selected.'

'I understand,' Mr Wilson said, as the dessert plates were removed, 'that everyone wishes to return to their tasks as soon as possible. So I propose to speak to you very briefly about one or two matters while we are served with coffee.' Standing, he smiled at Dick and Luke. 'First, on behalf of all of us trustees, may I thank you and all your colleagues for your dedication to vital work. Second, I would apologize to any of you guests who have been inconvenienced by what may seem to be unreasonable rules.' He paused as there was a rumble of agreement, not only from the professor. 'I am sure that our good hosts have explained that we have no choice. We are bound by the terms of his late lordship's will, which states unequivocally that, apart from Mrs Rowsley, no one – not even senior members of the staff, not even Mr Thatcher, who, with Mrs Rowsley, is responsible for the finances of the entire household, or Mr Rowsley, who has complete control over the estates here and across the country – can be alone in the library. No, the person to whom his late lordship entrusted the room and its precious contents is Mrs Rowsley. I am sure that at times she must wish this clause of the will to Jericho. But she is bound by it, as we are. Similarly, any decisions about removing anything at all from Thorncroft House or the estate have to be made by a full meeting of the trustees, and as the Croft family's lawyer, I am legally required to see that nothing is done to the detriment of the inheritance of the still missing heir, assuming, sadly, that the present Lord Croft's tragic illness will not respond for some time to the excellent treatment he is receiving.' His eyes narrowed as he heard a possibly critical voice. 'I can assure you all that his treatment is regularly reviewed by acknowledged experts in this field. Until we locate his lordship's heir, we have no option – no moral and no legal option – but to continue in this way. I might regret any inconvenience you suffer, but I do not apologize for his late lordship's will or the way it is implemented. And I request you in the strongest terms to desist from criticizing the trustees who are working so loyally.' Removing his spectacles with a strangely decisive gesture, he looked around the table. 'I trust I make myself clear.' He sat, as if absorbing a round of applause. Or as if he were a schoolmaster, dismissing a class. Certainly, the archaeologists started to drift away.

To my surprise, Professor Marchbanks dawdled, hesitating at the door and then turning back and approaching me. 'Clearly, I owe you an apology, ma'am. I did not fully understand the situation.'

I could either call him out as a liar, since he had actually seen the will for himself, or accept his words with a gracious smile. 'Let us hope for a few uninterrupted hours now, Professor. I must escort my poor husband to his bedchamber and then I will be delighted to unlock the library for you. Let us hope your wife is well enough to join us.'

Matthew held me back as everyone trailed out. 'While you were out, someone was brought to the Family wing as an emergency. Luke? Who is Doctor Page's new patient?'

'Everything happened in such a rush, sir, we've only got rumours to go on. The word is it's a man – maybe Ned Marples or Harry Tyler. But someone said it could be Mr Pounceman! Until they let us into the Family wing, we can't be certain. I'll seek you out as soon as I know.' He bowed to us in turn.

'Pounceman?' Matthew repeated stupidly. 'Either of those two hotheads I could have understood, but Pounceman?'

'That is just a rumour, sir. And, as you know, when there is an emergency, Nurse Webb permits no visitor whatsoever.'

White-faced Mrs Marchbanks might have been, but she insisted she was well enough to assist her husband in his endeavours, even if he had to carry all the books to her as she sat at a table. Since she dropped her pencil at least twice and fumbled the pages of her notebook, I was not convinced, but I was not going to be the one to ruffle the suddenly calm waters of our working relationship.

I had scanned no more than half a dozen pages of *The Woman in White* when Thatcher, his face at its most serious, tapped at the door. There was a note on the salver he offered. A quick glance at the Marchbankses and the most minute tap on the side of his nose explained why he did not simply tell me what he had written.

I am afraid that it is Mr Pounceman who is ill. He is in a comma, they say.

I clapped my hand to my mouth, staring; he nodded. 'We will discuss this when you serve tea,' I managed.

He bowed himself out. I felt a surge of pride. He could neither read nor write when he joined us; to get everything right but *coma* was an achievement.

I made little or no pretence to read, my mind churning with reasons why our rector should be so ill. If he had fallen unconscious yesterday, I would not have been surprised. But a whole day later? On my own, I could have paced about the room;

with this company, I felt obliged to remain at my desk, my face
impassive and revealing nothing of my horrified speculation.

As usual, we took tea in the muniment room, Mrs Marchbanks
sinking into the first chair she found as if she was dizzy. Luke
served us, lip-reading my anxious questions and responding in
kind: no, there was no further news, and Dr Page was still
in the building. I gestured: I would like to speak to the doctor
before he left. I doubt if the others even noticed our little
exchange – it was a skill every servant practised, knowing that
a servant, in addition to being well-nigh invisible, must be as
silent as the grave.

Certainly, the professor did not remark on it; once his thirst
was slaked, he went to great lengths to tell me what they had
done in the morning while I had been otherwise engaged, as
he delicately put it.

'Whoever worked here before made a good start,' he
conceded. 'But he lacked expertise.'

'He was all too aware of that. He took it up as a hobby,
really, to fill empty hours.' He had been very unpopular with
the rest of the staff and naturally preferred to avoid their sometimes open hostility. 'In fact, he's now become a sort of assistant
and apprentice to one of your colleagues, and his latest letter
tells me how much he's enjoying his new life.' This was information I had deliberately not passed on to the staff. Dick
Thatcher and Luke, usually the kindest young men, had taken
a great dislike to him. 'Did he find anything that you find
interesting?'

'Something that might help Mr Wilson find your missing
heir?' he asked.

Unable quite to work out his tone – if he was alluding to Mr
Wilson's speech earlier, it was hard to tell if he was being
humorous or ironic – I said, 'Anything like that. Discovering a
secret marriage might cause untold complications, however.' I
spoke lightly, but one in particular might destroy lives. What if
his lordship, who had seduced Maggie, one of the maids, secretly
married her before she was expelled from the House? Much as
I doubted it – he was a rackety young man even before his
illness struck – it was possible, perhaps even an act of defiance

to confound his mother, with whom he fought bitterly over the relationship. Where would that leave Lizzie, the child that had survived Maggie's death, who now lived as the daughter of a narrow-boat master? Her adoptive mother would petition the Queen rather than hand over a child she loved as much as those of her own flesh.

Once back in the library, before I could open my book, the professor asked, 'Did your late employer ever show you any books – apart from the Chaucer – that he particularly treasured?'

'People don't always treasure their most interesting or valuable possession, do they? Something speaks to us individually. For instance, I know that the first editions of Jane Austen's novels are nothing to some of the Elizabethan volumes as the world sees them, but should – heaven forbid – a fire break out here, I might save them first.' Why was I being so disingenuous? There was a Book of Hours tucked away somewhere, and somewhere, though I had never seen it, a gospel reputed to date back to Saxon times. I might even have mentioned them to him on his first evening here. But I wanted to be very sure I could trust him – wanted to see his reaction as he picked them off the shelves.

'Novels!' To my amazement, the sneer came from Mrs Marchbanks.

'Indeed. They are a window on the world, are they not, to those of us living secluded lives in the countryside? But I will not attempt an argument in their favour myself, when Jane Austen herself wrote a passionate defence of the form in *Northanger Abbey*: "Yes, novels . . . which have only genius, wit, and taste to recommend them."'

'Hmph.' She did not sound convinced, indicating by opening her notebook that she considered the conversation closed.

Her husband, however, looked almost approving: 'You have a good memory, Mrs Rowsley.'

'Such a thing is part of our training, sir,' I responded, hoping that my smile was not too self-deprecating.

We resumed where we had all left off. Ellis did not appear.

* * *

The rain the villagers had promised arrived at six, so there was no question of taking sherry on the terrace and not much hope for any smokers wishing to indulge there later. So it was easy for Thatcher to ease me unobtrusively from those gathered in the saloon to the quiet corner of the corridor where Ellis lurked.

'Mr Pounceman?' I asked without preamble.

'Still unconscious. He collapsed vomiting this morning; his servants had the sense to summon me. They believed – still do, I should imagine – that he has a stomach disorder.'

'He does not?'

'I believe it is a symptom of the concussion caused by yesterday's blow. Although I did not wish to move him, I felt he would be safer in Nurse Webb's more than capable hands. The blow from the picture frame must have been harder than I realized. Dear God!' His voice broke with anguish.

'But could you have done anything more? He seemed in perfect health and excellent spirits when you left together.'

'I could . . . I should . . .' He half turned, covering his face.

'You are not God, Ellis: you cannot know everything.' I put my hand on his arm. 'But you are a wonderful doctor, and if anyone can save him, you can. You know that.'

Shaking his head, he smiled sadly. 'I must return to my patient; I know you will understand if I do not join you this evening.'

'Of course. But we could send food up to you and Nurse Webb.' The wing now had its own kitchen, but I should imagine that the fare produced was mostly invalid slops. Nurse Webb insisted that the food offered to her and her staff was fresh and plain, and none of them wanted or expected better.

He smiled, then frowned. 'I had rather no one came into the Family wing. No one at all. I cannot understand why anyone should want to harm the man – a priest, for God's sake! – but should they want to make another attempt, those guards on the door are very conscientious.'

I took a deep breath. 'What if someone who appears to be a legitimate patient gains access and tries to kill him?'

He took a step back. 'You really suspect—?' Professor Fielding walked past, stopping to greet us. 'Are you a cricketer,

sir?' Ellis continued smoothly. 'Harriet tells me that she
suspects Matthew will insist on playing cricket on Saturday,
which he should not, and I would prefer to have a substitute
already in place.'

'Cricket? Never. I might hunt, shoot and, of course, fish, but
I never did like those nasty hard balls. Is Matthew well enough
to join us this evening?' he asked with his charming smile.

'Sadly, Harriet must dragoon him away to their quarters the
moment the dinner is over. And I shall rely on her to stand
guard over him. Forgive me – I need to give Harriet one more
instruction about my patient.' He waited while the professor
continued on his way. 'My dear, do you really think Mr
Pounceman was the intended target?'

'No. Nor do I think poor Milly was – Nurse Webb will tell
you about her. I'm not even sure that Matthew was. You recall
our conversation yesterday? I am sure there is a pattern that we
do not yet see. Destruction, perhaps – but not necessarily death.'

'But surely it cannot have been a coincidence that the picture
fell at the precise moment that Matthew and Mr Pounceman
walked past. I know you feel honour-bound not to retreat to
your own house, but can you at least lock your doors tonight?'

'George has found keys for our rooms and for Mr Wilson's.
He'll try to provide one for every bedchamber by tomorrow
evening. Oh, and there are now bolts on Mr Wilson's door and
ours, too.'

'I hope – I wish . . . No, I can see that you have to stay
here.' He hesitated. 'Have you seen anyone with a foot injury?'

'Only one I witnessed in the making. I made Mrs Briggs
jump as I went into the Room this morning and she dropped
her accounts book on her foot. She went pale with the pain.
And then she did exactly as I would have done – tried to walk
it off. I can't fault her dedication to work. And one of the maids
– Primrose – says her new boots are hurting her. Nothing unusual
in that.'

We went our troubled ways.

Locked and bolted in our room we might be, but neither of us
slept well. As we contemplated the day ahead, someone slid a
note under the door. It was sealed.

I sat down heavily beside Matthew to read it. And, to my surprise and horror, sobbed. 'Mr Pounceman survived the night.'

'Thank God! But why the tears?'

'He might have been on his deathbed. And you just as easily as him. You could both have been killed by that picture, Matthew. Any one of our colleagues could have been killed as they went about their daily duties. Any of our guests. And even if George gives us all keys, and makes all the pictures safe, that doesn't mean whoever wishes harm on the House and those in it won't find another way of inflicting it. There are the statues, the huge Chinese vases . . .'

He took my hand. Would he patronize me by denying what I had said, or by reassuring me that somehow all would be well? Thank God he did neither. 'Do we clear the House of guests? Send everyone packing?'

'How can we do that? Everyone is in the middle of their project. The remains . . . the library . . .'

'They are not human lives. Those are more important at the moment. Let us talk to Wilson. And also to Elias Pritchard. This can't wait till tomorrow's match. If he's not in court again, he needs to help us. I will send a note down to ask him if he can call on us at – say, a quarter to ten? Can you spare the time to join us?'

I relaxed slightly, my head against his shoulder. His arm around me, we sat in loving stillness for several minutes.

Then I straightened my shoulders. 'Dear me! The time. Breakfast! I dare leave it no longer. Jemima and Polly will be collecting their husband's wages at nine, won't they? I hope they can tell me that their husbands are behaving themselves at last.'

There was a tap on our door. I opened it to admit Ellis Page, grey with fatigue and unshaven. 'As you know, he still lives,' he said. 'But I would truly welcome a second opinion.'

'Send for whom you need. The estate will pay his fees.'

He nodded. 'Is there any servant who could be trusted to take a message to the telegraph office at the station?'

'I will take it myself,' Matthew declared, leaping into action – but then sitting down, trying not to let me see him clutch at his head. 'And one to the bishop to suggest we need a locum for Sunday. Esau will get me there and back within minutes.'

'He might,' I said, looking from him to Ellis. 'But he won't. Ellis has prescribed a quiet life for you. So I shall go. Robin will take me, before you ask. I'll be back in time to pay the girls. Would you pass me my hat, please?'

'Harry – behave himself? Yes, ma'am, indeed, ma'am,' Polly said, with a bob of a curtsy. She looked at Jemima, who had accompanied her.

'And Ned, too?'

'Not touched a drop, ma'am.'

'More to the point, he's not raised a hand in anger? Not hit you or little Frank? Polly, Harry's not struck you or little Flora?'

When they had worked as tweenies, the two young women – they were barely in their twenties – had been like twin dolls, smiling, nodding and shaking their heads in unison. They did it again now.

'They're good men really, ma'am,' Polly said.

'Just stupid,' Jemima added, who always was more realistic.

We talked for a while about their children, left with Polly's mother, apparently, and their hopes for a village school. Then another thought struck me. 'Will the men be able to behave themselves at the cricket match tomorrow?'

They looked at one another. Polly said, 'Constable Pritchard came to the cottages last night. Ours first, theirs next. Put the fear of God into the pair of them. Says he'll clap them both into the cells if he hears so much as a squeak.'

'Before, during or after the match,' Jemima added. 'Ma'am, is it true one of the gentlemen will pay for women to wash the stuff they dig up?'

'Because my mama will look after the babies for a few hours each day,' Polly said.

'I'll get Tom to take you along to the site and introduce you to Doctor Wells. Now, here are the wages – and Mrs Arden has put a few things in baskets for you.'

Twin smiles, twin curtsies, twin thanks. I sent them off and raised a silent prayer that the stupidity of their husbands would never spoil their friendship.

Mrs Briggs was hovering in the servants' hall as I left the Room, which I had borrowed for the few minutes it took me to talk to the girls.

'Thank you so much,' I said. 'That was very kind of you. I hope I've not delayed you too much.'

'There's always something to see to, isn't there?' she responded ambiguously. 'And how might Mr Rowsley be this morning?'

'He insists he's well enough to be back at his desk. Between ourselves, I think he's trying to prove he's fit for tomorrow's cricket match.'

My attempt at levity did not make her smile.

'How is your foot this morning?'

'Foot?'

'That accounts book must have hurt you a great deal.'

'We have to carry on, don't we?' she said. 'Now, I meant to ask you yesterday. The pictures. Apart from asking Mrs Arden to tell us not to dust them, what are you proposing to do?'

'What a good question.' Although I did not at all like the tone in which it had been asked. 'George is to rehang everything at risk, of course – but what else would you suggest?'

'You could get them all taken down. Then I could get the maids to give the place a proper, thorough clean. Or you could lock up most of the rooms. And you could stop that madman upstairs roaming around cutting them. Have him put in a strait-jacket, that's what I say.'

I nodded, as if I were taking her suggestion seriously. 'I will speak to Nurse Webb and Doctor Page today. Thank you for having the chapel floor cleaned, by the way. Mr Pounceman was very grateful.'

She gave me a look I could not read. 'I hear he saved your husband's life. Or was it the other way round?'

'Who knows?'

'Thank God no lasting harm was done,' she said.

'Amen! Now, another visitor is coming today, though he may well not appear in the main part of the House at all. One of the patients in the Family wing isn't responding to treatment, and Doctor Page has asked for a second opinion.'

'So does he need a room prepared?'

'I don't know. I assume if he needs to stay, it will be in the Family wing. But I will tell you if I hear to the contrary. Meanwhile, thank you for all you are doing. It's good to have everything in such conscientious hands.' Dear me, that was what her ladyship used to say to me. How had I come to speak as if I were mistress of the House? I must watch my tongue in future. I looked at the big clock. 'Heavens, I ought to be in the library, ready for Professor and Mrs Marchbanks.' And now I sounded like an apologetic tweeny.

We nodded our farewells.

'But what about the will? Even if there is some obscure clause in it that makes him a suitable guardian, Mr Wilson knows nothing about precious books,' Professor Marchbanks expostulated.

I suppressed a smile at the implication that I might indeed have had my uses and took my place at the desk. Mr Wilson arrived within moments, however, taking, with a grave bow, the key I handed over.

'To reiterate,' he said, his manner dryly pedantic, 'we take tea or coffee in the muniment room at eleven, the library being securely locked behind us. Instead of a footman attending us outside, you have arranged for a maid to be on duty, should Mrs Marchbanks have a recurrence of her most unfortunate faintness.' He bowed in her direction. 'We cease work at a quarter past twelve and adjourn for lunch. Given the beauty of the day, I would suggest that we join the gentlemen at the site for another al fresco repast.' Something about his smile always compelled obedience. It did not fail today. 'My dear Mrs Rowsley, it is therefore my honour to be your deputy for the day.'

FIFTEEN

Pritchard and I were drinking coffee in my office when Harriet came in; Luke had provided an extra cup – 'Just in case, sir!' I filled it. She seized on it as if it were nectar.

'We were talking about tomorrow's match, ma'am,' Elias said. 'I was wondering if Matthew would be well enough to play.'

She stared at me over the cup, raising an eyebrow.

'I think you should assume I won't,' I said ruefully. 'I'm sorry, Elias, but the team doesn't need a passenger.'

'True. We can try that nephew of Marty's. Tell you what, I'm worried about having both those hotheads, Ned and Harry, in the team. I want players to wrestle with the opposition, not fight each other.'

'I hear you've given them a good talking-to,' Harriet said, 'much to the relief of their wives.'

'I wish I could do the same for the maniac cutting your pictures down.'

She frowned. 'The *maniac*? I hope you're not referring to his lordship in such a way.'

He raised his hands in apology. 'No, I'm not, I promise you. I'm sorry if I sounded disrespectful.'

They exchanged a smile, Harriet's even more apologetic than his, I thought. What had made her so tetchy? I would no doubt find out later.

Elias continued, 'There are rumours about him, of course, in the village, as you'd expect. There always are. And in the House itself, I gather.' He grimaced. 'Which is why I made it my business when I arrived to speak to the guards on the door to the Family wing, and to Nurse Webb herself, of course. So I can scotch any more gossip.' He nodded firmly. 'Poor man. I was so sorry when her ladyship died, but at least she was spared seeing her grown son playing with children's nursery toys. So we need to find someone else to point the finger at.'

'Yes, indeed. And before someone is killed outright. Elias, have the rumours not reached you about the extra patient in the Family wing?'

'I've heard that the rector is ill with a stomach infection, of course.'

'Entirely between ourselves, Mr Pounceman is suffering from the effects of being struck on the head. No one knows if he will survive. It seems that that falling picture did more damage than anyone realized.'

'Dear God! This would be when you were hurt, Matthew?' He got to his feet. 'We may have manslaughter, even murder on our hands! I must notify Sergeant Burrows. All these people in the House and none of them safe!'

At last, Harriet smiled. 'We have taken one step to catch the perpetrator. Even catch him or her red-handed. George and I have a plan involving reddle.'

He laughed as she explained but added more sombrely, 'Even so, there's more than one way to skin a cat. What if someone starts pushing over vases and the like?'

'Exactly,' we said together.

'I think at the very least you might lock up some of the rooms.'

'That's what Mrs Briggs suggested,' she said, 'and I agree that we probably should. George has already found keys for our two rooms – has Matthew told you about a would-be visitor?'

He nodded gravely.

'But we can't lock the corridors and the staircases, which are as full of pictures and vases as any of the state rooms! I wish we could hire more footmen to stand guard – but with the hay harvest coming up . . .'

I said slowly, 'Why didn't I think of this before? What about employing more of our retired workers, the ones who are no longer strong or mobile enough to help with the harvest? They couldn't chase after a miscreant but their very presence might prevent any tampering. I'll go and talk to them myself: Joshua, Nathaniel, Alfred – they're all reliable men. Harriet, would you care to come with me?'

She hesitated, then said, 'I could take them a basket of food,' as if she needed an excuse for a pleasant walk.

'I can call on Joe Oates and Henry Carver on my way back to the village,' Elias said. 'Maybe old Tobias Smith?'

'Six more pairs of eyes would be wonderful – as long as we don't put their lives at risk. They deserve better of the estate than that,' Harriet said. 'But what about baskets for them? Can a constable risk his dignity?' she asked impishly. 'No, Elias, there's no need. If they come, they can carry them home themselves. All of them! I'll ask Dick Thatcher to organize some uniforms – though they may be the fancy old-style ones the men dislike so much.'

We had had to change the red and gold-braided ones for mourning, of course, which the footmen actually preferred: Thatcher said the men felt less like playing cards. I suspected that the words were more his than theirs, to be honest, and that possibly the old codgers would prefer a bit of familiar braid.

Thatcher given his instructions, we had a much-needed chance to stroll together, where whatever nonsense we might wish to utter would not be overheard. We soon recruited the old men, plus a couple of their cousins. Then, meeting Farmer Twiss by chance, we learned that Harry Tyler was not only behaving himself but working with a will – though he admitted that he was looking forward to the hay harvest, when his back might ache in different places. 'All in all, I'm hopeful he's learned his lesson. But if he doesn't—' Twiss jerked a gnarled thumb in the direction of the lane. Clearly, the young man would not get another chance.

We could continue our stroll. But our feet found their way to our own house. We let them. Why not? We had the excuse, if one were needed, that the place should be aired, and we joyously opened windows. And enjoyed, without fear of interruption, each other's company.

Should anyone discover our diversion, then the boxes we carried back to the House must convince them that we had been on urgent business. We locked them in my office as carefully and soberly as if they had not been empty.

All eight of the estate pensioners now togged out in the best-fitting livery Dick could find, and ready, after servants' dinner, to sit in crucial places, it was time to adjourn outside for luncheon. The spoil-heaps that had so enraged Francis were being further excavated with every shovelful of earth riddled and any shards retrieved. Hurley and Burford, who looked as if they would rather have been digging for golden statues, were painstakingly measuring and describing each piece, recording what they found in a surprisingly elegant copperplate.

Meanwhile, the nearest trench was now revealing a satisfactory amount of wall, looking as solid as it must have done when it was first built. But Francis was staring with frustration at one at right angles to it.

'There is so much less here – and I blame the church! The village church and those who built it, to be clear,' he added, nodding at Dr Wells and then Professor Marchbanks, 'not the Church as a whole. If you look at the foundations, particularly of the tower, you will find stone so like this that I am sure it was taken from here. Who knows what use other parts of the building – the buildings, indeed, since I am sure we have found a nymphaeum in that corner, where the stream runs into the site – have been put to.'

'You are concentrating on the exterior of the buildings?' Wilson asked.

'For now. I want to be sure of the general shape. I am not expecting it to be as large as Viroconium – what we now call Wroxeter. I suspect it is more likely to be an outlying villa or farm – like the one at Great Witcombe in Gloucestershire, perhaps – than any sort of military encampment.'

Professor Head, who had drifted over, was nodding, but the theory clearly did not appeal to Dr Wells. Within moments, they were in what one might describe euphemistically as an animated discussion. Fielding caught Harriet's eye and winked. She winked back, something I fancy he was not expecting.

As if prompted, the footmen whisked away the covers from the repast. Everyone, Harriet and myself included, turned towards the table. Except for one person, who seemingly regarded it as an interruption. Someone hissed – was it Wells? – 'Over my dead body – or, better still, over yours!' It might have been Head.

I whisked around – but the two undergraduates were shoulder

to shoulder behind me, and to have pushed my way back would
have been to give importance to something I trusted was just
acidulated academic banter.

We had not, of course, remembered to organize any cricket
bats and balls; Francis was tactful enough not to point out our
omission. In any case, it was not the best of his ideas. Hurley
and Burford stripped to their shirtsleeves and joined the
labourers in a game of football. It was clear that they were not
entirely accustomed to it, having played the eponymous game
at Rugby. Joe Sprue, as befitted the foreman, chose to referee
rather than play. There was soon plenty of laughter, not all
unkind.
    Wells and Fielding were arguing now.
    The Marchbankses were looking pointedly at their watches,
rather to the irritation of Wilson, who, rocking back in a chair,
was positively basking in the sun.
    Francis caught my eye and shrugged. He fished in a pocket
for a whistle. It was time for everyone to get back to work.
Even Harriet and me. But – ostensibly to see how all the work
was progressing – we dawdled our way round the perimeter,
asking questions here and making comments there. The men
were estate workers, by and large, and the women washing the
artefacts were all from the village; Harriet spoke to them all,
with a special word for Polly and Jemima, already hard at
work.
    As one, we decided to prolong our walk to see how the new
village was progressing. Its outskirts and the furthermost site
trenches almost touched, after all.
    One of the first workers we saw was Ned Marples, deep in
conversation with Joe Sprue, the site foreman. Amazingly, both
were nodding and smiling.
    Even more surprisingly, as we approached, Ned pulled his
forelock with a shy grin at Harriet, who responded with what
I could only describe as an official smile. There was some
warmth, but a decided hint of severity.
    Joe Sprue got a much warmer version – as did Ned when
his boss praised him highly. 'It's nice to see a young man try
to turn his life around,' he declared. 'Early days, I admit, but

he's been here before most of the others each day and not left till I've pretty well sent him home to his wife and child.'

'I'm glad to hear it, Ned. You won't let me or Mr Rowsley down, I'm sure – or Mr Sprue.'

Before the young man could respond, the foreman cut in, 'Moment he does, you'll hear of it, ma'am. No dead wood on any site of mine, I can tell you.'

'Ned?'

'I promised my Jemima, ma'am, and I promise you – to stay sober and not to raise my hand in anger.'

'Thank you. I hope you make us both proud of you.'

It was only as we walked away that she said quietly, 'If I had a pound for every young man who has sworn to reform, I should be a rich woman.' She stopped dead in her tracks. 'Matthew, I am a rich woman, aren't I? Thanks to her ladyship's will. Richer than I could ever have imagined. But what makes me rich beyond compare, Matthew, is you.'

SIXTEEN

R obin, the trap and I were on duty again within the hour, meeting Mr Kingsley-Ward, far too grand a physician to be addressed as 'doctor', apparently, at the little station on the estate. Apart from the reassuringly battered doctor's bag and overnight case which he insisted on carrying himself, grand he most certainly was in appearance, from the crown of his glossy top hat to the toes of his mirror-polished shoes. Even his hair, greying at the temples, added distinction. But he had good enough manners not to remark on the informal transport or the age and sex of the servant handling the reins. In the face of his forbearance, I gave a brief explanation – Matthew's head injury, our friendship with Ellis and, most important, the need for discretion. Hence, I was the only servant who knew about the problem; for his part, for safety's sake, he would enter Thorncroft House not through the grand front doors but via a much more modest entrance.

'This all smacks of what the good Mr Dickens would call "cloak and dagger"! Are all these precautions so necessary? Have I stepped into the pages of a Mrs Radcliffe novel?'

'I assure you that you have not. There is nothing of the supernatural in this. Just a living person who is seeking to upset the balance of everyday life.'

'But Doctor Page's telegraph mentioned a serious head injury. That is rather more than "upsetting the balance of everyday life".'

'It is indeed.' I would ignore the faint but perceptible sneer in his voice and treat it as common irony. 'The police are already investigating.'

'So I should hope! I must also hope that my patient makes a speedy recovery and that I may return to a place of safety!' And there was no irony at all in that.

'Until then, Nurse Webb will ensure you have every comfort. Hospital it may be, and as secure as a fort, but some of the rooms have been left in their original form – her late ladyship's sitting room and bedchamber amongst them. I trust you will find them comfortable. As you can imagine, the food is plain and wholesome, but you will find that there is tolerable wine on offer.' In fact, the wine was excellent, and the food, cooked by a woman Bea had trained, was as fresh as that Bea prepared – from the same source, too: the estate farm, the kitchen garden and the succession houses. But let him discover that for himself. We had arrived at the Family wing door.

Should anyone wonder why I had taken Robin out, I had a second errand – a more public one – distributing food to the poorest in the village. Bea had filled the baskets herself; now she helped me stow them in the trap. She even gave Robin an encouraging slap to set him in motion. Perhaps he was too affronted to respond.

'The trouble is,' Francis admitted, as the three of us talked privately in Matthew's office before dinner, 'that while one logically knows that "over my dead body" was just one of those clichés that people use in arguments, it sounded . . . quite threatening, didn't it?'

'Have you any idea who said it?' Matthew asked.

'One of the scholars, I fear. Wells? Head? Fielding? Heavens, they all bicker all the time. At least those labourers whom you sent to the rightabout made no bones about their animosity,' he added with an ironic grin at me. 'A decent fist fight clears the air more quickly than hidden mutterings. But how are you both? And this is no polite enquiry that demands no more than a dismissive smile. I see your turban is notably smaller, Matthew, but it's you, my dear, who have been looking quite careworn recently.'

Not knowing quite where to start, and knowing I must not mention my chief worry, Mr Pounceman's health, I shook my head and shrugged. 'I am well enough.'

'No. I told you that I was not making chit-chat.'

'I am tired,' I conceded. 'But having Mr Wilson here will make life easier. I hope.'

Matthew took my hand. 'She takes any failures of the household very personally. And, of course, notwithstanding Mrs

Briggs' efforts, ultimately the responsibility for everything falls
on her shoulders. As for the library . . .'

'The Marchbankses have made it a poisoned chalice, I fear.
I'm sorry: I made a bad mistake there. And I shall have to work
out a way to put it right – I'll have a word with Wilson who,
if I'm not mistaken, will enjoy a bit of subterfuge. If he can't
think of a good excuse for getting rid of them, I shall be very
surprised. Meanwhile, some of those academics may be duelling
to the death even as we speak; should we ride to the rescue?'

'Of course. Or I might have to get them to help clear Farmer
Twiss's manure,' I said, looking at my watch. 'Meanwhile, pray
excuse me. I need to write a note.'

Ushering Francis out, Matthew passed me his keys. I myself
delivered what I had written to Ellis Page, waiting for the reply.

It came in the form of Ellis himself. 'Pounceman lives. Mr
Kingsley-Ward approves of what we have done so far, but will
stay the night – Nurse Webb is having her late ladyship's suite
prepared for him. But he must leave tomorrow, on the early
train – all being well, of course. Might I – would it presume
too much on your kindness . . .?'

'He will need to leave here at a quarter to eight, won't he?
Robin and I will wait where I set him down.'

Dinner over, the consensus was that we would adjourn outside
again. One or two scholars evinced a desire to see the formal
gardens. Her ladyship had been so fond of them that the
gardeners maintained them as beautifully as if she would take
a stroll in them at any time. Thinking of her generosity to
me – tonight I wore a necklace she had given me when she
was alive – I led the way, our guests straggling behind me
and returning when they saw fit.

Despite the calm and general goodwill, Matthew locked and
bolted our door.

I was up betimes the following morning, ready to drive our
guest to the station. Mr Kingsley-Ward was not a man for
morning conversation, it seemed, taking his place with no more
than a nod. I was happy to indulge him – but first I wanted to
know how Mr Pounceman was. Was he even conscious yet?

'He is. However, he will need absolute rest in complete calm for a matter of weeks, in my opinion. I would not personally move him from his present location for a few days more – all the jolting it would involve – but then he might travel to a suitable nearby spa and extend his convalescence till the autumn. I thought of Cheltenham, perhaps, or Buxton—'

'My goodness. We must notify the bishop.'

'I should have added the words "in my opinion" again. Mr Pounceman declares he cannot leave his flock for so long. However, we have agreed on a compromise: I will ask a colleague where he is staying to examine him after six weeks' recuperation. Meanwhile, if there is any sign of a relapse, any at all, Doctor Page will summon me.'

'What a relief; we were all very worried indeed. Ah, here we are.' Robin had already stopped beside the youngest porter, who always had a sugar lump or two for him.

We exchanged polite goodbyes, and, as Jesse abandoned him to carry the physician's overnight bag, Robin had to accept that there would be no more sugar till he returned to his stable.

'Ned's never come home, Mrs Rowsley, ma'am. It's not like him, truly, ma'am!' Jemima sobbed. 'However much he's had to drink, he's always come home! And he's not drinking. He promised me. He promised little Frank. He promised *you*! It's after eight in the morning, and he's not home!'

We had arrived at the servants' entrance more or less together, me fresh from my early-morning drive. Taking her hands, I said, 'I'll organize a search party. Now, think of the baby and go and sit down. One of Mrs Arden's team will make you a cup of tea – Rosie? Good girl. Into the kitchen with you. Oh, where's little Frank?'

'Safe with Ma, Mrs Rowsley, ma'am.'

Dispatching one footman to the stables and another to the home farm – 'Everyone must report back here!' – I sent Luke to the breakfast room: surely some of the archaeologists would help. Dick Thatcher was already organizing the footmen into a team. Bea—

But there was suddenly no need for any searching. Joe Sprue, the foreman, appeared at the servants' entrance, grey-faced.

'There's been an accident over yonder, ma'am.' He pointed. 'Young Ned. It's very bad.'

'I'll deal with the men when they come here,' Bea said, slipping out.

'Doctor Page is here – I'll ask him—'

'Too late for that, ma'am, begging your pardon. His head's quite stove in. I've sent for Constable Pritchard.' He looked over my shoulder, horror rounding his eyes. 'My God, I didn't know his missus was here or—'

His words were drowned by her screams. She collapsed, holding her stomach.

Mrs Briggs appeared.

'Mrs Briggs – would you be kind enough to send someone up to the Family wing with her? She needs help.'

'Try slapping her face. That's what they recommend for hysterics.'

'She's with child,' Mr Sprue said, clearly shocked.

I knelt beside the girl while Primrose ran from the room; she'd know what to do. 'Thank you. There, Jemima, there.' I patted her forehead and cheeks. 'You need to be quiet for the baby's sake.' But my words weren't as effective as the cup of cold water Mrs Briggs threw over her face: there was immediate silence, broken only by snuffles. I mopped her face with my handkerchief, cradling her as best I could.

At last, Primrose returned with a bustling nurse, who waved us all clear of poor Jemima: 'Doctor Page is on his way.'

'That was quick,' Mrs Briggs observed.

'He is attending a patient in the Family wing,' I said.

Then Ellis himself appeared. 'Good morning, Doctor Page,' I greeted him. 'Thank God you were at hand. Jemima has had some very bad news and I fear for the safety of her baby.' I stepped into the yard. He had to follow. 'They've found Ned.'

'Dead as a doornail, Doctor, without a word of a lie,' Mr Sprue affirmed. 'Just at the edge of the new village, the Roman site side. Yes, near where we were when you and Mr Rowsley spoke to us, ma'am. I said not to move him till Constable Pritchard had seen him.'

'Excellent. I must see to Jemima and then I will join you.

Meanwhile, Mrs Rowsley, could you ask Sir Francis to come
too and bring his camera?'

'Ma'am . . . he's a mess. It ain't no sight for a lady.'

'I'll find Sir Francis.'

Was it heartless of me to abandon Jemima like that? Was I
rationalizing when I told myself the best cure she could have
was to know how – perhaps even why – her husband had died?
Or did I really want to see what had happened for myself?

As I strode along the corridor in search of Francis, I gave
orders to any footman I saw: would one locate Mr Wilson and
ask him to join me in Matthew's office so I could give him the
key to the library. Sir Francis, too – to Matthew's office with
his camera and tripod. We needed the dog cart – no, not pulled
by Robin; we needed a horse with more than one speed – brought
around to the front steps. Yes, the trap, too. Extra stable lads
to run errands if needs be. A stretcher. A sheet to cover the
poor body. A tarpaulin to cover the trench, if necessary.

And a maid – if I could find one – to bring me a hat.

Heavens, I was already wearing one, wasn't I?

We found Elias Pritchard calm and authoritative, spreading his
arms to keep everyone well away from the trench. Ned Marples
might lie face down in a parody of a grave, but his death had
become a drama it seemed half the village wanted to see.
Professor Head and Mr Burford joined us, other archaeologists
forming a half-moon on the far side of the trench from the
villagers. A subdued murmur announced the arrival of Ellis,
stripping to his shirtsleeves as he approached; within moments,
he was in the trench. Francis quietly offered his services to
Elias Pritchard and set up his tripod where the young constable
pointed. Matthew said a quiet prayer in the absence of Mr
Pounceman – an odd flutter of my brain hoped the rector would
be well enough to take Ned's funeral.

Ellis beckoned to the constable; they were to turn Ned over.
Their grunts apart, it was done in silence.

At last, Mr Sprue stepped forward, passing down the stretcher:
the body, its arms stretched out as if reaching for help, was laid
on it and covered with quiet reverence. Willing hands raised it
and laid it across the trap. A stable lad took the reins and, with

Mr Sprue and Ellis following in the trap, set off to Ellis's house. We all knew he would perform a post-mortem examination on it, but no one chose to mention it. And everyone knew who Elias Pritchard was looking for when he strode off in the direction of the home farm and Farmer Twiss.

Not all of our experts had been with us; some were hard at work on the site.

Wells observed tartly. 'One of the village women we were paying to clean the finds didn't turn up today. One of those you sent over, Mrs Rowsley.' The implication was that my judgement was at fault.

'Perhaps,' I said very quietly, nodding at the trench, 'it was because she was looking for her husband. Ned.'

'My God! I'm so sorry. I never thought – never realized. Please forgive me.' He looked genuinely penitent. I hoped he was.

Meanwhile, I had to speak to Jemima's best friend, Polly – Harry Tyler's wife.

She smiled at me, though she continued to work on a pot. 'This is what I'm doing, ma'am. I have a nice clean bowl with fresh water and I put a rag at the bottom so the pottery or whatever I'm working on doesn't get damaged if I drop it. And I use one of these little brushes – see?'

Poor woman: her husband was almost certainly under arrest by now. On suspicion of murder or at least manslaughter, Harry being the obvious suspect. Ned's death would destroy three other lives, wouldn't it?

'Just come here a moment, Polly,' I said, tucking my hand under the girl's arm and leading her away from the knot of men. What would I say? Probably just that Ned had died. I'd keep the details to a minimum – for the time being.

Polly screamed with horror. 'I must go to her, ma'am! At once!' She looked helplessly at the bowls of water. 'The Family wing? Will they let me in?'

'Tell them I sent you,' I said, hoping I sounded calmer than I felt. 'And I'll explain to Doctor Wells.' I watched her running off and turned to the archaeologists. 'They've always been like this.' I linked my index fingers. Then I covered my face;

this was probably the last time they would enjoy the uncomplicated friendship they had shared all the time I had known them.

I must not cry now. Taking a deep breath, I said, 'Doctor Wells, I am more than happy to pay her wages for the whole day. But please do not tell her the money is from me.'

'But she has barely worked an hour!' He seemed genuinely outraged.

'And if her husband hangs, she will soon be thrown on the parish,' Francis said sharply. 'Of course she must have her money, yes, and the widow, too. Dear God, her best friend.'

It was a very sober group of archaeologists who gathered round the tables for their lunchtime picnic repast. They had been quiet – but were reduced to complete silence when Constable Pritchard appeared. He stepped forward, saluting to show he was on official business.

'Good afternoon, ma'am.' His face was scarlet with sweat over his tight tunic collar

If he was formal, I must be, too. 'Good afternoon, Constable Pritchard. This is a hard day for you. Do you care for some lemonade? And other refreshment?' I smiled. 'Tell Tom here what you would like and he can prepare a tray.' He knew that anything he could not eat would be discreetly wrapped for him to take home. 'Matthew – shall we adjourn to your office?'

'Are you absolutely sure it was Harry who killed Ned?' I waited until Luke placed a tray of lemonade and a plate of sandwiches on the desk and left the room. I willed him to say 'No'.

'There's been this bad blood between them these last few years. Look at all the fights they've had.'

'But both men were going to become fathers again.' I sat down, gesturing for him to do so, too. 'And they were doing well, according to Farmer Twiss and Mr Sprue – neither had any complaint about their behaviour.'

'You sound like a defence lawyer, ma'am.' His helmet rocked gently on the desk.

'I will take that as a compliment! More lemonade?'

Matthew poured, looking from one of us to the other. 'What

does worry me is that Ned was felled from behind. They've always fought face to face before.'

'Harry could have knocked him out. He'd have a huge lump on his head if he landed on his back in the trench.'

'And a big lump on his chin where he was hit. His head wouldn't be stove in.' Matthew paused reflectively. 'Now, we didn't see the poor body close up – was there any sign of that? And were there any bruises on Harry's knuckles?'

'No – and the grazes he got last time he hit Ned seem to have healed over. Doctor Page will be able to tell you more, won't he?'

'Of course. Including what time Ned was killed, perhaps.'

'Ah, well – seems it could have been yesterday evening, only Doctor Page was saying it was warm last night and that made it hard to tell.'

'Yesterday evening?' Matthew repeated, shaking his head sadly. 'While we were all eating and drinking, the poor young man was being killed. How are people in the village taking the news?'

'The feeling is it was just a matter of time before one killed the other.' He looked at his watch. 'In fact, Harry's already halfway to Shrewsbury, by now. Yes, handcuffed to Sergeant Burrows and one of his town constables.'

'Not you? I'd have thought you'd be the one to question him.'

'Sergeant Burrows thought I'd have more than enough to do here. He'll be back as soon as he can, Matthew – Monday, probably, since he doesn't approve of Sabbath travel. He wants to talk to you about the picture-frame business.'

'Would he like his old room here? I could arrange—' I stopped short. 'I can *ask Mrs Briggs* to arrange it. And what better place to observe us than here?'

'There's been more trouble, ma'am?'

'No, thank God. But another pair of watchful eyes would be very welcome. Doctor Page probably told you he sent for advice from another doctor?'

'Indeed. Seems the rector's going to need a long convalescence.' Elias pulled a face. 'A village needs its rector, doesn't it? And him so – so much more Christian than he used to be, if you get my meaning.'

I nodded. I knew exactly what he meant. They said a blow on the head sometimes changed you. I just hoped that Mr Pounceman would not revert to his former aloof self.

'So what precautions are you taking?' Elias said, every inch a policeman again. 'Apart from telling people to be careful how they get hit on the head, that is?' His quizzical grin betrayed him.

'Locking our bedchamber and other doors, thanks to George, who has spent a lot of time finding keys that work. He's also fitted bolts to our door. And as you probably know, he's replacing all the picture cords.'

'Is that enough? Mr Pounceman could have been killed. Nearly was. As could you. As could anyone. Sergeant Burrows will no doubt have an opinion.' He might have set down his napkin with some force, but he looked longingly at the last sandwich.

'And we will take your advice and his,' I declared.

'If,' Matthew began slowly, 'falling on the back of his head might not have caused Ned's head to cave in, what else might have done? You know what, Elias, I do think a stroll out there would be a good idea.'

'When I'd locked Harry up, I popped back and roped the trench off,' Elias said defensively.

'It's a beautiful day. We've been denied our cricket, and I could do with a walk. Finish that last sandwich Elias, and we can be on our way.'

Of course, I was being unfair. We had no authority at all over the poor young man. He was an excellent village policeman. But I truly wanted him to be wrong this time. And I needed evidence to prove he might be.

'Constable Pritchard, sir!' Two of Mr Sprue's young labourers – lads no more than thirteen, by the size of them – sprang to something like attention and sketched a salute. One wriggled. 'Gaffer told us to mind the place, in case – you know – any folk come looking.'

'Evidence!' his friend added.

'Did he indeed?' Elias nodded as if he was impressed. 'What a good idea. Did you come on any *evidence* yourselves?' He looked keenly from one to the other. 'Empty your pockets, lads. Now.' He held out his hand. 'And don't think about trying to scarper. Mr Rowsley can outrun me, and Mrs Rowsley has a good turn of speed, too.'

I nodded. 'Your father was a young scamp, Arthur, and now it looks as if you might be the same. Let's hope you grow up to be a credit to the village as your father did and put any silliness behind you.'

Arthur and Edward exchanged glances, which slipped from the mutinous to the passably contrite. 'Weren't much, Constable.' Their eyes dropped to the still-outstretched hand, its fingers beckoning for instant obedience. 'There.'

'A handkerchief, eh? A handkerchief fit for a lady. And you thought you'd try to sell it for a penny or two? And you'd try washing it and ironing it as well as your mama could, because you know what she'd say if you asked her to do it? Or did you plan to come along to the police house and say, "Please, Constable Pritchard, we found this near where poor Ned Marples was murdered and wondered if the killer might have dropped it?"' He took the handkerchief with one hand and cuffed Arthur's ear with the other. 'Where did you find it? And while you're showing me, keep your eyes peeled for anything else that shouldn't be there. Understand? You come up with something useful and I might forget to tell your parents about this. Yes?' He cuffed Edward this time. 'Go and start looking.'

He pulled from his tunic a large black fabric bag, with a drawstring top. 'My wife made it for me to keep evidence in,' he explained proudly.

'That particular piece points the finger at me,' I said, wishing I did not have to. 'It looks very much like one of mine.' He held up obligingly. 'Yes. Lace but not very much. And that little pulled thread in the corner there. It's almost certainly mine.'

He frowned. 'But that looks like blood on it, ma'am. This smear, here.'

'It does, doesn't it? As if I had had to wipe a finger.' I wanted to stay silent – that or scream that I did not know how the blood had got there. Like Lady Macbeth, I stared at my hands. 'Constable, this is very awkward for you, isn't it?'

'Not really, Mrs Rowsley. Think about what Doctor Page

told me – that Ned must have been killed yesterday evening. And I doubt if you were on your own at any time.' He smiled. 'In any case— Now what are those pesky lads up to?' He ran towards them.

Matthew took my hand and we ran, too.

'Look what they've gone and found.'

Arthur held a large stone, smeared with blood and worse. Clutching his mouth, Edward bolted to a ditch.

Elias took it very carefully. 'Fits the hand nicely – if you've got a big hand like mine.' He cupped it and mimed a blow. 'Definitely one for the bag – but that handkerchief had best come out first or the one will rub off on the other. Still, that's what tunic pockets are for.' He grinned at Arthur. 'Well done. What else can you see?'

'Gaffer! Over yonder, gaffer!' Edward screamed from his ditch. He pointed at a thin plume of smoke just beyond the hedge. It was beginning to thicken. It blew this way. Flames crackled and leapt. Any moment now, the hedge would catch fire.

It took the men just moments to push through and stamp out the blaze. With all my petticoats, I had to find a gate, of course. In any case, with my skirt and petticoats I would not have dared to join in as the boys did with heroic gusto. I could at least peer on the ground for the cause – and there it was, perhaps. The remains of a pair of spectacles, sadly broken now.

'Well, well, well,' breathed Elias. 'Now, was losing those spectacles an accident – a complete coincidence – or did someone leave them there for the sun to come round and set a fire? In other words, hope to destroy the scene of the crime? I suppose we won't know whose they are and if they lost them. Or if someone stole them.'

The fire was out – I had made my way back through the gate while the men made sure that it could not accidentally restart.

'Now, what am I going to do with you lads?' Pritchard, arms akimbo, asked the two boys. 'You did wrong – no argument about that. And then you did right – no argument about that, either. So do we tell anyone about anything or do we keep our mouths shut? Myself, I think I go home with you and tell them almost the whole truth. We'll forget about the bit about your stealing the handkerchief – because stealing's what it was. But you were a help later on, and for that you deserve praise. What do you think?'

Arthur wriggled. 'Seems to me if you tell one bit of truth, you ought to tell the bad bits, too.'

'So you'll confess the bad bits, and I'll make sure they know all the good bits.'

I produced a couple of florins. 'And when your parents see these, they'll know how good the good bits are, won't they?' I handed them to Mr Pritchard. 'When you have a moment, we should talk about the evidence – to discuss who might just be trying to frame me.'

He nodded. 'But first, Mrs Rowsley, I must get the . . . weapon . . . to Doctor Page. He's the only one who can say for sure if it killed the lad.'

SEVENTEEN

We waited in my office till Pritchard returned, even hotter from his brisk walk than before and clearly grateful for the tea Luke brought.

At last, he spoke. 'Your handkerchief apart Mrs Rowsley – and you could have dropped it anywhere and at any time—'

'I might have dropped it in the servants' hall when I was with Jemima. Or later. I don't know.'

He jotted. 'Hmm. It'd be good if you could remember. As it is, the spectacles are the only clue we have, and they may be no clue at all. But it would be nice to know how many people in the House wear spectacles and if they still have them and if not, why not. You won't be offended if I start with you?'

Harriet, still pale, shook her head. 'I have . . . more than my share, shall I say?' She ticked them off on her fingers. 'The spectacles that live in the Room. Those in my chatelaine. Oh, and the pair that lurk here in the back of Matthew's pencil drawer. Three pairs.'

The young man laughed. 'Truly, I didn't know people might need so many.' Suddenly, he asked, 'Wouldn't you have a pair or so in your house, too?'

'My goodness, yes. Just one. In the library.'

'Just in case!' Pritchard grinned. 'I'm sure they're still safe and sound where they ought to be. And I'm equally sure you'll tell me if they are missing. Now, more important in my book: who else under this roof wears them? I shall need a list of guests and one of servants. More particularly, of course, someone who usually makes use of them but who hasn't recently. Confidential, of course.' He looked at her under his eyebrows. 'I will ask Mrs Briggs for one, which she can give to you, and I'd take it as a kindness if you'd list the guests for me. I know it's a forlorn hope, but I'd be failing in my duty if I didn't check.'

'And a young man's life may depend on it,' Harriet said.

'Don't look at me like that, Elias. I know you think Harry's guilty – which makes it all the more laudable that you're doing this. Thank you.'

He nodded. 'It sounds pompous, but it's what I took my police oath to do. To find the person who's guilty, which means keeping an open mind. And that handkerchief . . . No, neither of those men knows right from wrong, and either one could have snatched it. I don't know,' he groaned. 'It's been a long day, hasn't it? And a few hours still to go!'

'And an especially hard one for you,' she said. 'And you've had to do all that to-ing and fro-ing. But you were right to make sure that Doctor Page saw that stone as soon as he could, even though it meant extra miles on your feet . . . And we're grateful you came all the way back up here to keep us informed.'

He spread his hands: that was his job, wasn't it? Standing, he picked up his helmet. 'I'll bid you both good evening, then. Now, Matthew, I'm no doctor, but Harriet looks washed out. Look after her.'

'I will. Meanwhile, look at that clock, man – it's time you were with your family!' I urged.

'And one of us will speak to Mrs Briggs,' Harriet said.

I could spare Harriet one errand: I took it upon myself to go to the Room.

Mrs Briggs looked at me askance. 'What a strange request! Servants wearing spectacles? Servants losing spectacles? And why, may I ask, is such information necessary, Mr Rowsley?'

'I am afraid that though you may ask, I may not tell you. I'm sorry, Mrs Briggs, but it's information that Sergeant Burrows has requested from everyone,' I lied. 'Including your good self, I'm afraid.'

'A sergeant?' she repeated, clearly impressed by his rank.

'Indeed. And – though it is by no means certain – he may require his usual room here: the larger one in the block over-looking the stable yard. It's big enough to double as a bedchamber and an office, and he can pop in and out as he pleases. Now, could I just replace these for my wife in the drawer she keeps for her business in the Room?' I flourished her spectacles.

'No need for you to worry, sir – I'll pop them in when I go.'

'That would be kind – but I promised to take some papers back for her.' And to lock the drawer behind me. Just in case. She curtsied as I left, as did Primrose, laying the servants' hall table for supper.

I waited until all the guests, including Mrs Marchbanks, were on the terrace before stepping forward and nodding to Thatcher.

'Ladies and gentlemen, pray silence for Mr Rowsley. Mr Rowsley, sir,' he concluded, stepping back.

The quiet he achieved was somewhat ragged, but I moved into the middle of the group, catching eyes as I went, much as if I was my most feared schoolmaster.

'Good evening. Before we settle down to relax, may I remind you that a young man died in one of our trenches earlier today. A young man who was due to become a father. His widow is even still too shocked to speak and is in the care of the kind nurses upstairs. So I would like you to do one thing and consider doing another, too. I would ask you to stand in silence for a minute.' I made it two. 'Thank you. Now, Mr Thatcher will leave a bowl at the foot of the main stairs. Some of you might like to leave a donation in it – large or small, and entirely anonymously. Mr Wilson has offered to draw up a trust for the unborn baby and its brother. Thank you.'

'Oh, but – I mean, Rowsley, the man was just – well, an oik. A thieving oik.'

'A thief, Burford? How do you arrive at such a conclusion?'

'Well, he had a bad reputation – sacked the other day. It stands to reason. He was trying to run off with something!'

'A statue?' someone sniggered.

I looked Burford up and down. 'Reason, you say? What do they teach at Oxford these days, Burford? The only deduction my tutor would have let me reach is that he was lying dead in a trench!' I regretted the put-down immediately: he deserved it but not in public.

Before I could change the subject, Marchbanks jumped in. 'And another yokel is in jail already. Two bad lots.'

'So why are the police still asking questions?' Fielding asked.

'They have to be sure,' I said, 'that they have the right man.'

'Who else could it be if not him? We are all good Christian men, are we not?'

'Indeed, I hope we all deserve the adjective,' came a clear voice, 'if not the noun. Are we ready for dinner, Mr Thatcher?'

He was swift to beat the gong.

'A play-reading, Sir Francis?' Marchbanks repeated.

'Exactly,' our friend said affably. 'What better way to pass a summer evening? There are plenty of us, so we should not have to double too many roles, and it seems a good opportunity to have women's roles played by the appropriate sex.'

'Do I hear you aright, Palmer? You are expecting *ladies* to read parts?'

'Not expecting, perhaps, Professor. But certainly hoping. It has certainly been the custom as long as I have had the pleasure of staying here.' This was disingenuous, to say the least. Although he was now one of our most regular visitors, and certainly the most welcome, his visits only started when the Roman remains were first discovered a few months ago. As far as I knew, play-reading had not been one of the Family's regular occupations.

Harriet said limpidly, 'Her late ladyship always enjoyed the theatre.'

'Indeed. And am I to assume that you and she read plays together?'

'Alas, no. Her ladyship preferred to watch – or, in her later years, to be read aloud to. The books she and I got through together . . .' She smiled reminiscently.

Marchbanks was not to be deterred. 'Mrs Arden? Did you participate?'

'Dear me, no. Can you imagine my having time with a houseful of guests and their servants to cook for? Ah, such happy days – and such busy ones. Now things are less formal, however, and I have trained up some young women from the village, it's such a pleasure. One night an innocent girl, next a murderer,' she added with enthusiasm. She added, as if the presence of a well-respected doctor would clinch her argument,

'I understand that Ellis may be able to join us later, Francis, if that helps you choose the play.'

'Excellent.'

'So you insist on going ahead?'

Francis looked rightly puzzled. 'There is nothing to insist on, Marchbanks. It is simply an idea for entertaining us all – and as the immortal Mr Sleary would declare, "People muthst be amuthed."'

'Well, my dear wife will not wish to participate, whatever the other ladies might choose to do.'

Professor Head jumped in quickly. 'I know my own dear wife would have loved to read – I believe I said as much to Mrs Rowsley the other evening. I will be anything from an emperor to a clown – but not, emphatically, a clown who sings. Where will this entertainment take place?'

Francis responded with a smile that combined gratitude and enthusiasm. 'The terrace is the right size for the stage, of course – but you might prefer us to read indoors, Harriet?'

'It depends on midges – and on the moths we will attract when we light candles,' she said. 'Shall we be democratic?' she added with her most disarming smile. 'Except that for this vote, we women must have the suffrage, too! All in favour of an outdoor reading? The indoor reading? Very well, let us start outdoors. We can always adjourn inside if necessary.'

'Play-reading?' I muttered as our guests left the table. 'How did that come about?' For a moment I had the tiniest, most insidious fear that she might have told Francis about the spectacles and the fire. But then, why should she not?

'What will everyone need in order to read? People of my advanced years at least! I asked Francis how we might "amuthe" everyone, preferably something even those of us without musical talent might join in, and he came up with a play. It pleases *almost* everyone and no one has a clue that I am busily compiling my list of spectacle users. With one notable omission, of course.'

'What a strange pair they are.' I did not need to say whom.

'No wonder she looks so angry, so resentful. I almost think that her emotions choke her and cause her to swoon.'

'A sort of internal tight lacing?'

'Precisely. It's no use, is it? I must go and woo and cajole them to come and watch – not least because we don't want them wandering around where we can't keep an eye on them. I will promise more champagne . . .'

The terrace had become the Illyria of *Twelfth Night.* Young Hurley stepped into the role of Viola with great aplomb, saying almost apologetically that he had played the role at Harrow. Burford might have been inclined to sulk, for which I felt responsible, but was soon cajoled into the part of Viola's missing brother Sebastian. Bea and Harriet tossed a coin for Maria and Olivia. Wells was a surprisingly good Orsino, and Wilson, seeming to double in size, uproarious as Sir Toby. Slightly breathless – 'It's a boy!' he whispered – Page became Sir Andrew. To my frustration, even as we gathered round at the end of the play, a servant summoned him – an old lady had had a seizure.

'My apologies to you all,' he said with a bow, adding very quietly to me, 'I shall take young Jemima back to the village as I go: she wants to be with her mother.'

His departure signalled the end of the evening, now chilly under the bright moon. The brief enchantment was over.

'I must say it is good to see so many of the servants attending divine worship,' Professor Marchbanks declared, looking around the churchyard after the morning service. Almost dwarfed by a new bonnet – a construction of straw – his wife stood demurely beside him, head bowed as if she was still at prayer.

'Her late ladyship required it; we just encourage it,' I said. 'Several go to the nonconformist chapel or church in the village. Some just enjoy a little extra free time.'

'Indeed? And what does Mr Pounceman have to say about that?'

'He accepts it. And he and his fellow parsons work together in the matter of poor relief and so on.'

Ecumenical cooperation did not seem to attract him. 'I was disappointed not to hear him preach.'

'I understand he is still far from well,' I said, wondering how long it would remain a secret, the village grapevine being what it was. But his servants were now quite devoted to him and would surely reveal nothing deliberately. 'But I thought the curate's sermon was excellent. That passage from Luke is so hard to explain clearly, is it not? I thought he managed better than some. Ah, may I introduce you to Mr Roper, one of our churchwardens? I'm sure he will be able to explain how the church came to have that curious carving you asked about. Good morning, Mrs Davies; are you keeping well? Excellent! And Miss Davies?' This was after all a time to greet the estate tenants and the other villagers. 'Mr Jones, how good to see you. Is the new horse satisfactory?'

Harriet was deep in conversation with the haberdasher. Soon, however, I was sure she might drift towards Elias Pritchard, very smart in his Sunday-best uniform. Meanwhile, I was engaged with Farmer Twiss, whom I edged slightly away from the crowd.

'It's sad news about young Tyler,' I said.

'Just when I thought he was turning a corner,' he sighed. 'Mind you, like I told young Elias over there, I've no idea when the lad had time to go and commit such a foul crime. Kept him busy, dawn till dusk, I have. The manure heap's gone, and he's shown real promise with the stock – seems to be able to talk to the sheep, God bless us! Even Jess approves.' Jess was his prizewinning sheepdog. 'You know the best thing about him, gaffer? He comes to me on Friday morning and asks me to keep him working late.'

'I beg your pardon?'

'You heard aright. The lad says he always likes a drink on a Friday night, and for all Marty Baines has banned him, some of his mates will usually sneak out a glass of ale or two. So he wants to keep working till after the pub's shut, see. Well, as much to keep him busy as anything else, I got him to move the sheep from the top pasture down to the river meadow. I don't know what the sheep made of it, but Jess was tired out when they got back. Must have been ten, half past. I was waiting to lock up when they finally staggered in.'

So he could have continued over to the new village and killed Ned. But how would he have known Ned would be there? And why would Ned have been there anyway?

'What did Constable Pritchard make of the information?'

'He said something vague about time of death. But I tell you, I still can't see how the lad could have done it, and that's God's truth. Now I must bid you good day, gaffer; my good lady is trying to escape Miss Simms, the old gossip.' He mimed a rapidly opening and closing mouth.

Harriet too was trying to send a signal: she nodded in the direction of Mrs Tyler, Harry's mother, who had slipped into church late and had kept in the shadow, presumably hoping to escape public notice – and censure. She would get none of the latter from Harriet, at least. Yes, there they were, walking away from the rest of us, Harriet's arm now around the other woman's shoulders. Clearly, her conversation with Pritchard would have to wait.

'I'm glad Harriet's with her, poor woman.' Ellis's voice made me jump. 'Poor young Polly didn't dare leave her cottage, I'm told. As if she was in any way involved in her husband's crime!' We shook our heads as one.

'How's Jemima?' I asked.

'She was doing well when I called on her at her mother's earlier. I don't know if it's good or bad news: the baby is still hanging on, despite my earlier fears she would miscarry. How the girl – she's only nineteen, for goodness' sake – will survive with a child and a new baby and no support . . .'

'I have an idea that Harriet will find a job she can do.'

'And the children? They don't bring themselves up, you know!'

'What are grandmothers for? How many young women have to get their mothers to step in so they can do far more onerous work than Harriet will find for Jemima? Yes, and probably for Polly, too.'

'Not in the same house, surely to God!'

'That would be too much to ask of either girl, I agree. But there are farms all over the Croft estates – some not even in this county – that would welcome a hard-working young woman.'

'But not necessarily her children. It grieves me, Matthew, grieves me, that so many lives have been ruined by that one moment of madness!' This from a man who daily dealt with life and death. 'Ah, I think Doctor Wells is trying to catch your eye.'

He was.

I nodded politely in his direction but said to Ellis, 'Let him wait a second. Young Pritchard says Ned must have been killed yesterday evening. Presumably, modern medicine means you can work this out?'

'Yes. Rigor mortis. But it's still an inexact science, Matthew, as I told Pritchard. And I rarely come across the bodies of young men who have spent all night in the open air – especially on a warm night like Friday. I can say with some certainty, though, that it was a massive blow to the head that killed him – and yes, Pritchard showed me what I am sure is the weapon.' Even a doctor could wince. He touched the back of his head but realized other people might be watching and scratched vigorously. 'He was still breathing when he fell into the ditch, as it happens. I actually wonder if I can detect a second blow . . .'

'As if his killer jumped into the ditch after him and finished him off? My God.'

'It's not impossible.'

'Quite cold-blooded.'

'Or done in the white-hot heat of anger? Only the killer would be able to tell you. He might not even know himself. He might literally have forgotten – wiped it from his memory – because he is so horrified by what he did.' He gave a sad smile. 'Let us hope that Pritchard and his sergeant will be able to extract the truth from the young man. Or that the prison chaplain might. Speaking of men of the cloth, Pounceman is making decent progress. But somehow we have to spirit him out of the House before another picture comes adrift.' His eyes lit up as he caught sight of someone over my shoulder. Bea, no doubt. We nodded our goodbyes.

By now, Wells had buttonholed Head, so I was able to speak to Pritchard.

'Any more picture-frame incidents? No? Good. Now, have you discovered if anyone has lost their spectacles?' he asked.

'I've yet to receive Mrs Briggs' list; Harriet has hers in her reticule.' My account of how we discovered who still had them, at least, did not raise a smile. 'Mrs Marchbanks refused to join in?' he asked.

'Her husband refused on her behalf. So she did not need her spectacles.'

He shrugged. 'It's not a crime I would expect a woman to commit. Can you imagine a woman lifting a stone as heavy as the one we found and killing someone in cold blood?'

'Women are supposed to favour poison as a means of killing and that is singularly cold-blooded. But you are right – it would have to be someone both tall and strong. And cold-blooded.' I sighed. 'Young Harry and Ned struck me as the opposite – too hotheaded for their own good.'

'Hmph. It seems to me that Harry went to a great deal of trouble to set up an alibi,' he said dourly.

'I'm not sure that's how Twiss sees it. Nor the sheep, which were definitely moved. And though the two loathed each other, unless they agreed to meet, how could Harry have known Ned would be there? And would Ned ever have turned his back on Harry if he was in a rage?'

'Whose side are you on, Matthew?'

His anger took me aback. What had changed him overnight? 'On no one's. You know that. But I . . . I have doubts. Still, I'm sure you'll soon get the evidence you need, you and Burrows.' His lips tightened. Was that the problem? Tension between him and his sergeant? 'Look, the House guests are drifting away. Harriet is talking to one of the village women. I'd better go and pretend I'm in charge. You know where to find me if you need me.'

'Village woman? Not to Polly Tyler, I hope!'

'To Mrs Tyler senior, in fact. But she knows Polly as well as she knows Jemima, so I would not be surprised if later she popped in to see her. Jemima is with her mother.'

'It'd be better for her if she lost the baby, wouldn't it? And as for Polly – fancy giving birth to a murderer's offspring. Meanwhile, I have to say I think it would be better if your wife minded her own business at the moment.' He turned and strode off.

I would have liked to see him saying that to her face.

And perhaps I would. There was Harriet just coming back

to the village green. Pritchard could not avoid seeing her, especially as she waved to him, calling his name. It would be wrong
of me to sow discord between two people who liked and got
on well with each other, wrong to do anything except drift over
and offer her my support if she showed any signs of needing
it. As it was, I could not even eavesdrop: Dr Wells had finally
caught up with me. I wished him at the bottom of the duck
pond.

I heard the sound of laughter: Harriet's and the bass notes
of Pritchard's. Perhaps all was well. I very much hoped so.

EIGHTEEN

I'm in my Sunday best and a dog that has been chasing ducks comes and shakes itself dry – all over me and over Elias Pritchard, who had been heading towards me with a face like thunder.

'Dratted creature! No, don't come wagging your tail at me as if you've done something clever: be off with you,' I shouted. 'Oh, Elias, look at us! My new dress, too! And your Sunday uniform. What a pair we must look! Drat!' I dabbed ineffectually with my handkerchief.

Eventually, he reached for his and dried his face.

'I was hoping I would see you. This is the list of spectacle-wearers – you'll find most of us are of middle age and above.'

'Thank you. Mrs Marchbanks wasn't wearing hers last night, Matthew says.'

'Her husband disapproved of ladies acting.'

He laughed at the face I pulled. Perhaps now was the moment to take a risk. 'I've just been talking to poor Mrs Tyler; this business has struck her hard, of course. She blames herself for Harry's wild ways, as any mother would. She says his father was just as bad – did you know he simply walked out of the village one day and was never heard of again? And now this, poor woman.'

'Have you spoken to her daughter-in-law, too?' he asked stiffly.

I wrinkled my nose. 'Unsurprisingly, she didn't come to church, so I wasn't sure if I should call in. First, I might not have been welcome. And second – well, what would you have felt if I had done?'

My little challenge seemed to take him aback. 'I suppose it's not her fault. She felt his fist often enough. It's a pity Mr Pounceman's not well – it would have been a job for the rector really, wouldn't it?'

'Of course.' I sighed. 'It's a sad business, isn't it?' I looked around. Mrs Briggs was herding the servants as if they hadn't always made their own way back, sometimes reluctantly, true, but always with great self-discipline. Now it struck me that some were straggling deliberately. I took another risk, nodding in her direction. 'You've met Mrs Briggs; what do you make of her?'

'She's pleasant enough, isn't she? Just a little – on edge, shall I call it? To be honest, I wouldn't want to be in either of your shoes. You've ruled the roost nearly as long as I can remember – you and the rest of the servants have become a team. Yes, you've lost staff, but the newcomers seem to have found their place and fitted in. So you want it to stay that way. And she wants to make changes, maybe just to prove a point. Or is there something more than that?'

'It's just that . . . that *edge* you mentioned. I'm just not sure . . . Oh dear. What do I do?'

'What about her references? No, you wouldn't have considered anyone without good ones. I don't suppose you're acquainted with whoever employed her before?'

'No. It was a countess – yes, Elias, a countess! She lives in a mansion near Blenheim Palace and has a London residence, too. Not someone from my world at all – not the sort of person I could write to as an equal and ask for more information.'

'Why should she want to leave a post like that? I mean, it's very quiet round here, isn't it? Isn't that why Matthew's clerk left?'

'I'm afraid so. Yes, it's quiet for everyone in any country house. Unless, of course, there's a constant stream of visitors bringing their servants, as there used to be when Lady Croft was alive. Then it's hard work for all the staff, but there's a lot of fun and flirtation. And tips, of course. Mrs Briggs did very well in her interview, but so did the other candidate – that's why they'll both have a month's trial.'

'That can't be very nice for either of them.'

'Indeed, it isn't. But both seemed content with the idea – especially as the trustees are paying them both a month's wages for doing nothing while they wait for a verdict. And either is at absolute liberty to say she doesn't want to work here. She'll still get two-months' money.'

'That sounds generous. What if you have to sack one?'

'On the face of it, the same.'

'Whatever you sacked her for? Surely not! What if you find she – Mrs Briggs, of course – has been the one cutting the picture cords?'

I looked at him sharply.

'No, I've no evidence yet,' he said. 'But you can't have ruled it out, surely.'

'She isn't the only newcomer in the House – all those historians and archaeologists arrived at much the same time. And I've been accused in the past of all sorts of crimes simply because no one could imagine a *lady* or a *gentleman* doing wrong. So I'd hate to serve anyone else that sort of turn.' I grinned, my arms akimbo. 'Very well, whom do you suspect?'

He responded with a grin of his own. 'You don't want me to say Harry Tyler, do you?'

I looked him in the eye. 'What if the person who risked people's lives cutting the cords *was* the one who killed Ned? No, hear me out. It just could be. In the evenings, we don't sit everyone down together and watch their every move, much as we might want to. Some gentlemen like to go outside to smoke. Mrs Marchbanks often retires early to her room. Sometimes people like to look at the picture gallery or stroll in the long gallery. And, of course, before you ask, Mrs Briggs has her own room. She has a key to the servants' door. She could slip out unnoticed. Dick Thatcher could too, actually. And Ellis Page may have a murderous side we never dreamt of!'

We both laughed.

'Apart from that, you were serious, weren't you? You really don't want Harry Tyler punished!'

'On the contrary, indeed I do. If he's guilty. But I certainly would hate to see him hanged and – more to the point – the person who did do it get away scot-free. And you feel the same, don't you?' I patted his arm. 'Don't let that sergeant of yours jump to conclusions. He's a clever man – we both know that – but you know the people round here. And they trust you.' I took a risk. 'You know I've not spoken to Polly Tyler, but have you? You haven't, have you!'

'No point, really – she can't give evidence against her husband.'

'Jemima?'

'Have a heart, Harriet! Me question a widow, a pregnant widow at that, on my own!' He eyed me with suspicion. 'Why?'

'Jemima might know at least why Ned was out there in the middle of nowhere. That information can't do him any harm and might point us to his killer.'

He bit his lip. 'A woman might ask this – but not a man.'

'A woman might do it – but what she learned might not be evidence unless a man, a policeman, heard what the widow said.'

'Are you suggesting we work together?'

'I thought you were.'

'Today or tomorrow?'

'The Sabbath is supposed to be a day of rest. On the other hand, they start the hay harvest tomorrow and I can't imagine finding time for a delicate conversation. What time will you have finished your dinner, Elias?'

'Say three?'

'Robin and I will pick you up.'

I caught up with Primrose, right at the tail of Mrs Briggs' ragged procession: 'Are you enjoying working here?'

'Yes, ma'am. It's like having a family.' Her smile was sad – she had come to us as an orphan. 'Did you have a brother or sister, ma'am?'

'None that I ever knew of, I'm afraid – I was a workhouse child.'

'But now you're – you're you!'

'I was lucky. I was trained by good women. And I worked my way up.'

'That's why you want us all to be able to read and write.'

'Exactly. And why I want you girls to turn into capable women. That's easy enough, of course. It's more difficult to get men to recognize you're capable. Take some of our visitors now: they assume that because my husband is a man, he must know more about the House than I do, even though I've been here nearly twenty years and him less than two.'

She stopped in her tracks. 'Really? My . . . I thought he'd been here for years.'

Something in her voice told me it was important for her to know the facts. 'That would be the previous land agent, a man who grew fat at the estate's expense. My husband is trying to right those wrongs. The new village should have been built years ago – oh! What's going on?'

Even before we went through the servants' door, we could hear a quarrel. Primrose looked at me sideways and melted away.

I did not have that option. 'Mrs Briggs. Mr Thatcher. Raised voices on the Sabbath? And in front of your colleagues? Shame on you.'

Thatcher blushed to the ears and stepped backwards with a bow. Mrs Briggs' hands remained on her hips until she raised one of them to jab the air.

'Let us say nothing more until we are safely inside the Room, Mrs Briggs, or Mr Thatcher's office. In fact, we are less likely to be overheard there, I think, Mr Thatcher.' I led the way.

The young man had improved it a great deal since his predecessor's day, the trustees allowing him to choose furniture from never-used rooms in the rest of the house. His choice had been modest, appropriate – but good. The room was predictably clean and tidy, even to the books in the newly acquired bookcase. The only item that might cause Mrs Briggs to sneer was a newly oiled cricket bat propped up in one corner.

He installed us in the two chairs, fetching a third, slightly battered, from his bedchamber. He gestured slightly towards Mrs Briggs, inviting her to speak first.

'He's refusing to cooperate with me, Mrs Rowsley – again.'

'In what way, Mrs Briggs?'

'Yesterday, I wanted to get the silver polished. He tells me the servants will be helping with the hay harvest from tomorrow. So I wanted to get ahead. But he refuses to open the safe. And again this morning.'

Dick took a deep breath but said nothing until I asked him. Then he said, so quietly it was obvious he was trying hard to control himself, 'Ma'am, I tried to explain that the silverware is my responsibility, and, failing me, Luke's. I also said that

you helped me open the safe about a week before Mrs Briggs'
arrival, and that I cleaned it to your satisfaction, ma'am.'

'I am sorry you disagreed over this. And very sorry indeed
that you have disagreed publicly. You are responsible for the
discipline of all your colleagues. How will they behave if they
know you are squabbling? Especially at a time when many are
upset by the death of one and the arrest of another young man
they know well. I am afraid they will take sides in the matter,
and it is up to you two equally to make sure that any
disagreements do not bubble over into . . . regrettable behaviour.
We have a houseful of guests, and – you are both right – with
many of the footmen helping Farmer Twiss, the maids will be
under a great deal of pressure. Let us accept that we may not
always be able to meet some of our highest standards and
concentrate on doing a very good job of what we have to do.'
I smiled at them both. 'We have to think ahead, too. Since
some of the gentlemen will also be involved with the haymaking,
there will be extra laundry. And they will all want baths or
these new showers at the end of the day, so the boilers will
need extra stoking. Mrs Arden and her team will be busy
providing food and drink in the fields – to make life easier for
them, all our daytime meals and refreshments will be taken
outside.'

'All, ma'am? Even servants' dinner?'

'It will be a cold collation, Mrs Briggs, so it can be eaten
indoors or out. But all the guests will be served outside, either
in the fields or by the Roman site, which is where I shall invite
Professor and Mrs Marchbanks to eat. I can serve the guests
myself, but I might need just one footman, Mr Thatcher?'

'Of course, ma'am. I will arrange it. I will, of course, be in
the fields myself.'

'This sergeant you mentioned,' Mrs Briggs asked. 'What
about him?'

'I have no idea what time he will come. And as I told you,
he may not even wish to stay here, but whichever footman is
left on duty here should show him to his room.'

'That would be his usual room, ma'am?' Dick wasn't above
point-scoring.

'Yes, please. Mrs Briggs has had it made up for him.' I

hoped that she had. Or that she would see to it at once. 'Now, I need you both to lend a hand with whatever is needed, whether it's your normal work or not.' I stood. 'Mrs Briggs, I believe my husband asked you for a list. Will you make sure he has it before lunch, please? Thank you. Just to prevent any more unpleasantness, I will ask you both for your safe keys.' I waited while they unhooked them from their keyring and chatelaine respectively. 'Thank you. And may I also ask you both to remember Jemima and Polly and their children and even Harry Tyler in your prayers.' I left with a slight flourish – some might say I swept out. And why not? I wanted neither to chase after me to plead their case.

'I thought they were getting on better,' Matthew said as he locked the keys I had confiscated in his office safe.

'So did I. What I might do is something more subtle – Elias's suggestion, as it happens. I might write to Lady Bibury and ask for more information about why Mrs Briggs left her service. It's not unknown, is it, for an employer to write a good reference in order to get rid of a bad employee.' I paused. 'It's really a task for the lady of the house, of course – in fact, I wonder if it might come better from Mr Wilson, as chairman of the trustees.' Cowardly though I might be, it could spare me any gratuitous insults from an outraged aristocrat.

'You know, I think it might,' he said, as if he understood.

Of course he understood.

'And now I have to tell you what I've agreed to do this afternoon.'

Jemima kept baby Frank on her lap all the time we were there, more like a child hugging a toy for comfort than a mother nursing her infant. She accepted my explanation that although we knew nothing could bring him back, she might know something that might help bring his killer to justice.

'Everyone says Polly's Harry did it.'

'You must miss her,' I said. 'Your best friend. And if he didn't do it, you could be best friends again. Did Ned say why he was going out? What he was doing, if not going down to the Royal Oak?'

'He said to ask no questions, but he was going to make his fortune. Our fortune.'

'How?'

'Not stealing! Not Ned. The very idea!' She was genuinely if naively indignant. 'But he'd seen someone put something in one of the trenches. Bury it. Stamp it down good and hard. And he thought it must be worth something if someone wanted to hide it that much. So he was going to dig it up and claim the reward.' Tears dropped on to the baby's cap – one I recognized from the baby box that at her ladyship's behest supplied necessities for all new mothers in the village. 'That's all, ma'am, I promise.'

'Of course it is.' I passed her my handkerchief – twin of the one by the trench.

'Swore me to secrecy, ma'am – but he was going to give it to you, Mr Pritchard.'

'That would have been a very good idea,' he said gently, though not, I suspected, truthfully. 'I suppose he didn't tell you who buried whatever the treasure was?'

She shook her head. Was I convinced? I wasn't sure. 'Just that he had to be careful on account of it was someone from the House. That's all. No, he didn't even say if it was a lady or a gentleman.' She looked up. 'I don't suppose there'll be any reward in that, though, will there?'

'Not yet,' he said. 'But we'll see what we can do when we find what it is and who put it there.'

I dipped into my reticule. I'd put the coins in a screw of paper. 'These are your wages for cleaning the pottery. And there's a basket of food in the trap.'

'Oh, ma'am! I wish I was safe back working with Polly,' she sobbed.

NINETEEN

I t might be the first day of the harvest, but most of the archaeologists who should have been helping with the harvest were more interested in what was still in the ground, not growing from it, and had gathered around the tarpaulin-covered trenches. Elias Pritchard clearly had a sense of theatre and was waiting for the last archaeologist to struggle up. At some time, of course, Sergeant Burrows would add himself to the mix, but clearly the young man would not wait for him.

Stepping forward, he smiled at Palmer: 'Your assistance, please, Sir Francis.' They pulled as one man. He gestured – Francis was the expert here and should examine the trench and any contacts.

He did so with as much reverence as was possible when jumping down three or four feet. But he suddenly ducked out of sight, calling crisply – the effect was almost shocking – as soon as he was vertical again, 'My camera, if you please, Benton. Yes, here in the trench.'

The equipment used and returned to the surface, he called, 'Harriet, come and look at this – you too, Matthew. Head, Benton – I'd welcome your thoughts. And yours, of course, Wells,' he added as his colleague drifted up.

Obediently, we all stood beside the trench and peered down.

'Look. Just there.' Francis pointed at nothing more than a patch of earth, a marginally different colour from the rest. 'Let's see what a brush will do.' He squatted down. 'Ah! It's coming away quite easily – just as if it had been tamped down only last week, in fact.'

'That certainly fits in with what Jemima said,' Harriet whispered to me.

'We certainly didn't find anything of interest when we dug our test trenches. But here . . . Yes, there's something here. An artefact of some sort, not just a clod of earth. Look.' Some of the earth covering fell away. Was that gold?

Harriet gasped: 'Francis, might I have the honour of washing it?'

'Of course.' He passed it to her as tenderly as if it was an injured bird before scrambling up to join us. 'I would say you have more right than anyone else, wouldn't you, Head?'

'Of course.'

She ran gentle fingers over the object. A little more mud fell off.

Francis leaned closer. 'How interesting.'

Wells frowned. 'Are you thinking what I'm thinking, Palmer? May I suggest that you do wash it, Mrs Rowsley, before any of us handles it? It will be less likely to be damaged than if you scratch at it.'

Standing where Polly had stood yesterday, Harriet placed the object in a bowl, running water over it. She hesitated, as if uneasy to be enjoying herself with something that had caused a tragic death. However, she took her spectacles from her chatelaine. She donned them, squinting in the sun, and then, very tenderly, picked up the object again, dabbing it with a little brush. At last, she held it up. 'This must be gold, must it not? Such detail – what skill! And can these be pearls?'

'Indeed, ma'am,' Wells said. 'Clearly a jewel fit for an emperor. Caesar himself!'

'A jewel?' She placed it against her throat. But then she peered at it again, turning it from side to side. 'But how would one attach it? There's no pin. And in this little tube – I'm sure there's a technical term! – there's only one hole, not two for a chain. It would hang very oddly. No, nor a clip. But who would want to clip it against anything – look at the back, all that gold! You wouldn't want to hide it, however lovely the front is.'

'Forgive me, Wells,' Francis said, holding out his hand for it, 'but I need to photograph it, and our young scribe here needs to record it in the list of finds. Then everyone here will want a good look: I'm sure we all have theories about its origin despite it being placed in that ditch on purpose. After that, it will need a temporary home. A house this size must have a safe, Rowsley – is there room in it for this visitor?'

'Of course,' I said, wondering if it might be more secure in my office safe. Who would have the honour of taking it inside? It looked as if its natural habitat was a velvet cushion, born aloft by a knight to his lady. More prosaically, Francis slipped it into an inside pocket and headed to the finds table, where it was duly recorded.

At last, he and Pritchard led what became a ragged procession to the House.

'No, not through a mere side door,' I heard Wells cry. 'Through the front door! An emperor's jewel should be welcomed as if it were royalty!' Despite my efforts to remind him of Ned's violent death, he summoned a bemused footman with a thunderous bang with the huge knocker.

Francis appeared beside me. 'I fear he wants a massive display of bad taste, Matthew. I can only apologize for him. In mitigation, I can say it is the most amazing piece, you know. And people will want it laid where they can see it properly. It's the find of a lifetime, after all,' he said.

'A man lies dead because of it, Francis. Another is locked up. Is this the time or place?'

'Neither,' said Pritchard grimly. 'But the sooner everyone has seen it, the sooner we can lock it up and get back to reality.'

Still profoundly disagreeing with the notion of a celebration, I shrugged. 'Let's get it over and done with then. Champagne to the state saloon, if you please, Simon. And invite Mr Wilson and Professor and Mrs Marchbanks to join us.'

He smiled. 'I think it deserves one more sluice with warm water. I'm sure Harriet will do the honours.' He passed it to her.

In the absence of the velvet cushion I had imagined, a yellow silk one from a Regency sofa would have to suffice. I laid it ready on the central table, its gilding and its pietra dura top works of art in themselves. I did not hurry: if I knew Francis, he would carefully time Harriet's entrance to make the maximum effect. By now, all our guests were equipped with champagne – I noticed that Thatcher had selected the second-best set of glasses, still more impressive than most people would handle in a lifetime. And then I thought again of Ned, and what seemed a distasteful gathering now seemed almost obscene – especially as the killer was part of it.

Harriet slipped unobtrusively through the crowd of loud men and laid gently on the cushion a small box – it had once contained earrings I had given her. Slowly – yes, she had a sense of drama, too – she opened it. Even I could not forbear to gasp. Her ministrations had removed any residual earth and the jewel glowed – jewels, in fact, for it was clear that the little cross on the front was made of pearls. Cross? Even I knew enough about history to know that such a thing would be unusual in Roman Britain, risky even. Wasn't the Chi Rho the more usual symbol? I know Francis had hoped to find one on this dig, but considered it very unlikely.

The silence was sudden and complete.

It was followed by a cascade of chatter as the men jostled to see the treasure properly for themselves.

I suppose I should have expected Mrs Marchbanks' response. She fainted clean away.

My immediate thought was not for her health, but for the safety of the jewel while everyone's attention was elsewhere. 'The safe,' I mouthed to Francis, who responded with an approving nod. 'We'll take it there now. And I'll ask Bea if she can bring luncheon forward.'

'Outside? They're not dressed for indoors, after all. Your Mrs Briggs will kill when she sees all our footprints. On an Aubusson carpet, too!'

'We need to do two things,' Harriet said as we left the saloon via the service corridor. Apart from the complete absence of pictures on the walls, it was also the most direct route to the safe, and there was less chance of being waylaid by an expert demanding one more glimpse of the treasure. 'I want them to see the jewel.'

Pritchard stopped dead. 'You cannot be serious.'

'Never more. Seeing this won't make them feel any less sad about Ned's death, but it will remind them that we value them enough to show them something that excites all the guests they so diligently serve. His lordship shared his treasures with me; her ladyship left me all that priceless jewellery for my lifetime use. Do Bea and Dick, Luke and Primrose deserve any less?'

Pritchard looked at me, as if for guidance.

'When?' I had to give way, as I had done to Wells and Palmer.

'Now,' she said. 'Before the huge effort to get lunch served early and outside. It's a shame most people will be down in the fields, but those who are still on duty inside will be in or near the servants' hall. They have to be assembled to hear the announcement. Second, I want them also to see you lock the jewel in the safe – except they won't, of course.' She produced a second little box, identical to the first. Pritchard nodded slowly. 'They'll just think that it's locked in there, so if any of our guests should ask, that is the answer they will get. Guests and anyone else,' she added.

'Swapping boxes? I'm no conjurer!'

'You have two inside pockets, Matthew,' she pointed out, patting my chest. 'All you have to remember is which box is in which.'

'All!'

'You can always swap them later, man,' Pritchard grunted. 'Now, I want to watch everyone's faces. That might tell us something.'

Having retrieved the keys she had confiscated yesterday, we walked into the servants' hall together.

'Now,' I began, raising my voice, 'I'm sure the village is abuzz with rumours about the murder. I suspect it will soon be equally busy with rumours about something the archaeologists found this morning. So we thought you should see it for yourselves,' I said, studiously avoiding Harriet's eye. 'May we have a clean tablecloth, please, Mrs Briggs? Thank you. Now, we know this is very old indeed, and probably very fragile. So would you all stand clear? Shortest at the front, tallest at the back, please.'

'You were right,' I said, as Harriet and I made our way back to my office and the much more anonymous safe there. Pritchard had opted to drink tea in the servants' hall and keep his eyes and ears open. 'Though I was terrified I had picked the wrong box.' My hand was shaking as I opened the one I had kept in my jacket. Even now, the sight still made me gasp. I passed it to Harriet while I opened the safe, burrowing amongst the bundles and folders of dry-as-dust documents. At last, I was satisfied that no one who was not actively looking for it would find it in less than ten minutes.

'Phew.' Stepping into her arms, I leaned my forehead against hers.

'Right about what?' she asked at last.

'Showing it to the staff. Absolutely right. Though not everyone was impressed, I fancy.'

'They would have been if it had been bigger and more sparkly. Anyway, you struck just the right tone. And you have proved to be a talented conjurer.'

'Do you think I should show it again this evening? So no one is left out?'

'If you have the energy, we'll have to go and join the workers in the field after lunch. Except,' she added, narrowing her eyes and peering at me, 'I think you should be excused – you've got another headache, haven't you?'

'A little. But I should show my face, shouldn't I?'

TWENTY

All the archaeologists who had seen the jewel were now outside, eating lunch, with the exception of Mrs Marchbanks, who was still indisposed. I made sure I expressed all the correct concern; inside, I was cold with fear that she might be roaming free in the Family wing. I was ashamed of myself. If ever a woman deserved the adjectives 'poor' and 'downtrodden' it was she. And yet . . . and yet . . .

It seemed I had suddenly become something of a celebrity. How had I cleaned the treasure, how long did it take, when could they see it again? The answer to the last question was easy, since Francis stepped in to remind everyone that the find had to be reported to the coroner as treasure trove.

'Some little Roman trinket?' someone asked.

Professor Head joined in. 'Apart from its brief interment, it doesn't seem to me that it was ever put in the ground to save it from others,' he said. 'You recall the Cuerdale Hoard? It's nothing like that – no evidence of it being deliberately buried.'

'Except by some recent malefactor,' Wells observed tartly. 'But who knows where he got it from before he buried it?'

This was the most important question, surely – but the theories bounced on, as if everyone thought it must have been found originally in the Roman area.

'In any case, it's hardly a trinket,' someone else pointed out. 'With that Christian symbolism, it's pretty rare.'

'Indeed, you'd not have expected such an overt display. We've seen nothing, nothing at all, to suggest that this was anything other than a heathen camp.'

'Villa!'

The talk surged around us – over my head in more than one sense. Francis left them to it, edging me to one side. 'It's not often you look bemused, my dear.'

I smiled. 'Professor Fielding warned me about the bitterness of experts' quarrels – yet he's bickering away with the rest of them. Francis, I trust your judgement. Where did it come from and what is it?'

'I genuinely do not know the answer to either of those questions. Not for sure. Everyone assumes it was uncovered during our dig. And where else could it have emerged from? You know, there is something not at all dissimilar in the Ashmolean. What I would dearly like to do is take ours and place it alongside the Alfred Jewel – but I can't imagine Mr Wilson and you trustees agreeing to that.'

'Indeed not,' said Mr Wilson, appearing on cue. 'I think you would need the coroner's authorization. You could bring the other jewel, the Oxford one, here?'

'My dear sir, you joke!' Francis seemed genuinely outraged.

Mr Wilson smiled enigmatically. 'Did I hear someone allude to a hoard? Not here, surely.'

'The Cuerdale Hoard? It was a wonderful Viking hoard – all sorts of precious metal and jewellery jumbled together. It seemed as if it might once have been placed in bags which were then put in a box together – no, only the metalware was found, because anything organic like wood or leather would rot.'

'So the original intention of whoever left it there was to come back and retrieve it?'

'Exactly. This may simply have been dropped a long time ago coincidentally in an historic area. A millennium ago, indeed. And then someone found it recently and reinterred it. Why?' He shrugged. 'Ironically, it turned out that the owner of the Cuerdale land was Queen Victoria herself.'

'I suspect she has enough treasure,' Mr Wilson said. 'Now, if you will excuse me, I believe Professor Marchbanks is tapping his watch. It is not the way I am used to being summoned, but perhaps anxiety for his wife has made him forget his manners.' He bowed and left us.

It was time to load up the trays and return the detritus of lunch to the scullery.

'Mrs Rowsley! Mrs Rowsley!'

I had never expected Sergeant Burrows's voice to be medicinal. I turned towards him, smiling and offering my hand. 'Welcome to Thorncroft House, Sergeant.'

'Thank you, ma'am. And what lovely weather it is for a day in the country. Half a day,' he corrected himself.

Half a day. So he did not intend to take up our offer of hospitality. Perhaps I was relieved. Or perhaps I would have liked his reassuring presence overnight.

'Indeed. And wonderful weather for the hay harvest; you'll find almost everyone in the fields.'

'I've found one person I wanted to talk to, at least, ma'am. You.'

'In that case, may I offer you some refreshment? A cup of tea, perhaps? And I have a very great deal to tell you – there was much excitement this morning!' I led the way back through the servants' door; everyone would know of his presence within five minutes anyway, so he might as well make a nice public entrance – except, of course, that the servants' hall was deserted. So was the kitchen.

He looked around in disbelief.

'It's time for the midday break in the fields, so all the staff who aren't helping with the actual harvest are ministering to those who are. But it's not beyond my powers to fill a kettle and make tea.'

He followed me into the kitchen. 'My, this is all very smart, isn't it? All this new-fangled stuff?'

'It was one of the last changes made in her ladyship's time, and very grateful Mrs Arden is too that it saves so much work – especially as we have fewer staff now. It's still a hot place, on a day like this, though.'

He insisted on carrying the tray, looking nonplussed when I asked him to put it down on the servants' table. I placed a tray of biscuits beside it.

'Maybe we should talk in the Room? You know, just in case anyone comes in.'

'The Room is now Mrs Briggs' territory,' I said. What if she was still inside?

He seemed to approve of my short explanation. 'You can't expect to do everything,' he said. 'Now, you are obviously going out somewhere—'

'The fields – to serve the haymakers beer.'

'I'll try not to keep you very long, then,' he laughed. 'You

know that Harry Tyler is under arrest and held in Shrewsbury
Gaol. I want to keep him where he is for a bit – in a village
like this, there may be bad feeling, and we don't want it spilling
over at a time when men have nice sharp scythes to play with.
So I hope it's a case of out of sight, out of mind.'

'Actually, they're probably talking of nothing else, when
they have breath to talk – but at least they can neither lynch
him nor march to the lock-up to demand his release, so I think
your decision was very wise. But I'm not convinced that he
is guilty.'

He nodded. 'If Tyler didn't kill him, who did, in your
opinion?'

'Perhaps we should talk in my husband's office, Sergeant.'

Gallantly, he picked up the tray again – and put it down so
he could make room on it for the tray of biscuits. Then we set
off. Looking ironically up and down the deserted corridor, he
said, 'I think it's safe for you to answer my question, don't
you?'

'Very well. The murderer is someone tall and strong enough
to hit him with that large stone. Someone who may have tried to
destroy any evidence by using their spectacles to set a fire.
Someone who may have used someone else's spectacles to
suggest they were the killer. But spectacles are not common
amongst the villagers, and in any case, Ned's widow told
Constable Pritchard and me that the person reburying the jewel
was living – or staying – under this roof. And then, of course,
there is the problem of the severed picture cords. I assume
Constable Pritchard has told you about this?'

'Yes, and about the reddle. Your rector's still lying low in
– what do you call your hospital? – the Family wing, that's it?'

'Still very unwell. Still not allowed visitors – though that's
probably to keep him safe in case the man who tried to kill
him and Matthew makes another attempt.'

'Or woman, of course.' I had forgotten how shrewd his
eyes were. 'But you wouldn't want to think of a woman doing
such vile things. You'd be surprised, though, Mrs Rowsley,
surprised.'

I shook my head. 'I know women can be truly evil. But
women here? In this house? Please! No! But . . .'

'You're frightened, you're angry, you're suspicious. Of someone.'

I made him wait as I unlocked the room and made a space on Matthew's desk. Files on the floor? I gathered them up.

He stared at the heaps of paper. 'Busy man, your husband.'

'Very. But not usually this untidy.' I frowned. 'Sergeant Burrows, I jump like a cat when I see anything unusual. I fear that every picture will fall, that every piece of sculpture will topple. And when I see Matthew's desk like this, I instantly fear that someone has been in and has searched for something.'

'Who could get in? The door was locked, Mrs Rowsley.'

'Both the butler and the housekeeper could, if they needed to for some reason, unlock the key cupboard and remove whatever key they wanted.' My face felt very stiff.

'What would either of them want in here? I should have thought a land agent's life was full of dry-as-dust contracts and orders.'

'Yes, but—' Ready to panic, I shook my head. Then I forced out the words, 'The key to the safe.'

'Which is still locked.' He tried the handle.

'I know I am being stupid. Heavens, the key is on Matthew's ring, which is always clipped to his belt. What am I thinking of? I'm so sorry – I'm being stupid!'

'Come on, ma'am. This isn't like you. Take a deep breath, sit yourself down and have a cup of tea. I'll be mother, as they say. There, now.'

We drank in silence for a few minutes, him helping himself enthusiastically to biscuits. At last, I could smile and ask, 'Have I answered all your questions? Because I need to tell you about this morning – unless Constable Pritchard did?'

'He left a note with the stationmaster: you've found something that was placed deliberately in one of the trenches, causing a lot of bickering amongst these here scholars. But I'd like to hear your view of it all. And I'll interrupt if I have any more questions.'

He listened to my account, merely nodding as I went.

'Pretty well. You didn't reply when I asked you who you suspected, did you? But though you may not know it, you've

given me a good deal of information I didn't ask for. Yes, in
view of what his widow said, you believe that whoever killed
Marples is, one way or another, living under this roof. And now
I know that you believe that the find kept in that safe is connected
to it, and that one of the people in this House might steal it
from this safe.' He frowned. 'If it's that precious, though,
wouldn't it be hard to sell it? Everyone who might want to buy
it would know it was stolen.'

'He might just want to possess it. To keep in his private
collection. To let no one else see.'

'That's crazy. If you don't mind my saying so.'

'It's not very sane to go around cutting picture cords, is
it?' I countered. 'I wonder if it's hard for people like us –
people who have to work for their living and scrimp and save
for everything they want – to understand dedicated collectors.
His late lordship bought even more books for a library so
full that no one could possibly know what was there. Towards
the end of his life, he had a change of heart: he wanted other
people – scholars in particular – to be able to study and
appreciate, to help other people appreciate, his finest posses-
sions. He didn't want to give them away, mind. He wanted
to keep them in the family. But he did want some to go on
display in museums, some to go to specialist libraries. This
meant they had to be properly assessed and catalogued. That's
why two of our guests are here – Professor and Mrs
Marchbanks. They are in the library even now, supervised by
Mr Wilson.'

'Ah, I shall be pleased to renew my acquaintance with him.
But supervised? Are two scholars really likely to steal some
old book? Even given what you say about collecting things like
magpies.'

I told him about his lordship's will and my new role.

'I see. Heavens, I wouldn't like having to work with someone
peering over my shoulder all the time. Not that you would, I'm
sure.'

'They certainly don't like it. There has been . . . friction.
Which is why Mr Wilson kindly offered to take my place from
time to time. I'm very grateful – apart from anything else, I've
got many other duties.'

'Isn't that new housekeeper – Mrs Biggs? Ah, yes, Mrs Briggs – doing those?'

I pulled a face. 'There's no lady of the house, Sergeant. So I have had to take on some of her late ladyship's responsibilities. Charity in the village. Acting as hostess to all our guests. Not much, but all of them time-consuming. Like helping to serve refreshments to everyone toiling in the fields.'

He got to his feet, smiling. 'You must be wishing me at Jericho, ma'am.'

I rose, too. Then I surprised myself. 'On the contrary. You have no idea how good it is to talk to someone on the outside. Someone not involved – except in the murder, of course. Even Constable Pritchard knows everyone in the village. Where is he, by the way?'

'I told him to go and help the haymakers. On the face of it, to help. In fact, to question as many people as he can. Especially the labourers the archaeologists employ. Especially them. And even more especially the experts themselves.' He set down his cup and saucer with some finality. He did not want any questions from me.

I got to my feet. 'Now, who would you like to talk to? I can introduce you to anyone here.'

'Thank you. Who would you start with, if you were me?'

The sergeant stayed long enough to watch Matthew repeat his lunchtime performance with the jewel. There were far more staff to watch, but most of them were bone-tired and showed the most perfunctory interest. Mrs Briggs, however, bustled up as he was about to replace the jewel in the safe. 'I really can't imagine the state of the silver, Mrs Rowsley, after all this time.'

I should imagine my smile was as weary as hers. 'We won't even look at it till after the harvest, I promise you. But we can make sure that if ever we have another formal dinner – and that might not be till Mr Wilson finds the heir – you can inspect it when Mr Thatcher has polished it. Now, go and put your feet up; that's all I want to do.' I waited until her back was turned before turning to Matthew.

Soon we were back in his office and the jewel was locked in that safe. And then, far from putting my feet up, I had to take Sergeant Burrows back to the station. For once, I could completely identify with Robin. At least he did not have to spend the next two hours smiling and nodding at our distinguished guests as they squabbled like fractious children.

TWENTY-ONE

When he arrived slightly late for breakfast on Tuesday morning, Francis looked as if someone had lit a candle behind his face; apart from that, his behaviour differed not a jot from normal. Harriet too looked happier than she had for days; she had already spoken to Wilson, who approved what we had done with the keys, with one proviso: he would privately take possession of one of them. He agreed with apparent pleasure to write the letter to Lady Bibury that she requested. Burford and Hurley, who had stayed on the Roman site yesterday, were already dressed for their stint in the hayfields in what they conceived to be bucolic wear, though I doubted if the young men they would work alongside would recognize it. Farmer Twiss would surely be wise to keep them away from the freshly honed sickles and scythes. They could do much less harm, and conceivably a lot of good, binding and stacking the sheaves alongside the older men such as myself. The labourers from the building site, trained for the harvest almost since infancy, would be cutting alongside the regular farm labourers. There would be no dragging the senior archae-ologists from the site, not with the hope of more treasures awaiting their trowels; as for the Marchbankses, they would no doubt continue their work in the library, under the aegis of Wilson. Thatcher would nominate a footman or two – probably retired retainers – since he and all the young men would be toiling in the fields, where Harriet, Bea, Mrs Briggs and most of the maids would be serving refreshments.

At some time, of course, Sergeant Burrows would add himself to the mix.

Harvest or not, I still had responsibilities to all the Croft lands: as soon as I had surrendered a key to Wilson, I would have to deal with a problem with a tenant farmer near Droitwich. There was an immediate tap on my door: Francis.

'I've taken the liberty of asking Harriet to join us here,' he said without preamble. 'I have something I would like you both to see,' he added, producing a letter from an inside pocket. 'Ah, good morning, little sister! Look at this! I telegraphed a friend yesterday and this is what he sent – I got one of the stable lads to collect it from the post office as soon as it opened.'

He laid on my desk a line drawing, complete with the dimensions of the object depicted: front, back and depth. 'The Alfred Jewel,' he said reverently. 'Tell me if it reminds you of anything. This is the obverse.' He laid another drawing beside the first.'

'The jewel from the trench, of course,' Harriet said. 'But isn't this one a little larger? And there's no cross, only that man with big eyes and those staffs in his funny little hands.'

'Show a bit of respect, my love,' I said. 'I think – if this is the Alfred Jewel – that may be Alfred the Great you're mocking. Let me guess why you've brought this here, Palmer: you want to compare it with the one in the safe. Wait a moment. There! My God!' Mine was not the only intake of breath. We gazed in awe at the actual jewel before trying to control our emotions and to engage our critical faculties 'We'd better summon Wilson to see this.'

'He's already in the library with the Marchbankses, I should imagine. I'll go and take his place,' she said reluctantly. She visibly set her shoulders, gave the jewel one last loving look and slipped out of the room.

Eventually, Palmer spoke. 'If this is what I am sure it is – an aestel – then it is simply beyond price.'

There was a tap on the door.

'Drat!'

I thrust a ledger over the jewel. 'I don't want even Luke or Thatcher to know I keep it here.' And I was just in time. Luke announced Wilson.

'How dear Mrs Rowsley endures that pedantic pair I do not know!' he snapped as a greeting the moment the door was closed. 'Ah, before I forget, here is the letter she requested.' He laid it on the blotter. 'I assume someone will take it to the post, despite all the agricultural activity?'

If I asked any of the staff, someone might guess what was happening. 'I'll take it myself before I join the others.'

'Working in the sun despite your head injury? My dear
Rowsley, is that wise? What did Page say, and Harriet?'

I pulled a face. 'I had to promise that I will do very little,
but I must show myself there.'

'Hmm.' Taking a deep breath, Wilson continued, 'Do you
know, their task nowhere near completed, the Marchbankses
are talking about packing up and going home? Going home! I
made it clear that they could not leave until we had received
their written report on what they had found so far, and their
recommendations on what books we trustees should lend to a
learned institution.'

'And, of course,' I said, 'though Constable Pritchard has
not stated it formally, I can't imagine him letting potential
witnesses leave for Oxford. I admit it is unlikely but he and
Sergeant Burrows might want to interview everyone in the
area. Everyone. Not just the villagers.' Especially if Twiss told
Burrows what he had told me, and if Pritchard accepted what
Harriet had said yesterday after their joint soaking.

Wilson was quick to nod. 'Of course, I could have told them
that. But one doesn't want to fire all one's ammunition at once,
does one? Now, gentlemen, how can I help you?'

Palmer smiled. 'I would like you to look at this drawing.'
He laid it on my blotter.

'If it is a sketch of what I think might be called the Croft
Jewel, then it is not very accurate – ah! It is not the Croft Jewel,
is it?'

'It's the Alfred Jewel, now in the Ashmolean Museum. And
this is – yes, the Croft Jewel.' He removed it carefully from its
hiding place and put it beside the sketch.

I have never seen so much emotion on Wilson's face. 'May
I?' He picked it up as gently as if it were a butterfly. 'This is
– let me see – Anglo-Saxon? Not Roman at all? Made by people
who form part of our common Christian ancestry? Thank you.'
He polished, then replaced, his spectacles. 'If you, as an experienced archaeologist, were unsure of its provenance, does this
mean it is a very rare item? Very rare indeed?'

'Vanishingly rare. An aestel, I believe. We are not entirely
sure what such devices were used for, but scholars speculate
that one was held when reading aloud. Instead of tracing the

text – probably illuminated, certainly very precious – with a human digit, a monk would use this jewel as a pointer: think of a schoolmaster pointing at his blackboard with a cane.' He gestured. 'And perhaps a quill or something was fixed in this little tube so the gold didn't scrape the vellum. See that little hole there? For a tiny pin or peg, perhaps.'

'Dear me. Dear me. So old. So precious.' He swallowed. His voice changed. 'As a lawyer, I must ask where you keep it.'

'Everyone believes it is in the House safe, alongside all the silver and gold plate and her ladyship's jewellery.'

He raised a finger. 'Lady Croft wanted your wife to use the jewellery, Rowsley. I hope she does.'

I pulled a face. 'Rarely. It is very grand – too grand for the comparatively mundane life we live. And on occasions when she has worn something – the jet mourning parure, for example – she has been accused of theft, not to put too fine a point on it. As you probably recall, it takes two keys to open the safe – the butler's and the housekeeper's. I suspect Harriet feels that to ask Mrs Briggs to open it would be tactless, perhaps. In any case, to prevent a row on Sunday, Harriet confiscated both keys, so while they may believe the aestel is in the main safe, they can't check.'

He shook his head in irritation. 'I will speak to Harriet later. Meanwhile, my apologies for the digression. If this jewel does not live in the main safe, I trust its hiding place is secure.'

'We thought it might be safer to keep it here.' I touched the office safe. 'As you can see, this is a fairly recent Chubb. If it was unlockable during the Great Exhibition, it should be unlockable now.'

'Alas, Matthew, did not one Mr Hobbs manage to open it? Admittedly, lock pickers of his calibre are mercifully rare, and probably not found in Shropshire. So let us assume it is a good safe. But if anyone does open it?'

'The jewel's not in an obvious box or tin; it's just in a little box hidden amongst documents. Many, chaotic documents.'

'You have a clerk, do you not? I hope he doesn't have access. Dear me, I forgot: he is no longer employed here.'

'Sadly not. He was a huge asset and made my life very much easier. But he found Thorncroft too isolated for his taste and has taken a post in Exeter, working for the bishop. I should be interviewing new applicants next week. If we make an appointment, we may have to think of a new home for it.'

'Indeed. You trustees have an interesting decision to make,' Palmer said. 'Assuming the coroner does not consider it treasure trove and it reverts to the estate, do you lend it to the British Museum or the Ashmolean? More to the point, how do you transport it there in complete safety?'

Wilson looked at his watch. 'I should be relieving Harriet, and unless the Marchbankses decide to make a small contribution of their own to the harvest effort, I shall spend the day in the library – luncheon apart? I assume that, as usual, we will have the pleasure of eating *en plein air*? In answer to your questions, sufficient unto the day is the evil thereof. Good day to you both.'

'I must go, too,' Palmer said. 'Those of us left at the site will be extra keen today. Who knows what treasure we shall find? I for one will not be expecting an aestel, but in the trenches in which we are working there will still be Roman artefacts – and even a battered coin or a broken comb is precious to a genuine archaeologist. As for the aestel trench – someone will want to explore further, but I'm sure to no avail. Actually, I have another question: how on earth, given that Shropshire is not particularly known for Saxon artefacts, did the Croft Jewel come to light here?'

TWENTY-TWO

I t could not be said that the professor and his wife greeted me with any obvious enthusiasm, and my reminder that everyone would again be eating al fresco today aroused even less. However, they continued purposefully about their task.

I allowed myself the privilege of browsing the shelves. How many times had I used the softest of feather dusters, even an artist's delicate brush, on those volumes? Or wished I might touch the books that looked as old as the world? How many times had his lordship invited me to share with him the pleasure of a well-turned phrase – 'It takes a great writer to choose the precise adjective, the exact noun' – or to look at an illustration so beautiful it might well have been in a frame and hung for all to see? Did I dare look without him at my side?

Almost as if he himself spoke, I heard the words, 'Of course you can. You are the guardian of all this. It is your duty to get to know the books – and more than just their faded or non-existent spines. Your duty.'

But it would be such a private moment, almost like kneeling in a great church, that I did not want it shared by anyone else. Not by the Marchbankses, at least. Heavens, she would probably faint. But I would come back at a time when they would not be here. But not, alas, today – I knew how busy we women would be. All the same . . . I reached for one—

'I have put those in order; do not undo my good work, if you please,' Mrs Marchbanks snapped, not so much making a request as giving a command in a tone I would be reluctant to use even to the most junior tweeny.

Perhaps she expected an apologetic curtsy. But I stood tall, looking her in the eye, my right eyebrow raised. Sometimes I had reduced even impertinent house visitors to a stuttering apology with that eyebrow. There had been days, however, when I had had to add an icy 'Indeed?' Today was one such day.

'Indeed!' she spat back. 'All this giving yourself airs – and

you are nothing but a jumped-up housekeeper. And not a very
good one at that. All this trouble with the pictures – what sort
of housekeeper allows picture cords to rot? And here you are
pretending to know all about books.'

I let the silence grow. Surely she would realize that she had
gone too far. Surely her husband did. But neither spoke.

Someone else did. Mr Wilson. How much of this had he
observed from his viewpoint in the doorway? 'It is precisely
because Mrs Rowsley knows less than she likes about books
that you are here, Mrs Marchbanks. She herself does not employ
you, so she cannot dismiss you as she might well wish. Neither
can I. It takes all the trustees to end your contract – actually,
your husband's, one gathers – one which pays you a very good
salary—'

'I prefer the term *emolument*,' the professor said.

'Whatever term you prefer, sir, you are in receipt of monies
for carrying out a task, namely cataloguing the books in this
room. You know that it is not in Mrs Rowsley's power, nor
mine, to leave this room unattended while anyone is in it. You
might consider his late lordship to have been over-stringent in
his will. I might myself. So, on a glorious day like this, when
she has pressing duties elsewhere, might Mrs Rowsley. But she
does have one right: as the legal guardian of every book on
every shelf, she may touch and examine any and every book
she fancies. I trust I make myself clear? And I must make it
equally clear that she is entitled to an apology for your
insolence.'

I kept my head high, inclining it slightly to the right – and
waited, eyebrow raised again.

A dairymaid would have made a better job of a few mumbled
words. But I had nothing to gain from drawing out the moment.
With a dismissive curtsy, I left the room.

In the privacy of our bedchamber, I stared at myself in the
mirror. Why was I shaking? Why was I ready to weep? All my
life, I had dealt with insolence in one form or another; on
numerous occasions, someone else had stepped in to defend
me. So why had this incident affected me so deeply?

A number of inchoate reasons churned in my head. But I

knew from experience that the best way to deal with pain was simply to work through it. And there was enough work ahead. Selecting a broad-brimmed hat – almost a bergère – I pinned it at a jaunty angle: no one would see even a vestige of my tears. Then I would head out to take my place in the fields. Usually, I picked up news of families I had not seen for months, and, in turn, could talk about the progress of the new village. Today, however, I suspected that what most people wanted to talk about was the murder. I must try to do what seemed to come naturally to Elias Pritchard: elicit information that people did not even know they were revealing. And, in turn, I must give nothing away that Elias wanted to be kept secret. Even as I locked the bedchamber door, I stopped. Had Mrs Briggs ever given Matthew the list he'd asked for? He hadn't mentioned receiving it. But I must ask him before I asked her.

I caught him still at his desk. He narrowed his eyes. 'What's happened?'

'I'll tell you later.' Hands on my hips, I looked about me. 'You know, even Sergeant Burrows was shocked by this mess. We thought you'd had intruders! We even checked to see if the safe was still locked. This isn't like you, Matthew. But at least tidying it will be better for you than working in the fields, won't it?'

He nodded, finger to his mouth as if he were a guilty schoolboy.

'Now, did Mrs Briggs ever give you the list you wanted?'

'The spectacles!' He smote his forehead dramatically. 'No. I'll go and ask her myself.' But he looked hopefully at me. 'I don't suppose you—?'

'I would – but I really don't want another fight today. I managed not to lose my temper just half an hour ago. I might not succeed this time.'

'The Marchbankses? I'm sorry. I was wrong to ask you.' Despite the hat, he kissed me. 'I'll see you in the fields.'

'I beg your pardon? What would Ellis say?'

'I did ask him. He said an hour should not hurt. In any case, I'm taking this to the post. Wilson's letter to Lady Bibury. I thought it best to be extra discreet. And yes, I shall walk, not take Esau.'

'You could always take Robin?' I suggested.

'So I could. And be there in time for *tomorrow*'s post.'

'Now, I shall keep an eye on you – to make sure you don't try to do too much!'

'Yes, my love,' he replied, pretending to look hangdog and earning another kiss. 'And I'll come back and tidy my desk.'

It was time to do our duty.

TWENTY-THREE

Sometimes I would walk through the entrance hall for the sheer pleasure of it. Today, although I was dressed for the fields, I had another reason – to make sure that the retired retainer was happy in his new role. I was reassured by the way he leapt up to open the door for me – and kept it open for a group of Palmer's colleagues striding up behind me. Despite my disreputable hat, the sun blinded me as I stepped from the stately gloom inside. Wilson's letter fluttered from my grasp. Hurley and Burford scuttled after it, joined by Head, apparently intent on proving he was as lithe as men half his age. Fielding watched the proceedings with some disdain.

At last, Head returned the letter, which I tucked into my inside jacket pocket.

Fielding said, 'You cannot mean to work in the fields after your injury? Surely, it is most unwise. And I presume you intend to go to the village post office, too? Could not a servant—?'

I shook my head. 'The harvest takes precedence over everything. But you will all be fed and watered as you should be, even if you find maidservants offering you coffee and luncheon instead of the usual footmen. Please assure your colleagues that you will not starve. What do you hope to find today?'

'Everyone wants to trump Saturday's find, of course,' Head declared. 'I hope we find evidence to support Palmer's theory that we are working on a villa, not a fort.'

'I'm afraid it will be slow and routine, sir,' Burford said. But he couldn't sound dignified and sensible for long. 'Wouldn't it be ripping to find – oh, I don't know – gold coins or a bracelet?'

'Not that we'll get a chance,' Hurley reflected. 'Not us scribes.'

'Not even scribes today,' Burford pointed out. 'Labourers. Oh, what I'd give to be let loose with a trowel! I suppose if we get the hay in quickly . . .'

'If you impress Farmer Twiss, you might be let loose with

a scythe – but you must treat it exactly as he tells you. A scythe can kill, lads, remember that. And then you'd never get to use a trowel.'

Fielding laughed. 'As if to scrape with a trowel brings instant treasure. Ah, the young, God bless them,' he added as they cantered off.

Although I'd only been working half an hour, I was already looking forward to the next break, not least because I was worried about Harriet; she'd been unusually grim and I was sure she had been crying. She had not been out with the last team of women, who had now returned to the kitchen; if she wasn't with them when they came back with our picnic lunch, I would go in search of her. Meanwhile, I had to concentrate on what I was doing: Twiss's scythes were, as he said, wondrous sharp. No wonder he had dispatched all the archaeologist volunteers to start tedding in the bottom meadow, where I noticed they were joined by Pritchard.

Heavens, I was tired. If only I could have asked Hurley or Burford to go to the village for me; it would have been a lark for them but had become disconcertingly like a trudge for me. My head was beginning to thump. Yes, I must stop.

To my huge relief, someone spotted Bea's team and a cheer went up. No, Harriet wasn't in this group, either. Then I remembered she was helping serve the older archaeologists still on their site. If she was unhappy, Palmer was better than I was at restoring her good humour, something of which I was greatly ashamed.

Joining the decidedly disorderly queue, at last I had a chance to speak to Bea. She motioned me to one side.

'You know she's taken charge of the archaeologists' luncheon. Matthew, something's upset her and she won't say what. Well, we've not had time to chat.' She gestured to the laden tables.

'I don't suppose you've seen Mrs Briggs, have you?'

'She was here a while back, but we were both working flat out so we didn't have time to talk. She gave Dick a strange look. But I don't think they've had another tiff. In fact, they've both been minding their P's and Q's.'

'She'd have been hard put to even speak to him – he's been

down here all morning, working his socks off, according to Mr Twiss. Over there.'

'Dear me, he's caught the sun already, silly lad. And you, Matthew. God knows what you're doing here after that bang on the head.'

'Ellis said an hour or so wouldn't hurt.'

'Well, mind it's no more. You all think you've got hide as tough as these lads who are out in all weather. Put your shirt and hat on, do, or you'll end up with heat stroke.'

I obeyed with alacrity – not because of her advice, excellent though it was, but because I suddenly remembered I had tucked Mrs Briggs' list into my inside jacket pocket. I had reasoned it would be safe at the side of the field since I was paying Sprue's grandson, Walter, who was too small yet to help in the field, to guard everyone's coats. I hadn't reckoned on it becoming a goalpost in a game of football. I was about to rebuke him roundly when he said, 'Please, gaffer, this man came down to see you. Said he needed to leave a note for you, so which was your coat. So I said I'd take the note and give it to you. No, he had to put it in your pocket. Nothing else would do. So I said did he know which it was, 'cos I didn't, though of course I did. And he offered me a tanner to show him, and I said even for a florin I didn't know. He started to look for it himself, gaffer, that he did, which I suspicioned was strange. That's when I said to Bert we should play football and I'd be goalie. Didn't I, Bert?'

'Yes, gaffer. Though Walter can't save a ball for toffee.'

'Liar!'

'Can't so.'

'Liar, liar, pants on fire!'

Who hit whom first?

'Enough!' But I was so pleased to find the list where I'd left it that I said, 'I bet I could beat the pair of you. Come on, give me the ball.' Bouncing it, I asked casually, 'This man – did he give his name so you could give me a message?'

'No, gaffer. I tried to ask, but he didn't seem to hear,' Walter said. He looked genuinely puzzled.

Was he telling the truth? Or after an extra tip? 'Was he old or young?'

'Not old.'

'No, nor young, neither,' Bert chipped in.

'How tall was he?'

'A bit more than you, maybe.'

'So quite tall. And what did he look like?'

'Well, like a gentleman.' The boys looked at each other with matching don't-know expressions. 'Didn't see his face, see, gaffer. He's got this big straw hat. Like a lot of the gentlemen have. And such a runny nose, like harvest gives some folk. Had this big hanky to his face all the time. And sneezes fit to burst.'

'Clothes? Light? Dark?'

'The colour of your jacket. Like all the gentlemen wear.'

Linen, then. 'Anything else?'

'Talked like a gentleman, too – sort of. No, it was funny – not quite like you, gaffer. But not like us either.'

'Well done. And if you think of anything else, tell me or Constable Pritchard straightaway.'

I dug in my pockets. A shilling each? Why not? It would soften the blow of my scoring an easy goal. I ruffled two tousled heads and went to look for Twiss to excuse myself for an hour or so.

'Ah,' he said dryly. 'Saw you just now. You know what we say, gaffer: *one boy's a boy; two boys are half a boy; three boys are no boy at all.*' He nodded at me: I was the third boy, wasn't I?

'Guilty as charged,' I said with a grin, as I slipped on my jacket. 'But young Bert's already gone back to work. And Walter – he earned his corn this morning when someone wanted to get hold of my jacket – look, he's back on guard, too. He'll do well, that lad.'

'Ah. You'll be after him for this school of yours, no doubt.'

'Probably! But that cock won't fight any more, Twiss, and I've got an office job to do. I'll be back within the hour, with luck.'

He narrowed his eyes. 'Maybe best make it two or three hours; you look done in, if you don't mind my saying, gaffer. You have to watch those bangs on the head, you know.'

*   *   *

As I walked back, longing for the cool of my office, I tried to think, cursing the fog that filled my brain. Who had been trying to find my jacket? And why? Was it something to do with the list Mrs Briggs had given me? My own list? Or was it to leave me a note accusing someone?

I headed for the nearest door, the servants' entrance.

And pulled up short. There was someone on guard.

'Good afternoon, Billy. What are you doing here?'

Yes, it was a stupid question. Billy, known almost universally as Boots, was a youngster of seven, perhaps eight, whose lameness kept him from the fields.

'Afternoon, gaffer. Mr Thatcher told me to keep an eye on things while everyone else was in the fields.'

Poor child: no football for him.

'So I thought if I brought this here table out, I could do my blacking' – he held out an immaculate boot, one of many lined up beside him – 'and keep an eye on things at the same time. The comings and goings, gaffer.'

I nodded, seriously. 'That was an excellent idea, Billy. Well done. Is everything as it should be?'

'Yes, gaffer. Seen no strangers, that's to say. All the maids have been to-ing and fro-ing, Mrs Arden, too. And that there Mrs Briggs. She came back half an hour since.'

'What about the guests?'

'Coming out this way, gaffer? Be the front door for them.'

'True. Now, Billy, if you want to be a footman, you need to practise calling men "sir", not "gaffer". It's more the thing, you know.'

His lip wobbled. 'But now they say cripples can't be footmen. And I shall be thrown on the parish.'

'"They"? Billy, you know Mrs Rowsley and I promised you a job. And we always keep our promises.' Even to boys with a club foot as bad as Byron's. Tall and broad-shouldered he might never be, but Harriet would make sure he had some responsible role in the household. 'Understand?'

'Yes – yes, sir!'

Another lad who deserved to be at school . . . Meanwhile, I pressed a shilling into his hand.

*   *   *

Reluctantly accepting that I should not return to the fields, I changed into my office wear and went to look outside, hoping that Harriet would not be too busy to speak to me.

The few archaeologists left on the Roman site were still at lunch. Head was regaling the Marchbankses with details of the morning's work. Wilson was deep in conversation with Sergeant Burrows, both laughing freely. Harriet? Where might she be? What if she had gone to find me just as I was looking for her?

'I knew you wouldn't recognize me,' she said quietly.

I wheeled around to find her offering me lemonade. 'Why are you dressed as a maid?'

She laughed. 'The disguise has worked before, hasn't it? Oh, do you remember your cousin's face when he realized who had been dusting and sweeping his house? Anyway, I agreed with Bea and Mrs Briggs that I would take charge here – didn't Bea tell you?'

'Yes, but not that you would be dressed like this.'

'You've no idea how much cooler a print dress is. And more practical. Especially if you're serving food and drink. And—'

'And?'

'I'll explain later. Did you say you had that list for Sergeant Burrows?'

'Yes – thanks to young Walter,' I added. 'I have a suspicion someone – possibly a gentleman – might have been looking for it, but while he might have guarded my coat well, neither Arthur nor his friend could give a decent description of him.'

'I bet the good sergeant will be interested in that, too. Oh, there he is! Now, is your desk any tidier?'

'Not much. But the moment I've given this to Burrows, I'll get back to it.'

'Not the fields? So you've seen sense at last! Thank goodness for that.'

I cupped her face and kissed her on the lips. 'And when I've tidied my desk, we'll talk about that "and" – promise?'

'Promise. Now there is dessert to be served.' Before my eyes, she became a servant again.

Palmer joined me, separating me slightly from the others. 'What amazing courage she has. And such wonderful panache – what better way to challenge that dratted Marchbanks woman's snobbish insults than by embracing them? Oh, Harriet'll explain, I'm sure. If not, Wilson will.' He looked at his watch. 'It's more than time we resumed work. However, before we do, I think that we gentlemen, all of us, should help Harriet carry the remains of the picnic back to the kitchen.'

No one, not even the Marchbankses argued, though it was obvious some might have wished to.

Our trays delivered, Burrows buttonholed me. 'A word in private, if you please.'

'Of course. I can give you the list I mentioned. And tell you of an odd occurrence in the hayfield.'

Burrows looked around him as I let him into my office: 'This is a bit better, sir, if I may say so.'

'Yes. A bit. Harriet told me off, you understand. Meanwhile, here is the list I asked Mrs Briggs to compile. And the list for the guests.'

'Thank you. This might be a complete waste of time. If you've used your spectacles to try to set a fire, would you admit to it? But Pritchard can work his way through it.'

'And he might be able to identify a mysterious gentleman who tried for some reason to find my jacket in the field today. He was thwarted by a little boy who lied to his back teeth that he didn't know which it was. And created a neat diversionary tactic, too,' I explained, to be rewarded with a smile.

'There are those who don't hold by education for everyone, but a bright lad like that – well, it makes you think, doesn't it? And I know what I want for my sons . . . Now, I need to talk to all your scholars and archaeologists, but I'm going to find that hard, aren't I, with them being scattered everywhere. I need to do it quickly because my train departs at half past six.'

'You could stay. I believe your usual room's been made ready.'

He shook his head. 'My wife's near her time. I know giving birth's her job, but – well, I feel I should be in the House to run errands at least. More to the point, if I'm not, she'll kill me. But I'll come back tomorrow, all being well. Not that I'm expecting otherwise; it's our fourth.'

Having said all that was proper, I added, 'If I were you, I'd start with the Marchbankses. They've been making life unpleasant for Harriet, especially today, though I don't know the details. And you'll find them guarded by Mr Wilson.'

'Ah, Mr Wilson – my sort of man, Mr Wilson, though I've never had much time for lawyers before, doing all they can to help knaves and scoundrels escape just punishment.'

'He's as straight as a die. I used to respect him; now I like him, too. Do you remember how to reach the library or shall I take you there?'

He looked at me shrewdly. 'If I were you, I'd take a break from this deskwork. You've set an example in the fields. Now show some common sense here, man.'

My aching head told me he was right. 'I'll take you there and then just go and close my eyes for a bit. And yes, I'll lock up behind us.' I produced the key and turned it.

TWENTY-FOUR

The procession of tray-carrying gentlemen had stunned the occupants of the servants' hall. Stunned – and, in one case, offended.

'Are they suggesting my women can't do their job properly, Mrs Rowsley? Are you?' Mrs Briggs added, looking me up and down. 'Dressing like that and all?'

'It's a good job I did, isn't it?' I responded, laughing. 'Look, tea all down my pinny. And strawberry jam. As for the guests' behaviour, I'm as surprised as you are.' Francis' idea, I would imagine. 'Now, Mr Wilson will work in the library this afternoon, so I can do my proper share in the fields.'

'That's my job. And Mrs Arden's.'

'In this household, it's always been everyone's job,' I said gently. 'Even Lord and Lady Croft – and the present Lord Croft, when he was well – would always lend a hand. They would even invite their town friends to come along for the corn harvest and all the Harvest Home celebrations. Oh, the aching backs and the blisters – I bet we'll have some of those today, since it's the first time some of the archaeologists have been in the fields. And some sunburn, though at least they always seem to wear hats, don't they? Thank goodness for Nurse Webb and her team. It used to be our job—'

'Ma'am, we've surely got enough to do!'

'Exactly. Especially as we've only half the staff as in the old days. This is why the system changed when we got a nurse on the premises. Heavens, I should be on my way to the fields already,' I fibbed, not wanting any more conflict today.

'It's a real relief, ma'am, I can tell you, to be doing the job I'm meant to do,' Dan, the stable lad said, cajoling Robin between the shafts so that I could collect Sergeant Burrows and take him to the station.

'It's a relief to have you here. Robin point-blank refused to let me harness him. Idle creature, aren't you, Robin!'

The wretched animal seemed to take it as a compliment.

Of course, the sergeant could have walked – he had made his way up, after all – but driving him gave me a chance to question him. And to give him a basket of fruit and vegetables for his family.

He eyed it suspiciously. 'This isn't a bribe, is it, ma'am?'

'It's not for you, Sergeant. It's for your wife and family. And I won't ask any questions. But if you ask me anything, I'll answer.'

'In that case, I can say thank you and tell you it's very timely. My wife's about to give birth any moment now. Our fourth. We'll be needing another maid, my wife tells me. And I think she may be right.'

I said all that was proper.

'Thank you. Now, if you're not asking questions, I am. Do you trust Sir Francis Palmer?'

I gasped. 'With my life! He's my oldest friend, Sergeant. But I would dearly love to ask why you might doubt him. Though I know I said I wouldn't.'

He laughed. 'I wondered how long that would last. Very well. I have no reason to suspect him of anything. Yet. Do you trust his friends?'

'I've not really met any – just the colleagues he's brought here.'

'Not friends?'

'I don't think these men are his friends. They don't behave like friends, at any rate, especially with each other. For all they're experts, they're like badly behaved children with their tiffs and spats. And the trustees are paying them to behave like grown-ups!'

'A strange mixture, those I've encountered. And some making hay, of course, while the sun shines.'

'Are you implying some are making hay in both senses?'

'I might be. You, for instance, think that this Professor Marchbanks and his wife are making notes on what they are doing. What would you say if I told you she can't write? Maybe not read?'

'Can't read and write? Never!' My jerk on the reins brought Robin to an unauthorized halt. I clicked him into reluctant action again. 'I assumed . . . How on earth did you discover such a thing?'

'I made it my business to pay the library a visit. And to look at the books. And to look at their jottings. She doesn't write down what her husband says. She just makes strange lines and squiggles. They might mean something to the Man in the Moon but not to me, I can tell you. She rattled off a list of books and authors just as if she was reading from the page, mind – so she must have an amazing memory,' he admitted. 'But exactly what she's doing in your library, goodness knows.'

'I'd no idea. Absolutely none. She's always been so industrious.'

'And that pinafore of hers, too – well, he's got one, hasn't he? Have you checked what they put in their pockets?'

'I've never seen a suspicious bulge. They know that their luggage will be inspected when they leave. And no parcels have been sent from here.'

'Hmm. Well, that's something. You don't just sit and read, either you or Mr Wilson?'

'I did at first. But . . . did she faint while you were talking to her, by any chance? I'm sorry. I shouldn't have asked.'

I felt his eyes on my face as I manoeuvred round the last tight bend before the station. 'Why did you?'

'Because she swoons so regularly.'

'Ah. And what does he do while she lies lifeless at your feet?'

'He calls for help at my behest. He upbraids me if I am heartless enough to lock up bookcases before I attend to her.'

'Where does she go when she's had one of these swoons?'

'Once or twice to the Family wing, for medical attention. Usually to her bedchamber. And – Sergeant, I've just remembered – early on in her stay, she was found insensible, apparently with drink, on the dining-room floor.'

'And you've never questioned her?'

'Things are bad enough between us without my risking that.'

'Hmph. And you still think no books have disappeared?'

'Don't think I haven't checked for gaps on the shelves! And I confine the Marchbankses to the muniment room when I have to leave the library.'

Expecting a sugar lump from the youngest porter, Robin speeded up.

'Isn't that risky, too? There must be all sorts of important documents in there. Mrs Rowsley, I've already told Mr Wilson that this nipcheese approach to preserving valuable property isn't good enough, with or without the Marchbankses. You need a few ex-constables on guard, that's what you need. Ah, is that my train? Good day, Mrs Rowsley. I hope to see you tomorrow. One last thing: if anyone, anyone at all, tries to leave before I get back, get young Pritchard to arrest them.'

I had to run after him with the basket, for the sheer pleasure of imagining him striding through the ancient streets of Shrewsbury pretending he was carrying nothing.

'Thank goodness you are here,' I said. 'Though we ought to be changing for dinner.'

Matthew looked up from a slightly tidier desk. 'Here as in *alive*, here as in *not harvesting hay* or here as in *in this room*?'

I snorted. 'All three! But we need to talk about the Marchbankses. The fact, for instance, that Sergeant Burrows believes she can't read or write.'

'What?' He sprang to his feet.

'Yes! I remember showing her his lordship's will – she just held it, as if it was meaningless. And there's something else. When she was so rude to me' – I explained, as I had promised I would – 'her outburst was provoked by my approaching some books she said she'd just put in order. What if there are some missing and she's afraid I'd know?'

'And would you?'

'All those books shoved higgledy-piggledy wherever his lordship could find a space? I wish I could. But guests or not, I am going to look at those books today. Could you come with me?'

'Of course. But I think you need an impartial witness.

Wilson, of course. Yes?' he snapped as someone tapped the door.

'We have tesserae!' Francis said, opening his hand to reveal two coloured cubes, perhaps the size of gaming dice. 'What I've been waiting for all this time! Can you send someone for Wilson? And the Marchbankses, I suppose.'

'I would if there were anyone to send,' Matthew said. 'Everyone will be under the yard pump or having a quick sluice or already changed and at work in the kitchen.'

'Oh.' He sounded truly disconcerted. How dare Thorncroft House let him down? He gave an impish smile. 'Well, you're the only ones I really wanted. Come and see! Oh,' he added as I tapped my watch, 'please come. Please. It will only take five minutes. That can't hurt.'

How little my dear friend knew about running a kitchen and having food ready – and not overcooked – for the time guests would expect a meal. But he was as excited as a puppy. What could we do but follow him?

'What is a tesserae?' I asked Matthew quietly as we followed Francis.

'Tesserae is plural, the plural of tessera,' he said.

I nodded. 'One tessera, two tesserae.'

'Exactly. And I believe they are very small tiles used to make mosaics. But let him explain. He'd rather. Heavens, if he had a tail, it would wag him off his feet. Look at him!'

Not all the experts were as overjoyed as Francis. Dr Wells was already marching off, making pointed remarks about changing into civilized clothes. Professor Head appeared beside us. 'Did I not say as much? However, do not let someone's pique spoil Palmer's moment. Look!'

He pointed into the trench Francis had leapt into. A brightly coloured picture was emerging. Yellow, red, a lovely blue. Surely it was a flower? Several flowers. All buried and now seen for the first time in centuries.

He looked up. 'I'm sorry – as soon as you have had your fill, I must cover it again to protect it. I'll cover the whole trench, in fact, in case a badger decides it is a ready-made sett.'

We watched as he pushed the earth gently back, reaching for the tarpaulin Mr Burford passed him. 'There.' He weighed it down.

'Am I right in thinking this calls for champagne?' I asked. But I spoke with only muted joy, for I knew I could not go to the library tonight.

TWENTY-FIVE

How Bea and her team managed to present us with any dinner at all, I do not know. Neither, perhaps, did Thatcher or Luke, who were serving us.

Although the plentiful champagne should have relaxed everyone into a state of tolerant benevolence, Wells publicly considered the chicken curry too spicy, and Marchbanks did not enjoy the texture of the dhal. But Head and Fielding, both of whom now boasted of spending time in India, assured us that both dishes were authentic, as were the accompaniments. Hurley went so far as to propose a toast, congratulating the cook. Bea smiled modestly. When her face was in repose, however, it was clear she was exhausted – as were most of us.

'I wish I were a nanny so that I could send our guests to bed early,' I muttered to Harriet.

'Perhaps the gnats will do the job for us. I will suggest we take our coffee outside once more.'

Fielding, finding that no one wanted to read Shakespeare, proposed charades instead. 'Book titles,' he added. 'And we simply draw an imaginary line – here – through the circle we're sitting in. Wells, will you captain Team A, and Head, will you lead Team B? Ah, Luke, could you bring me two pads of paper and two pencils? Thank you.'

How the young man was still on his feet, I did not know. But he did as he was bid, even managing a polite – if very stiff – bow. Absently, Fielding nodded his thanks and passed them to the reluctant team captains.

'But now, Luke,' I said, intending everyone to hear, 'you and all your colleagues should stand down. Yes, all of you. Everyone has worked very hard indeed and there is more to do tomorrow. We are quite capable of gathering our cups and glasses and taking them to the scullery. Go!'

Even as he left, someone – was it Benton? – muttered, 'But he is a servant!'

'Well done, Luke,' Palmer cried, almost drowning out the carping tone. 'And will you pass on our thanks to all your colleagues? You have worked wonders.' He led a round of applause.

Then Fielding took over. Here were the rules. This is what we had to do. We did it.

Enthusiasm dwindled palpably. Mrs Marchbanks declined to play any longer, accusing Wells of choosing too obscure a title. Wells's apology was little more than a sneer. Fielding was sharp to both.

Palmer looked ostentatiously at his watch. 'I'm afraid we all have to rise early tomorrow, as the harvest and the dig continue. So I propose to declare this a tie – we can always conclude the game tomorrow if you wish. Meanwhile, it's time for us stay-at-home scholars to pull our weight.' He loaded the tray, carrying it to the door, which Wilson opened with a flourish, declaring, 'No, Bea! You have worked harder than any of us. Goodnight and God bless you all.'

With some embarrassment, Burford and Hurley got up and followed them. As for the others, they needed to retire at once or smoke a last cigar. Harriet and I were left to gather the remaining china and glasses.

In fact, the best part of the evening was to come. We were greeted as we entered the servants' hall by the sound of laughter from the scullery.

'Dear Lord, they're washing up!' Harriet squeaked. 'And I don't suppose a single one of them has ever done it before! How many breakages will there be?'

'More if we interfere now. Let's leave them to it,' I whispered in her ear.

'Let's! No. We can't. We can't abandon poor Mr Wilson.'

'Damn and blast. How long can it take to wash and dry a dozen cups?'

'We shall soon find out.'

The men were still laughing when they emerged. They had had the sense to remove their jackets, but not to roll up their sleeves or don pinafores.

'Look! More!' Hurley crowed as he saw what we had brought. 'Bags I wipe, this time. I'm soaked to the skin. Your turn, Wilson!'

Harriet said, 'You could always ask me.'

'No, indeed, Mrs Rowsley. This is men's work!' Burford shouted.

Soon it felt far more like a game than the one we had just played. There was laughter. There was fun. Bea emerged from her rooms to join in. She produced some of her special damson cordial, pouring each of us a thimbleful.

'Ma'am, it's nectar!' Hurley declared.

'But don't, like Oliver Twist, ask for more,' I warned him. 'Or you'll sleep till noon.'

Wednesday morning followed Tuesday's pattern. Most people would be working outside again, but the possibility of a court case against one of the tenant farmers meant I would be tied up in my office with a particularly turgid document for most of the day.

I was interrupted by a knock on the door.

'Please, sir,' piped a child's voice, 'Constable Pritchard for you.'

'Thank you, Billy.'

'Good lad,' Pritchard said. He waited till the door closed. 'I had to lead him here, but he said he must announce me.'

'We should find him some sort of uniform. I can't see him ever becoming a footman, but we will find a post here, using his brains, not his body.'

Pritchard nodded. 'Good. As it happens, I've come about another boy. Sprue's grandson. Walter.'

'Ah, the footballer.'

'That's the one. He came to my house first thing. Said he found a hat in a hawthorn hedge – a straw one like that worn by the man who wanted to see your jacket. Tucked away, he said, where he couldn't quite reach it. But when he took me to show me where it was, it had gone. At first, I thought he was spinning a tale. Then I looked, and there were some bits of straw caught on the thorns. You could see where they'd been woven – parts were bent or flattened – or I'd have thought they were odd bits blown from the fields. But it does pose a question: why should anyone hide a hat and then go and retrieve it?'

'Assuming it was the same person, of course. A decent hat, in a hedge or not, would be a great temptation to anyone finding it.'

He looked crestfallen. 'And finding's not stealing, of course. Yes, you're right. I'll make some enquiries in the village.' He straightened his shoulders. 'How are you, by the way? Out in all that sun?'

'It was foolish of me. Don't tell anyone, but I got a pounding headache. Which is why I'm here, getting a different sort of headache.' I nodded at the paperwork.

'Your friend Sir Francis might get one, too. Those experts of his – snarling like stray dogs, they are. Should be ashamed of themselves if you ask me.'

'Should I stroll down? I'd like to see that pavement again. And, in fact, yes, you *must* see it. It's a miracle it's been preserved so well.'

'Haven't you got enough to worry about here? Let them get on with it, say I.'

'I can spare five minutes – and so should you. This is something to tell your children about!'

His camera already on its tripod beside him, Palmer was holding forth in a most uncharacteristic way when we arrived. 'This is just not good enough, gentlemen. It is not professional. Yes, the sun is shining, yes, you've been working hard for several days. But on the day when we are going to be working on a find of perhaps national importance, you – distinguished scholars! – drift here late like idle schoolboys who haven't done their prep. Now, please – start work. You know what you have to do: do it!'

He jumped when he saw us. 'My apologies, gentlemen – how can I help you?'

'I brought Constable Pritchard here to see the mosaic. And to see it again myself,' I added with a grin. Yet I had a sudden frisson of fear: what if one of those disaffected experts had chosen to damage it to spoil Palmer's theories?

It was intact. Palmer was soon explaining in some detail how one was made. Pritchard was engrossed, asking intelligent questions. But as they both straightened and it seemed that he was going to take his leave, Pritchard asked him an altogether different question: 'These gentlemen who were late this morning – will you provide me with a list, please?'

Palmer bridled. 'They are not factory workers, Constable, having to clock in every day.'

'You spoke to them as if they were children earlier, sir. And I am speaking to you as an officer of the law. As I shall be speaking to them, as soon as I know who they are. Have you got a room I can use, Mr Rowsley?'

'Several dozen,' I said dryly. 'What sort of room would suit you best?'

'Somewhere on the ground floor. Quick in, quick out.'

'We'll find one. Follow me.'

'One moment.' He raised his voice. 'You are all to stay here. All of you. No excuses. Sir Francis will take note of anyone straying away for whatever reason. Do you understand?' He turned to me. 'What if I borrow young Billy to escort the gentlemen in and out and summon the next one?'

'Of course. I hope there are a few women left in the kitchen: we need that uniform now, don't we? And someone to make it fit him. It'll take a bit of doing, of course,' I added doubtfully.

Even newly scrubbed, Billy looked what he was: a short, slight boy with a bad limp. Just as I was despairing, Primrose arrived in the servants' hall. She took in the problem at a glance, retrieving from the uniform store a pageboy's uniform – old-fashioned, but not much too big.

'Just the shirt, waistcoat and breeches,' she suggested. 'There'll be pins in the sewing room.'

'Which would make an excellent base for you, Constable,' I said.

She took the boy's hand. 'Come on. No, Billy, I won't stab you, not if you stand still. I'll make you look really smart.' They headed for the door.

'And what, may I ask, is going on here?' came Mrs Briggs' voice.

Before I could speak, Primrose bobbed a curtsy. 'Constable Pritchard wants a reliable manservant to help him. Billy will do it very well – yes, Billy?'

'Yes, ma'am,' he said with a bow.

Mrs Briggs turned to me. 'And what about their normal duties? When we're all working every hour God sends?'

'I can assure you that Billy will be doing what Mr Thatcher wanted him to do: he will deputize for the absent footmen.'

'Please, ma'am, I've done all the boots already,' Billy answered.

'And I'll be back before you can say knife,' Primrose said, sweeping him off.

Pritchard waited until they had gone. 'Surely, ma'am, you understand that solving a heinous crime is even more important than cutting hay.' Saluting, he marched off.

'I will be in my office, Mrs Briggs,' I said, wishing I had matched the simple dignity all three of the others had achieved.

TWENTY-SIX

Much as I wanted to spend time alone this morning in the library, it would be impossible. I had the same duties as the previous day's, of course – though at least I knew that Matthew would be safe in his office, not attempting heroics in the field. And I drew a certain amount of comfort knowing, from a few whispered words from Primrose, that Constable Pritchard was in the building.

Since the men would be harvesting fields further from the House but easily accessible by the lane to the village, I had also commandeered Robin and the dog cart for the day. It would make the work of us women much easier. Whether Robin would see this as an advantage I doubted, but Dan certainly did, though he assured me he knew his place was really with the other men. I easily found him a task to do at midday while Robin rested between shifts: he would help me carry out the experts' luncheon. He demurred that he might smell of horse and be clumsy, but brightened up when I told him he might take any leftovers back to his mother and grandmama.

That agreed, I walked back across the yard – but I didn't step into the servants' hall. I became a silent and unobserved witness to a scene being enacted by Matthew, Constable Pritchard, Primrose and Billy, with Mrs Briggs cast as the villain. Since she might well be smarting in defeat, I slipped up the back stairs to change into my print dress to give her time to recover. In fact, I was packing baskets of food in the servants' hall when I heard her voice: 'Ah, Mrs Rowsley. Good morning.'

'Good morning, Mrs Briggs.' I kept my voice light, unlike hers, which was heavy with portent. 'I hope you weren't disturbed last night. The young gentlemen insisted on washing up – imagine, they saw it as a great treat! – and things got jolly, did they not?'

'If "jolly" is the word you choose to use . . . It wouldn't be my choice, as it happens. I heard female voices, too. I assume

you would like me to find out who broke the lights-out rule
and came down to . . . to be *jolly.*'

Whatever I said, she had put me in the wrong very efficiently.
Bea and I were, of course, the wicked women. 'I'm sorry if we
disturbed you. Naturally, Mrs Arden and I had to stay to supervise the gentlemen.'

'It doesn't set a good example to the girls. They have a
lights-out time, after all.'

Did they indeed? 'Her late ladyship never had such a thing.
She said that if they worked hard enough, they would go to
sleep without being told.'

'Her ladyship isn't running the household now.'

I returned to packing the baskets. 'Alas, no. Oh, Mrs Briggs,
when I think of this place in its prime! Guests all the time,
except when we went to one of the other Croft residences. The
Mayfair property – she employed a French chef for parties and
balls, you know. Such times . . . But all this reminiscing won't
bring back the past, will it? We must just pray the heir is found
soon. Now, I should be on my way with all this food. Did I
tell you I was driving Robin today? I could make room in the
dog cart for you if you like.'

She spread her hands: she still had too much to do.

'Of course. Now, I will be back in time to serve the experts
their luncheon, so that's one thing you don't have to worry
about.'

'I could do that if you wanted to stay in the fields.'

'Of course – but I want to come back to make sure Matthew
isn't working too hard after that accident: he overdid it yesterday.
Since Robin will be in his stable, Dan will act as footman. We
can't expect Billy the Boots to do that yet.' More baskets ready
to go.

'It's not fair, Mrs Rowsley, and I'd be wrong not to say it:
your husband is playing that boy along something shocking.
Making believe he can be a footman, indeed, and tricking him
out in some strange costume. The boy's a cripple, Mrs Rowsley,
and that's the truth, whether he likes it or not. I'm sorry, because
he's a nice enough child, but one day, whether we like it or
not, he'll be in a workhouse, where such folk belong.'

A workhouse, where such a person as myself once belonged.

I hoped my deep breath did not show. 'Have you heard of the poet, Lord Byron, Mrs Briggs? The famous poet with the club foot?'

'That wicked man! I'm surprised his name passes your lips!'

'Wicked he most certainly was, but he was also one of our greatest poets, a scholar and a soldier. There. All done,' I declared, running an eye over the baskets.

'That's all very well, but he was a gentleman. And that young Billy is not.'

That was unanswerable. I gathered up two of the baskets. 'Will you excuse me if I take these to the stable? Perhaps you might even help load up if I bring the dog cart to the door?'

I resolved to visit the library before my luncheon stint. With Mr Wilson supervising the Marchbankses, surely I might legitimately investigate the books that had attracted Mrs Marchbanks' attention when I had touched them. In fact, my visit coincided with their morning break, taken outside with the archaeologists to make life easier for the servant on duty – in this case, Primrose again. Mr Wilson was just locking up when I appeared.

'My dear Mrs Rowsley, I did not expect you!'

'I am shirking for a few minutes. I wanted to check something here – preferably with a witness. Would you mind staying here for a very few minutes?'

'Of course not.' He opened the door with a flourish and locked it behind us. 'How may I help?'

I laughed. 'Just by watching me. I don't know what I am looking at, let alone looking for. But if someone doesn't want me to touch something, I am perverse enough to want to handle it. But only with gloves on.' I reached into the drawer in what had become my official desk – to find none. 'There are some in the muniment room,' I said.

He bowed. 'In that case, so that we keep to the very letter of the will, I will leave you here and go and fetch them. Where exactly are they?'

'Thank you. In the main drawer of the central table.'

He was back within the minute, shaking his head. 'None.'

'The Marchbankses must have used them all, then. They must be in the laundry bag. I'll ask when I see them.'

'How many pairs, my dear Mrs Rowsley, would that be?'

'Only five or six. Handling old books is dirty work, and you would want clean ones each day.'

'Might anything else have left gloves dirty?'

I looked him straight in the eye. 'Handling a bloodstained stone. I need to talk to Constable Pritchard, do I not? But first, *first*, I really must look at those books, gloves or no gloves.'

They fitted snugly on the shelf, so there was no sense of one having gone missing.

'They seem a fairly random selection, if I may say so. Though I suppose that is why the professor is here – eventually to put them into some sort of order.'

'Exactly. But he will catalogue them first. And, if some go to another library, then the resulting empty shelf or shelves will make it easier physically to reorganize them. Now, let me think: where were these before?' No, I couldn't recall. But they shared one theme – there were four books of sermons – including a 1649 collection of Donne's, a writer his lordship much admired. For some reason, it was cheek by jowl with a wonderful fifteenth-century Book of Hours. Imagine, to be holding it again after all this time.

I put them all back – yes, again they fitted closely. Surely none had been removed. And yet . . . and yet . . .

I looked at the shelves around them. And there, quite high up, was a shelf on which a group of books seemed much further forward than the others.

Mr Wilson passed me on the library steps. 'I sense that you would prefer to investigate yourself, but I do think I might be safer.' I acquiesced as he passed me the offending volumes. 'Aha! Please take this very carefully, Harriet. I myself fear to handle it.'

So did I. It was old, fragile to the point that the binding was disintegrating. But I had to open it. I placed it on a nearby table. 'I can't even decipher the writing,' I said, helping Mr Wilson down. 'And where I can make an educated guess, I can't understand the words.'

'From the illustrations, decorations, whatever they called, this must be a gospel, surely,' he breathed. 'Oh, drat and damnation!'

A loud banging announced the return of the Marchbankses. Mr Wilson admitted them.

'Dear God, you are touching that priceless tome without gloves?' he screamed.

'Because there are no gloves, Professor,' I said. 'Perhaps you forgot to inform me when the supply needed replenishing.'

'Is it my job to do a servant's task?'

'Only if a servant had no idea that you'd used them all. What have you done with the soiled ones?'

'Disposed of them, of course. And before you ask, we placed them in the bin in our bedchamber, not in here since you will admit no servants, and they have been duly placed with the other rubbish, I presume.'

'How very unfortunate.' There should still be plenty of pairs in the linen room, but for once I did not want to imply that their attitude was acceptable. I wanted them to know that they were in the wrong. 'If you would be kind enough to give me today's when you come down for dinner, I will ensure that they are washed and dried in time for you to start tomorrow. Meanwhile, could you tell me something about this volume? Surely it is very old?'

I was in time to catch Mrs Marchbanks as she swooned. 'Dear me, I don't have my smelling salts about me!' I said untruthfully. 'Excuse me – I will go and find some.' As the professor alternately patted her cheeks and chafed her hands, I did something almost sacrilegious. I slipped the ancient book into my pinafore pocket. 'The safe!' I mouthed to Mr Wilson.

As I ran – against every rule – along the corridor to Matthew's office, I saw him locking up and walking away. 'Matthew! Matthew!' I had never screamed like that in all my years.

'What on earth's the matter, my love?'

'Just lock us in your office. Thank you. Matthew, I have taken this from the library. I think it explains Francis' aestel. But I can't explain how until he and Elias are here. Mr Wilson, too. Heavens, Mrs Marchbanks needs my smelling salts – I must go back to the library. Please, if you can, just stay here.'

'I'll put this in the safe and lock myself in. And you'll find Pritchard in the small sewing room.'

*   *   *

Probably, it took no more than ten minutes to locate everyone and herd them into Matthew's office. For once, I was glad that Mrs Marchbanks was unwell – and this time she genuinely looked very pale and was quite breathless. The professor accepted my suggestion that she should lie down on her bed and escorted her out. She might be even paler soon.

Mr Wilson carrying the bookrest, I sent him on his way, locking up punctiliously, of course. Next, I located Elias, and lastly Francis, who was so busy with his tesserae that he was reluctant to leave them. 'You will come if I have to drag you,' I hissed at him.

By the time we were all assembled, I was shaking so much that Matthew had to place the ancient work on the bookrest. Only then could I touch it.

'I should not be handling this, should I?' I said. 'But I need to open it just here. Now, what do you see?'

I thought Francis himself might faint. 'Dear God, it's the imprint of the aestel. It's been there so long – so many centuries – that it's deformed the vellum.' He looked straight at Pritchard. 'This surely means that someone who had access to the library found it – found the aestel – in this . . . this niche. And stole it.'

'And buried it in that builder's trench,' Pritchard concluded for him.

'Where are you going, Pritchard?' Matthew asked.

'Where do you think? To find my chief suspects and arrest them. Mrs Rowsley, I don't think this is a job for young Billy; will you take me up to their bedchamber? Now.'

TWENTY-SEVEN

'What an anticlimax,' Palmer said, when Harriet returned with the news that the Marchbankses had not been arrested because they were not in their room. 'They have flown already?'

'If they have, they have left all their belongings behind. I wonder if Mrs Marchbanks was genuinely ill when she collapsed this time – she was very pale and could hardly breathe. She is in the Family wing. Constable Pritchard is already there. Meanwhile, if you are well enough to risk riding down to the village, my love, he would like a telegraph sent to Sergeant Burrows asking him to come as quickly as he can.'

'Of course.' I checked the safe was locked. 'Palmer, when you return to your tesserae, could you make sure no one leaves the site without a good excuse?'

'I hope I can – they are grown men, you know. But I think gathering everyone together for luncheon would help me.'

'I'll arrange for it to be brought out as soon as possible,' Harriet said. 'But first I have to warn the stationmaster not to let anyone from here board a train at the halt – Constable Pritchard's orders. I shan't employ Robin – I need Paragon, a horse that actually moves! – but you still may have to serve yourselves until I arrive.'

Within moments, the office was empty. And firmly locked. My note on the door for Pritchard asked him to seek out Palmer. I nearly added the words 'for information', but had a sudden and irrational fear that should the wrong person read it, our friend would be at risk.

Everything looked remarkably normal when I returned from my quite exhilarating errand – Esau always loved a good gallop – and, mercifully free of a headache, belatedly I joined the archaeologists and Wilson for their picnic luncheon. My arrival coincided with that of Harriet, pink-cheeked from driving the spirited Paragon.

She took me to one side. 'I asked Joe Oates and Henry Carver to seat themselves in your office corridor – but not directly outside your door. If anyone asks why they're there, they're to say that one of the experts thinks that hideous statue might be valuable and that there's a rumour someone wishes to steal it.'

'Personally, I would wrap it up and tie the parcel with red ribbon to get rid of it – but perhaps, since none of these people have yet inspected it, I had better not. On the other hand, Francis must have walked past it times without number – but he's never had a eureka moment: "Aha! I see a Roman relic!"'

'Not my period, I'm afraid,' he said, making us both jump. 'It's much later – Renaissance, I'd say. It might appease Wells, who's very knowledgeable about Italian sculpture, if you were to ask him: he's very tetchy. That's what I came to say: the good constable's questioning has irritated my colleagues. To be fair to them, I disliked intensely having even to ask them why they were late this morning– what sort of answers did the constable expect? "I was planning to steal a treasure"? More likely, "I was using the new facilities" or "I could not find my spectacles"! I take it there was a genuine reason connected with the crime – one of the crimes – committed here?'

'Pritchard is conscientious to a fault, as you know. He would not ask you to do something if he did not have to. Trust him.'

'Funnily enough, I do. But I won't tell my colleagues that. They are far more vocal when they think he is no more than a hayseed – and may give something away, either to me or to him.'

'Here he is – heavens, he looks very solemn.'

Palmer backed discreetly out of earshot as Elias headed straight to me. 'Mrs Marchbanks appears to have had a heart attack, quite a serious one.'

Harriet gasped. 'Dear God! Was it – could it have been the . . . the unpleasantness . . . between us?'

'Or,' he responded seriously, 'guilt? Fear of being exposed? I don't think you should blame yourself, Mrs Rowsley. I really don't. We'll know more when Doctor Page has examined her – but until he has, Nurse Webb won't let me question her. And, of course, Professor Marchbanks is too upset to talk to anyone. Damn and blast!' He drove his fist hard into his palm. 'Sorry, ma'am.'

She shook her head, touching him lightly on the arm.

'So what do I do now?' He sounded like a lost schoolboy.

'It is more what Doctor Page must do. Not with her, but with Mr Pounceman. Someone tried to kill him – or Matthew, of course.' She smiled briefly at me. 'That someone could be Mr or even Mrs Marchbanks. Granted, if she really is ill, she can't try again, but he might have time on his hands . . . Elias, I don't know what to do, any more than you do.'

He straightened his spine. 'I should be present in the Family wing till Doctor Page appears and then discuss with him what is to be done.'

'Excellent,' I said. 'And – this is just a suggestion to keep the archaeologists here – I think perhaps you should make a very neutral announcement to them saying that she has had another fainting fit and he is by her side. And rather than labour the point that none of them can leave or you'll arrest them, perhaps you could speculate that this warm spell might end in a storm. That would spur Sir Francis to urge them to make an even greater effort.'

'It might indeed end in a storm,' Harriet said dryly.

He scanned the still cloudless horizon and looked at her, narrowing his eyes in doubt. Then he grinned. 'Ah! I see what you mean.' He strode off. But before he could speak to Francis, he was intercepted by Wells, soon eagerly gesticulating and pointing towards the house. Perhaps he was putting forward his suggestion that a small group of experts should be allowed to examine the aestel under his supervision. Now Wells was beckoning Wilson with some fervour. Wilson obeyed with rather less.

It was very pleasant to stand aside in companionable silence and sip lemonade and watch the discussion, which was becoming increasingly animated. Soon, however, Head strode towards us, and Harriet was on duty again, her professional smile in place.

'Have you had a successful morning?' she asked, ready to serve him his selection from the array before him.

'Very possibly. I believe we may have found a hypocaust. Perhaps you would care to see it?'

'As soon as I am off duty here, I would love to. As I am sure Matthew would.' That sounded curiously like a distress signal. Was it because, like me, she had no idea what he was talking about? Or was she reluctant to spend time alone in the company of any of the experts? I moved closer. 'More pâté, Professor? A little salmagundi? One of Bea's specialities.'

'What have you found that suggests a hypocaust?' I asked. I was soon so well informed that I might have written a short essay on Roman heating systems, though I would rather have been eavesdropping on others' conversations.

One of which was about to be interrupted. Young Billy, in his somewhat doubtful grandeur, was hobbling purposefully towards us.

'Please, sir, I have a message for Constable Pritchard.'

'He's just over there, Billy.'

He pulled a face. 'Will he mind being interrupted, sir?'

'Is it an important message?'

He frowned, as if trying to remember a lesson he'd not fully grasped. 'So . . . so I am given to . . . I think so, sir.'

'In that case, he will want to be interrupted.'

'Thank you, sir.'

'So you are reduced to employing cripples and dwarfs,' Head remarked.

'We are pleased to employ a youngster with no advantage in the world except initiative, Head,' I retorted. 'And – look – he has achieved his mission.'

Pritchard raised an apologetic hand to the two men and stepped aside to read the note the boy had brought. Nodding, he tucked it carefully in his tunic pocket and, fitting his speed to Billy's, walked away from us. Then he swung him on to his back and broke into a run. Their laughter rang out.

'Another good job done,' Palmer declared, looking at the trays waiting for the scullery maid's attention. Whether he referred to the catering or the way the experts had stacked the china and glass was not clear. 'I suppose you have no news I can share with the others.'

'We have no news at all,' Harriet said firmly – and very clearly; there were, after all, many servants around, including Mrs Briggs. 'I must rejoin the team in a few minutes – but I would so like a cup of tea first. Shall we take it in your office, Matthew?'

'Might we be permitted to join you?' Wilson asked.

I suspected she might have preferred a few minutes' quiet, but we could hardly refuse.

'I feel – and I think Wilson shares my sentiments,' Palmer began, a few minutes later, accepting the cup she offered, 'that we are in a state of limbo – tossed around on a sea of ignorance, not knowing whom to trust. I beg your pardon – I mixed my metaphors there!'

If he expected sympathy from Harriet, he was to be disappointed. 'We are all in the same boat, Francis, if you will forgive me continuing your second image. His late lordship may have put his faith in me – but I really . . . I don't feel competent . . . I'm not qualified to do what he asked.' She swallowed hard. 'The couple supposed to help me have been nothing but a thorn in my side, and now may well be found to have stolen a priceless object and killed an innocent young man in order to keep it. And now it turns out that the woman can't read or write – I'm sorry, hasn't Sergeant Burrows told you yet? She makes strange scribbles on the page. What if she's too ill to confess? She may get off scot-free.' Her voice broke. 'Is it she who cut the picture cords and might have killed three innocent people? A woman? A mother? Or is she simply a very unhappy accomplice? Or is she genuinely ill and someone else has been manipulating the situation to throw the blame away from himself?' She dashed away tears. 'Forgive me. I'm not making much sense, am I?' With a valiant attempt at irony, she concluded, 'I really do need that cup of tea, don't I!'

Palmer poured it himself. The hand passing her the cup shook as much as the one taking it. 'I am truly sorry, Harriet. Truly. You are my dearest friend and I do not know how I let all this come about. One day you may be able to forgive me, but I don't think I shall ever forgive myself.'

'I think you'll find you are forgiven as soon as I've drunk this,' she said, accepting a pristine handkerchief from Wilson and mopping her eyes.

There was a vehement knock on the door. Billy appeared. 'Constable Pritchard, sir. Sirs. Oh, and ma'am.' Billy flushed scarlet.

'Confusing, isn't it? We'll talk about that later, Billy. Meanwhile, you'll find some lemonade in the servants' hall and probably cake and biscuits. Ask Mrs Briggs first, mind!' I said. 'Oh, and ask Primrose to bring fresh tea and another cup.'

The door firmly shut, Pritchard sank to the chair Wilson pushed forward. 'Mrs Marchbanks is still alive and demanding to go home. Doctor Page has told her and her husband very clearly that she is too ill, and that he will not answer for the consequences if she tries to make the journey. But if she insists, do I arrest her? It all feels a bit beyond me – but I'd only be doing what I was ordered to do.'

'It all feels a bit beyond us, too,' Harriet said. 'The sooner your sergeant arrives here the better. But there is something – probably too trivial to burden you with . . .'

'Suppose you let me be the judge of that,' he said with a mixture of kindness and authority. 'Just tell me.'

'The Marchbankses have taken it upon themselves to throw away all the cotton gloves they have been using in the library.'

'Cotton gloves? Oh, so that you wouldn't get your hands dirty handling old books.'

'Or get old books dirty with modern sweat,' Palmer suggested. 'But why throw the things away, not just wash them?'

'Because there is a stain on them that wouldn't wash out? Like blood?' Harriet said quietly. 'They may still be in with the rubbish. Or they may be in with the laundry, if a housemaid has been especially efficient.'

'Which means they will already have been washed, of course,' Pritchard pointed out. 'I'll go through it all, rubbish and laundry, when Sergeant Burrows arrives.'

Palmer said suddenly, 'I am due for some penance, Constable. Allow me to do it alongside you. Under your supervision.'

'Really? There's no need for you to do it, and if you did, no reason for me to supervise you, sir—'

'There is – just in case,' he added with a smile at Harriet. 'Seriously, if it became known, rumours would swirl around that I was trying to hide something I had hidden, something incriminating. So please, keep an eye on me.'

Wilson said slowly, 'Someone else you might want to keep an eye on is Professor Head.'

'And why might that be, Mr Wilson?'

Harriet might have been drooping a little, but now she was upright and alert.

'It concerns my recent shopping expedition in Shrewsbury. There I briefly encountered a gentleman I did not know – a chance jostle in the street – but whom I recognized immediately when I was introduced to him here. Professor Head. He responded with an entirely blank face. Manners forbade me to press him.'

'Was he carrying anything? Anything at all?'

'Not that I recall.'

Pritchard frowned. 'I could ask Sergeant Burrows to spare a couple of men to ask shopkeepers if a strange gentleman visited them – but that might mean a lot of shops, and all for a very small possibility.'

There was another loud knock on the door. I hoped, against all logic, that it was Burrows himself. It wasn't, of course. It was Billy, pushing, of all things, a tea cart. Goodness knows where he had found it: I had never seen it in use. 'Your tea, sir,' he declared. 'Please, ma'am, I know I should wear gloves but I don't know where they are.'

Harriet smiled. 'Shall we go to the linen cupboard together and find some?'

TWENTY-EIGHT

'Good evening, Harriet,' Ellis Page greeted me as I walked with the newly gloved Billy to the servants' hall. 'How are you in the midst of this organized chaos?'

'About the same as you, I should think. Very tired, but driven by a mixture of duty and determination. And,' I added, smiling at her over my shoulder, 'Bea would probably say the same.'

He laughed but added, 'How much longer before the hay is all stacked?'

'Another couple of days, I should think. It's a matter of Farmer Twiss being happy that it's dry, of course.' I looked around. Apart from Bea, no one was within earshot. 'Might I ask how your patients are?'

As Mrs Briggs passed, he said, 'Poor Samuel is feeling the heat – he's inclined to be tetchy, especially as Dick Thatcher is too worn out to spend as much time reading to him as usual. He fell asleep reading Hebrews to him last night, apparently – one of Samuel's favourite passages, too. Young Amos Phipps got too enthusiastic with his sickle and has a badly cut thumb – trying the blade to see if it was sharp enough, the young idiot.' Only when we were alone again did he continue, 'As for my younger male patient, a visit would be welcomed, I think. He is still confined to bed and Mr Kingsley-Ward's instructions were that he could read but only for a very short period at a time. Consequently, he is – to put not too fine a point on it – bored. Could you spare just a few minutes?' he cajoled me, catching me looking up at the clock. 'Thank you.'

'Might I ask where your latest female patient is? Not to mention her perfectly well husband?'

'I knew you would ask. Pritchard made it clear that until we find the picture assailant, no guest, no member of the household even, could be in the wing while Pounceman is there. So, ill though she is, she is back in her chamber, bedbound. She is certainly not well enough to travel – in fact, she needs a great deal of rest. I'm afraid this information made her – and her husband – very agitated, so I had to find something to soothe her. She was asleep when I left. To do him justice, he has remained at her side all afternoon. To his chagrin and probably yours, I would not let Pritchard speak to either of them. *Could not.* I am just about to ask Bea and Mrs Briggs if their meals can for the moment be served in their room.'

'And I will ask Dick Thatcher – who looks dead on his feet, bless him – to move one of our retired footmen to keep a discreet eye on them.'

Mr Pounceman greeted me and my hastily picked bunch of flowers with every show of pleasure. 'My dear Mrs Rowsley, I am amazed you can spare the time to come up here. With the haymaking in full swing! And all your guests!'

'The only reason I have not come before,' I said with imperfect truth, 'is that we understood you were too unwell for visitors.'

'Pray, do sit down. Yes, I have been ill – I seem to have missed two whole days since the accident. The incident, I might rather call it, since I have a very real sense of human agency in the unpleasant business. Doctor Page tells me that recalling the moments before you are knocked senseless is fairly unusual, but I clearly recall sounds when your husband and I were in the chapel – a surprisingly clean chapel, though I suspected rats might be skulking there . . . Ugh.' His smile was self-deprecating. 'And I *felt* rather than saw movement the instant before Matthew threw himself on me. Doctor Page tells me he is doing well?'

'He is, thank God.'

'Amen. I understand the bishop sent an adequate curate for Sunday. This Mr Kingsley-Ward may be a most brilliant physician, but he does not understand the needs of a parish, Mrs Rowsley. I cannot, simply cannot, leave my flock till the autumn, can I? Come,' he added with a smile, 'in my place, you would not. And I have never, I fear, been as conscientious as you are.'

'In your place,' I said carefully, 'I would try to balance the short-term needs of the village with the long-term needs: in other words, if you come back too soon, you may take much longer to recover completely.' I leaned forward. 'This is a very abrupt change of subject, and I hope you will forgive me.'

'Of course. I know how pressed you are at this time of day.'

'Thank you. You spoke of your memory of the – can I call it an attack? – a moment ago. That memory, Mr Pounceman – did it come with sounds?'

'Sounds?'

'The slam of a door, say, or the swish of a skirt or the tread of a leather shoe on stone?'

For a moment, I thought I had overtaxed him, as he leaned back on his pillows, closing his eyes with a frown. But he raised a finger, as if asking me to wait. 'Could I have heard a grunt? The noise you would make if you were pushing or pulling something heavy? And a sharp intake of breath as it fell?' He opened his eyes. 'I probably would, wouldn't I, if someone was trying to pull something as big as that picture down? So perhaps I think I would have heard . . . No. I do recall it. Whether it was male or female breath . . . I don't want to say something for the sake of it – the good doctor tells me that it is better to let a memory come to you of its own will, as it were, than to try to force it into your mind. Oh, Mrs Rowsley, you do not know how frustrating this all is! I have the Lord's work to do – and all I can do is lie here and think. And there are periods when I can't even think!' he wailed. He composed himself. 'I can pray, however – and I have been praying for the widow of the young man who was killed. Tell me, if you have time, how the investigation is going.'

A young nurse appeared with a little bell. Its tinkle might have been irritating, but it saved me the embarrassment of having to refuse. 'I see that my time is over. But I promise you, Mr Pounceman, that if Doctor Page permits, I will return tomorrow.' I stood to take my leave.

'Wait – just one moment, if you please, Nurse. In private, if I may? Thank you.'

She picked up the flowers and slipped out.

I moved closer again.

'Height. I have a recollection of something . . . perhaps I confuse it with that statue . . . of a sound of fabric.'

'A woman?' I tried not to squeak.

He pressed his forehead. 'If only things were clearer!'

And, the nurse returning with the flowers in a vase, with that I had to be content.

'I hear that your husband is puzzled by a statue,' Wells said over sherry that evening. I had arrived after most of our guests: would any of them notice that I had had to change from being a maid to being their hostess in no more than six minutes? 'Why do we not gather round it after dinner and give you our opinions? God knows it would be more useful than sitting around playing foolish parlour games.'

'It could well be – provided everyone agrees,' I said, thinking that unlikely. 'What did Constable Pritchard think of your suggestion for examining the aestel, by the way?'

'He expressed what I might describe as cautious assent. But he has made no immediate commitment – he said something about the approval of his sergeant, who has not deigned to put in even a perfunctory appearance today.'

'I'm sure he has many other duties,' I murmured, thinking of his wife. Before I could say more – and I would not mention his private circumstances – Billy appeared with an envelope on the appropriate silver salver. He might have been a very small adult. When he winked and touched his nose, however, he was a ten-year-old again. 'Thank you, Billy,' I said, pocketing the note – from Elias Pritchard, judging by the handwriting, and therefore not to be read in public. 'Could you explain how the hypocaust I've heard about works, Doctor Wells? And if it's so good at heating, why don't we have them now?'

'That is a remarkably pertinent question, Mrs Rowsley. Let us begin with the principle of the hypocaust first, then you have a better chance of understanding the system and thus why it has fallen into desuetude.'

'Except, of course, Wells,' Francis said, with a surreptitious wink at me, 'it was revived by a manufacturer of note in Birmingham, was it not? A member of the Lunar Society, no less. Surely you are aware that Matthew Boulton equipped his home, Soho House, with a hot-air system—'

'No, not at all the same. Surely you realize . . .'

Professor Head joined them. Very soon, it was not a discussion but an argument. I might have murmured my excuses, but none of them gave any sign that they heard. I could withdraw to a quiet corner. Elias was happier to talk than to write, but what he said was clear enough. Sergeant Burrows would be back tomorrow. His wife had given birth to a girl. A village lad had found a straw hat and brought it to the police house. He would present himself here again tomorrow. He had told Francis not to say anything about searching the linen baskets and the rubbish bins, but he supposed he couldn't stop him talking to me.

I did not swallow the sheet of paper but did the next best thing: I slipped it down inside my bodice.

There was no wind, which should have made sitting outside after dinner a pleasure. However, the air was so thick with harvest dust, which was making several of the guests sneeze and complain of sore eyes, that I suggested we adjourn for tea and coffee to the yellow drawing room instead. The last thing I wanted, of course, was a visit to evaluate an ugly statue which was really no one's business. I did not want charades. I did not want Shakespeare. I did not want anything more to do with those braying, self-confident, opinionated men.

'But I thought we were to discuss that statue!' Wells said, even as I mentioned the drawing room.

And here we were with an argument even before we left the dining table. The dissenting voices surely outweighed those in favour.

I heard myself speak again. 'On evenings like this, his late lordship would often invite his guests up to the long gallery to play skittles. I might be able to find them for those of you who would enjoy it.'

'My goodness,' Matthew said, as he collapsed beside me, both of us still dressed, on our bed some two hours later, 'where did you get the energy? More to the point, how did you learn to play like that?'

'His lordship liked to practise against someone. Will I ever move again?' I groaned. It was one thing playing as a young woman in a maid's loose dress, quite another to do it in one's middle years and – more to the point – tightly encased in a corset and a gown better suited to polite conversation. 'But at least I had a chance to speak to Francis. His search for gloves. He found a couple of dozen pairs in the laundry baskets – Dick's and Luke's, I presume. And in the rubbish, due to be burned, of course, another dozen pairs – including one bloodstained pair. So I should imagine that tomorrow will see Sergeant Burrows and Elias playing a real-life version of Cinderella and the glass slipper. I just hope I wake up in time to see it . . .'

'I hope so.' He sat up suddenly. 'Where did you put his note?'

'If you release me from this instrument of torture, I will do more than tell you – I will show you.'

TWENTY-NINE

I f Harriet had imagined a macabre morning watching grown
men trying on a bloodied glove, she was to be disappointed.
Sergeant Burrows would not arrive until twenty past ten, so
I had time to prepare for a meeting later on with Tertius
Newcombe, a fellow trustee who ran the biggest farm in the
area. Harriet popped her head around the office door.

'I'm just going to meet the sergeant's train. Elias is still not
able to talk to either of the Marchbankses, and I think he's
hoping that Sergeant Burrows is going to override Ellis's veto
and insist on questioning them. I suspect he won't. He respects
authority too much, doesn't he? I just hope that Robin accepts
that he lives with us to do a job, not simply to eat! I have to
get back in time to serve the archaeologists their luncheon!'

'I will have a personal word with the animal.' And use the
opportunity to walk quietly with my wife and hand her into the
dog cart. 'Or you could always take Paragon.'

'Wrestle with him, more like.'

I had just waved her off when I saw Wilson.

'I expected the sergeant to be on the early train,' he said. 'I
do hope the reason for his tardiness is that he has been checking
Shrewsbury's emporia, not because his wife is unwell. Puerperal
fever carried off both my sisters, Rowsley – a terrible illness,
terrible. And the poor widower is required to carry on with his
work as if nothing had happened – sometimes with a newborn
baby to worry about. Fortunately, I was in a position to pay for
wet nurses for my niece and my nephew. But it was a sad, sad
business.'

'My dear friend, I am so sorry for your loss, your double
loss.' Harriet would have embraced him; all I dared offer was
a prolonged handshake. Was that why he had never married?
He had been sweet on Bea at one time, but nothing came of it.

Our footsteps took us to the Roman site, where another
hypocaust pillar was appearing.

'Imagine walking around on heated floors,' I said. 'Would they not transform our lives if we had them?'

'But not if we had to endure endless explanations about how they worked, only to hear countless counter explanations. Ah, Professor Head, it seems as if progress is being made!'

'There would have been far more had it not been for the labourers we need so much being drafted in to help that farmer – not to mention that officious yokel of a policeman who now has an obsession with straw hats. I have a good mind to write to the chief constable. And his sergeant – where is he? I have a good mind to pack up and go home!'

Telling him that this would cause his certain arrest would not improve his temper. Wilson touched my arm lightly: he would deal with this. 'The trouble with precipitate departures is the nagging worry that one might miss something important, is it not? Imagine if one of your colleagues found a treasure, not you! Now, could you give me your views on Sir Francis' belief that there is a temple – a shrine perhaps – by that spring?' He drifted him away.

Mrs Briggs was outside my office when I returned.

'I hope I have not kept you waiting,' I said mildly, although I had not expected to see her. I unlocked the door, gesturing for her to precede me. 'How can I help you? Oh, please sit down.'

She hesitated. 'It's about that young cripple.'

I feared that my voice was about to be less gentle. 'Billy Walker?'

'He upsets the staff, him hobbling around like that.'

'I'm sorry to hear that – after all, most of them have known him since he was tiny. And he certainly tries his best.'

'I can't argue with that. But as I said to your wife, you're raising his hopes. And he'll never be the footman he wants to be, will he? Best to let him go now.'

I shook my head slowly. 'In fact, I'm the wrong person to talk to, aren't I? Mr Thatcher hires and fires the male staff, within reason. Mrs Briggs, you are in a very difficult position; please don't think I don't know that. I was on probation myself when I took up my position here. You feel that someone is

watching your every move, don't you? And they are, only in
our case we are watching to see that you are happy here. It's
a very strange place to work in, isn't it? So far from towns,
quite a long walk to the village, even.' I smiled. 'And now we're
at sixes and sevens with the harvest and the excavations and
the murder, of course. What a baptism of fire!'

'I never thought I'd be serving labourers with their ale, I can
tell you. It's not what I'm used to . . .'

'Of course. And I promise you that – as soon as tomorrow
– things will return to normal.'

'Well, I hope so. I really do hope so.' She got to her feet.
'Or I can't see myself staying beyond my month.'

'Really? I'm very sorry to hear that. We know how hard
you're working, and as I said, life will soon return to normal.
I do hope you'll find it in you to stay a little longer.'

The extra-loud rap on my door must be Billy's. I opened the
door before he could fling it wide. 'Just one moment, Billy.'
Closing it, I turned back to Mrs Briggs. 'But you need to bear
one thing in mind, Mrs Briggs,' I said as gently as I could.
'Until the murderer has been identified and arrested, no one
will be allowed to leave here. None of us. Not me or Mrs
Rowsley. Not even Mr Wilson or the archaeologists. Not one
of us.'

She opened her mouth, then shut it again. 'But—' She
straightened. 'Thank you, sir. I'll bear that in mind.' She curtsied
and left the room.

It was Billy's turn again. He flung open the door with some
panache. 'Sergeant Burrows, sir.'

'Thank you, Billy. Could you bring us some tea, please – or
would you prefer coffee, Sergeant? – and some biscuits if there
are any. Thank you.'

He closed the door as quietly as if he were a reincarnation
of old Samuel.

'How are you, Sergeant?'

'I'm very well – and so is young Harriet, if you think your
wife won't mind.'

'Your daughter? I'm sure she'll be delighted, honoured.' I
shook his hand vigorously. 'And your wife?' Was I right to ask?

'She's as right as ninepence, thank God. Except you always

worry, don't you? Even though that nag of yours would lose in a race with a snail, I bet you worry every time your wife drives that little dog cart of hers. She's off picking up Pritchard, though I wager he'd walk faster. Now, what I'm interested in is – Ah! Mrs Rowsley. And Constable Pritchard.'

The latter saluted smartly, pressing a bunch of flowers into his surprised sergeant's hand. 'For your wife from mine, sir.'

'Billy is bringing extra cups – we met him in the corridor,' Harriet said gaily. 'Ah, that will be him now – he needs to oil the wheels again, but see what he's unearthed, Sergeant!'

Sitting after Harriet had taken her place, Pritchard waited till Billy and his contraption had squeaked down the corridor again. 'When can we talk to Mrs Marchbanks, that's what I want to know, sir. This not reading or writing business – not to mention the hollow in that beautiful book – there's got to be a very good explanation, I'd say.'

'So there has – but we have to tread carefully, Pritchard. It really wouldn't do to have a suspect keel over and die, would it? Not unless they confessed first, at least.' Burrows laughed again. 'What I have in mind is this. We ask Doctor Page to sit in the room while we talk to her. Or that stern nurse.'

'And what about her husband?' Harriet asked. 'Will you allow him to stay in the room?'

Burrows blinked. 'He's her husband! It's his duty, surely!'

'He's also a domineering bully who will speak over her and correct her. As I know from experience,' she said, chin up.

'Mrs Rowsley is right, sir. We need to interview them separately and, if possible, at the same time. Though it would be difficult,' Pritchard conceded as his sergeant glowered.

'As far as I know, neither of us can be in two places at once. I don't think I can legally lock either of them up here – but we can shove the professor in the lock-up, can't we? He won't enjoy it, and I'll wager he'll complain to the chief constable, but I can see no way around it, can you? Unless you want him to do some more work in the library? Under your supervision and Mr Wilson's, Mrs Rowsley?'

'You wish me to invite Guy Fawkes into a gunpowder factory?' she asked coolly.

'Very well. The lock-up it is. May I borrow your dog cart,

Mrs Rowsley? But not that Robin, if you don't mind.' He
scratched his head. 'Getting the doctor up here and all – it's
going to take a bit of organizing, isn't it?'

She bit her lip. 'What I am about to say may sound . . .
Look, upstairs there is a sick woman who may need urgent
medical assistance. Why do we not ask Doctor Page if it is safe
to move Mr Pounceman at least to our house here in the grounds,
or preferably to his own home, where his staff would care for
him and he would be even closer to Doctor Page himself – they
live no more than a hundred yards apart. There is no more
gentle pony than Robin . . .' She paused ironically and was
rewarded with laughter.

'But everyone would know within two minutes what was
happening,' Burrows objected.

'Not if I drove him, and he was wearing a bonnet and was
swathed in a shawl? It could not be the first time that I've
returned a patient to his or her home.'

'If you agree, I can ride down to the village,' I said, 'to speed
things up.'

Before Burrows could speak, there was another Billy knock
on the door. 'Might Mrs Rowsley favour me with a word,
please, sir?'

As she leapt to her feet, Harriet and I exchanged a glance
– pride at his grasp of formal language and bemusement in
equal measure. Stepping outside, she pulled the door to – but
not completely shut, so we could eavesdrop.

'What is it, Billy? How can I help?'

'Please, ma'am, I'm sorry, ma'am, but I . . . Can I tell you
something, ma'am? A big secret, like?'

'Of course. It's something important, isn't it?'

Silence. He was nodding, perhaps, his eyes wide open with
anxiety.

'You know you can tell me anything – or Mr Rowsley, of
course.'

'That's what Mr Thatcher said. It's about something Lottie
said—'

'That's your sister – the new scullery maid, isn't it? She's a
very sensible girl, so I'd like to hear it, whatever it is.'

'She said as how . . . She said that she saw Mrs Briggs come into the kitchen when everyone was in the fields – she was left to wash up, my sister, that is – and open the range. Lottie thought she was going to stoke it, which Mrs Briggs didn't need to do because Mrs Arden had seen to it before she took dinner to the men, and she was going to tell Mrs Briggs, but you know what she's like, so Lottie just carried on with the dishes. Only when Mrs Briggs had gone, she had a very quick peep and she saw something white beginning to burn. With red on it.'

'Red?'

'Did I do right, ma'am? I don't want to get Lottie into trouble.'

'No one gets into trouble with me for telling the truth, Billy. Now, this is for Lottie, and this is for you – but take care no one knows. It's our little secret. Off you go – and well done!'

She closed the door gently but firmly as she returned. 'Well, well, well,' she said.

'I couldn't have put it better myself, Mrs Rowsley,' Burrows said. 'I'd best have a talk with this Lottie – and with Mrs Briggs.'

I shook my head. 'Now, how can you approach this without alerting Mrs Briggs? We need to protect Lottie if she is telling the truth, and if she isn't – well, Mrs Briggs seems very unsettled this morning and might . . . Well, we don't want anyone wreaking vengeance on the child.'

Burrows opened his mouth to reply, but there was another vehement knock on the door. 'Professor Marchbanks,' Billy announced.

Burrows swore, not entirely under his breath. What he had thought of as a bit of organizing had just become bigger.

Marchbanks jabbed a finger in the sergeant's direction. 'I demand to speak to you.'

'And so you shall, sir,' Burrows said affably. 'You'll have my full attention, I assure you, when I interview you.'

'Interview me? How dare you!'

Burrows stood, suddenly bigger and more authoritative than he had seemed five minutes ago. 'Professor Marchbanks, if you don't behave yourself, I shall be forced to arrest you.'

'On what grounds?'

'For a start, on suspicion of stealing a valuable object from the Thorncroft House library.'

THIRTY

'This is your doing!' the professor said, wheeling around and pointing at me, his hand quivering with his rage. 'Yours!'

Sergeant Burrows stepped between us. 'Enough of that! Intimidating a possible witness won't help you, professor, will it, now? And it could lead to my arresting you.' He sounded both avuncular and vaguely threatening. 'Mr Rowsley, thank you for your kind offer.'

Matthew nodded. 'I'll leave my spare key with you, Sergeant.' And, unfastening it from his ring, he was gone.

The sergeant continued, 'Mrs Rowsley, I was going to ask you to take us down to the lock-up in your trap, but I can see why you might not want to.'

'The lock-up? I'm not some common criminal!'

'I hope not, sir. That's why we want to talk to you, just to make sure you're not. It doesn't have to be an arrest and the lock-up, not if you behave nicely. Mrs Rowsley, can you perhaps think of a suitable room on these premises where we could talk to this gentleman?'

Did I detect a touch of sarcastic stress on the noun? Suddenly, I wanted to laugh. Instead, I responded, very seriously, 'We have a number of rooms, Sergeant. One you might consider is the sewing room in which Constable Pritchard spoke to the archaeologists the other day.' Elias nodded. 'And – though Professor Marchbanks hasn't asked for a lawyer to be present – I wonder if he would like me to locate Mr Wilson.'

'One of your allies!' the professor snarled at me.

'I've warned you, sir. Yes, Mrs Rowsley, I think that's an excellent idea – if the gentleman is prepared to, of course. In fact, I want a word with him myself – about interviewing your good lady, Professor.'

'You must not – you dare not! She is a very sick woman.'

'Which is why I need to get advice. Don't you worry. Now,

why don't you just calm down while Constable Pritchard and
Mrs Rowsley see if this sewing room is unoccupied.'

Of course it was. 'This will do nicely, Mrs Rowsley, with
an extra couple of chairs, if that's all right,' Elias said. 'It
worked for the historical experts, didn't it, and I don't see
why it shouldn't work for him. Especially if he fancies a bit
of plain sewing. It'll prepare him nicely for making mail-bags,
won't it?'

Elias's calm, prosaic observations and dark joke calmed me
enough to start thinking again. 'I'm not sure Sergeant Burrows
is right to talk about interviewing Mrs Marchbanks, even if he
does consult Mr Wilson first. It ought to be Doctor Page, surely,
that he speaks to first – which should be possible if he comes
back with my husband. Meanwhile, the poor woman is lying
ill in her bedchamber not knowing what has happened to her
husband.'

He pulled a face. 'I know what you're thinking: someone
must go to her – and I bet you can think of no one but
yourself.'

I nodded. 'But what should I say to her? What could I say?
I certainly don't want to be responsible for another of her
attacks. At the very least, I'd need the presence of someone like
Nurse Webb when I told her anything.'

'Why not Nurse Webb herself?' he asked, adding with a grin,
'unless we wait until Doctor Page arrives. I'd wait, if it was up
to me. But first – could you do me a big favour? I've no idea
where to look for Mr Wilson. Could you find him and bring
him here?'

I needed no second bidding. Was there anyone calmer in a
potential crisis than Mr Wilson? Or, just at the moment, more
elusive – not in his rooms, not in any public room.

To my amazement, I eventually found him out in the sunshine
with the archaeologists, busily recording their finds.

'It took two young men to do this,' Francis laughed. 'But
Wilson is faster and more accurate. He's a joy to work with.'

'I'm afraid I may have to borrow him for a few minutes –
maybe longer. No, I can't explain. Not now. Perhaps when I
bring your morning refreshments . . .'

*   *   *

'You realize how irregular this would be,' Mr Wilson said. 'Lawyers are supposed to be invited by their clients to act for them, not be wished upon them by others.'

'At the very least, you can say that in front of Sergeant Burrows.'

'I can. And I can find out beforehand what he's discovered about Professor Head's shopping expedition in Shrewsbury, which may well have a bearing on the way he questions my putative client.' To my amazement, he put his hand on my arm. 'Harriet, this will all be sorted out, you know.'

'Will it?'

'Of course. You are a strong, rational woman: engage your brain.'

'I wish I could,' I said, without any enthusiasm since I felt none. 'Mr Wilson, all I can think of is Mrs Marchbanks worrying why her husband doesn't return. I'm on my way to discuss her situation with Nurse Webb.'

'Of course. But remember, if you can't find me, ask Billy.' He sucked his teeth. 'Could you possibly ask Nurse Webb if the lady in question is well enough to be spoken to by our police friends? I would be present to ensure it is a conversation, not an interrogation.'

'At the moment, I don't even know if she's well enough to learn what's happening to her husband.' With that, I almost ran up the stairs to the Family wing, where Nurse Webb was sitting in her office, a pile of files as high as Matthew's before her. She nodded me to the seat opposite, listening intently as I explained the situation.

'Should I simply tell her that her husband is having a long chat with Sergeant Burrows?' I asked.

Ellis Page's voice, coming from behind me, responded, 'Well, saying her husband might be a thief and – could he be the murderer, too? – won't help her health, will it? I'm sorry if I made you both jump. Harriet, Matthew suggests I have a word with Nurse Webb and Mr Pounceman.'

I nodded, ready to leave.

'As for Mrs Marchbanks, a kindly lie, I'd say, Harriet. On a prosaic level, how will the household deal with her meals? I can't imagine there are any maidservants available.'

I shook my head. 'I never even thought of that! Though I think I can conjure up a manservant . . . How will she pass what may be an interminable time? I know she doesn't like novels, but perhaps devotional books . . . sermons? Though there is a rumour that she can't read.'

'Really? I wonder what people do without books or conversation . . . Perhaps she's a needlewoman. What do you think, Nurse?'

'Leave it all to me, Doctor. We're quite slack in the Family wing just now – I could always suggest she come up here to wait for him.'

I glanced at Ellis.

'You can't seriously think that a sick woman can be any threat to him!' Nurse Webb laughed.

I looked her in the eye. 'I seriously don't know what to think about anything that's going on now. What would you say, Ellis?'

'Give me a few minutes with Mr Pounceman first, and then Nurse Webb and I can come to a decision. Where will you be? In your quarters here?'

'Outside, serving the archaeologists their mid-morning refreshments.'

'Excellent.'

When they all had cups in their hands, Francis drew me to one side. 'Harriet – there is a rumour that an arrest has been made.'

'Where on earth did that spring from?'

'The fact that the sewing room curtains are drawn. Come, our two worthy plods are closeted with someone in there, are they not? It's not one of our team, you and Wilson are both swanning around outside the library – who else could it be but Marchbanks or his wife? Or is it Marchbanks *and* his wife?'

'The sergeant and Elias could, of course, be having a conversation with Professor Marchbanks.'

'Hmm. What about his sick wife?'

'I believe Ellis might be discussing her with Nurse Webb even as we speak.'

He looked very serious. 'I didn't quite mean that. Are you

sure that they arrested the right Marchbanks? It seems remarkable that she times her swoons to the most critical moments.
Think about it.'

'Do you think I haven't? But it may be that it's the stress of
such moments that makes her faint.'

'It's unlike you to fence with me, little sister. Or do you
suspect me?'

'Should I? Oh, Francis, you are my rock. I can't imagine
ever suspecting you of anything criminal.'

He gave a sad laugh. 'We both know that there is one aspect
of my life that could result in incarceration. But I do draw the
line at killing young men – heavens, think of it! I might have
propositioned Ned, been rebuffed and retaliated angrily, might
I not?' he asked melodramatically.

He might indeed. 'Not if you thought he'd fall into the trench
and damage a possible find,' I said as flatly as possible. Then
I did something I had never done before. I took his hands.
'Francis, I am lost and confused in my own home. And
frightened that I can't cope with it all. So much danger. So
much fear. So much information I mustn't speak of to anyone.
Not even myself,' I added with a shaky laugh.

He held me tightly, kissing the top of my head before releasing
me. 'Matthew will always be here. I will always be here. And
we both need a cup of tea after all this emotion.'

'You shall have one. And one of Bea's biscuits.' I looked
over the whole site – all those bent backs and bowed heads . . .
and hats. Why had I never thought to look at them while I
served their owners? We knew someone's was damaged after
a sojourn in the hedge. Would it be here, on an academic head?
Was it matched with one of those linen jackets that young Arthur
had noticed when he guarded Matthew's coat? With one of
those strong hands that had struck young Ned not once but
twice with a heavy stone?

Most of the gentlemen were sporting not rustic straw hats
but smart Panamas, none at all battered. Their owners all
seemed to be going out of their way to be polite and even
charming this morning as they flocked towards me for their
refreshments.

'Do you want my advice, Harriet? The moment they are all

fed and watered, discover an urgent errand that will get you away from us all – even for an hour!'

'I suppose someone should take all the letters down to the post office and collect ours at the same time.'

He took one of my fingers. 'Cut this and you would find the word "duty" running through. Just go for a jaunt. Please!'

There was Ellis, waving to me. 'I might indeed, Francis.'

A knock on the sewing room door brought the sergeant out, a frown on his face. 'Leaving for the village? Why?'

'Who else could drive a former patient back home?' I asked very quietly. 'I will be back as soon as I can. If you need me, leave a message with Billy.'

He nodded and went back into the sewing room.

My gardening bonnet, a blanket and a shawl ready for the poor box would have deceived no one taking a close look, but Ellis and Mr Pounceman were satisfied with the transformation, given that almost all the staff were in the fields anyway. Robin was as docile as he had ever been and delivered his precious cargo to the rectory without incident. Ellis would see him settled and then return to examine Mrs Marchbanks before the police could speak to her.

What next? The post office, of course, where I handed over one bag of letters and collected another. I had a sudden yearning to call at the haberdashers for something – anything – that would be a reminder of normality in a world of chaos. And I might hear – but not share – some useful gossip there. But – rational I might be, but I knew, *knew*, I had to return. I just hoped Ellis would be ready for me to collect him. He was.

Our journey back took me past the field where they were stacking the hay. Dick Thatcher was working close by; he ran over in response to my wave.

Ellis excused himself – it would probably be quicker to abandon Robin and walk from there. I did not argue.

As he waved and set out, I bent to talk to Dick. 'I don't want to interrupt your good work, but I wanted to thank you for keeping an eye on young Billy.'

'Someone needs to. He's a good lad, but people – it's his limp, isn't it? I don't know why she – why *people* should be afraid of him. Yes, afraid of a child, for goodness' sake!' He shook his head.

'Perhaps they think limps are somehow catching, like a cold,' I said sarcastically. 'He needs an occupation. Later, a proper job. And God knows his mother needs the few pence we give him a week.' I looked him in the eye. 'You said "she" – you meant Mrs Briggs?'

'I'm afraid I did. It's – it's as if she's two people. Most of the time she's really good now; we've worked quite well together since . . . Yes, quite well. But sometimes it's as if she's another person. I know you never encourage gossip, but . . .' He grinned boyishly.

'But today I might make an exception.'

Although there was no one within twenty yards of us, he dropped his voice. 'They say she's got a fancy man – one of the experts.'

'Really? Which one? No, I shouldn't even ask you that.'

He said in a tone remarkably like Francis' at his most mocking, 'I won't tell if you don't. In fact, I don't know. Not for sure. But Primrose swears she's seen her talking ever so secretly with Doctor Wells, yes, and with Professor Head. Though someone said he was looking for a housekeeper, maybe, since he's a widower.' Yes, he'd told me how hard he'd found it to get someone who suited him. 'And she's what you might call a fine-looking woman, isn't she – for her age, of course.' I tried not to wince – it was youth speaking, after all. 'So she may not be staying beyond her month. Interesting.'

'Very interesting.'

'It's a bit naughty of a guest to try to poach staff, though, isn't it?' he mused. 'No, maybe I'm jealous – no one's ever tried to poach me.' He eased his back and sighed. 'I'd best get back to work, hadn't I? Heavens, I shall be glad to get back to being a butler.'

'This should be your last day in the field, shouldn't it?'

'With a bit of luck, as they say, and the wind behind us.'

'Actually,' I said slowly, 'I could add a fresh breeze myself. Dick, I need you and Luke to help me – now, if possible. I want you to do a job that's beneath you. But I need someone to do it whom I can trust absolutely. I'll deal with Farmer Twiss. Could you find Luke and make your way back? As fast as you can?'

He narrowed his eyes. 'Would you rather we just snuck in? And used the service stairs and corridors? Mrs Briggs hardly ever does. She likes the public ones.'

'Let's just say that if anyone sees you and questions you, you can say you are no longer needed here and you are to return to normal duties. You need not add that you are going to be my eyes and ears. And please don't change into your livery. I'm afraid you'll be getting very dirty.'

'Dirty?'

'To the point of filthy. You know that everything in the chapel is covered with dust sheets. I want you to look under each one – yes, replace it afterwards – to see if anything unexpected lurks underneath. As I said, I could only ask someone I could trust implicitly and who would make a good witness if necessary.'

'Witness? In a court?' he almost squeaked.

'Yes – and you have to be alive to do it.' We exchanged a grin. 'Seriously, Mr Pounceman and my husband could have been killed. I really don't want you two dead.'

'I'm pleased to hear that, ma'am.' His voice was serious but his eyes were full of amusement.

'You must . . . This could be dangerous, Dick. You understand? Excellent. I'll go and speak to Farmer Twiss now.'

At least Robin's pace and his knowledge that his stable awaited him meant I could concentrate on the task in hand. The chapel floor. Why had I never once asked Mrs Briggs why it had been cleaned when I had made it clear it was never used? Now, the answer seemed to scream at me: if the floor was clean, people could go in and out without leaving footprints. Why had I never once wondered if Matthew and Mr Pounceman had, in fact, been targets? Had their being in the chapel alarmed someone enough to seal their fate? Because of the damage to the other pictures, of course. They couldn't have targeted anyone in particular. Surely, however, no one had planned to get those two men there and kill them? Surely someone – perhaps there coincidentally – had seen an opportunity to kill two possible witnesses and prevent them from reporting . . . what? Here logic and instinct fought a vicious battle. But logic kept hitting back with the unarguable fact that a floor which I expected to be dirty had been not just swept but mopped. Had something been removed from the chapel – in which case, where was it? Or had something been hidden under all the sheets?

Meanwhile, where was Dick's fine-looking woman? Nowhere in any of the fields I drove past. She must be indoors somewhere; I would ask her to serve the picnic luncheon for the archaeologists so that I might observe her with Dr Wells, Professor Head and any other eligible bachelor or widower. In a word, I would spy. I would need a good reason to ask her about the chapel, of course – why was I not able to? Matthew might have some ideas – but when I reached his firmly locked office, I found a note on his desk reminding me he had gone back to the village for a meeting at Mr Newcombe's and was not sure when he might return. I must find an excuse of my own. First of all, I sorted out the post I had collected. A lot for Matthew of course. One on very fine paper for Mr Wilson. One or two for most of the archaeologists, including Mr Hurley and Mr Burford, currently toiling for Farmer Twiss. One for Mrs Briggs. And soon – for as I locked the door behind me, Mrs Briggs almost collided with me.

'Good morning,' she said, sounding at least as disconcerted as I was. She certainly looked askance at me, as if I should not have been alone in Matthew's office. 'I didn't think to see you here.'

'Nor I you,' I responded. 'But I'm very glad I have. I've just picked up the post and there's a letter for you.' I slipped back into the room and picked it up. I could have wished she hadn't followed me, peering at the other envelopes. 'There's another thing. My husband has asked me to do an urgent task, so as you're not feeding the farm workers, I wonder if you would have time to take over my duties on the Roman site? For just a few minutes, I hope.'

'I suppose I could,' she said doubtfully. 'At least it won't be as dusty as those fields.'

'I'll take no longer than I have to,' I promised. I waited till she had left before I locked Matthew's letters in his desk and stowed the others in my pocket to distribute as I went around the building, sliding them under doors. I would put into his own hand the one to Mr Wilson. Just in case.

My errand took a very few minutes. Soon I was descending the staircase nearest the sewing room. There was silence within and no response to my knock. Billy would no doubt have a note for me. It was time to change into working clothes.

THIRTY-ONE

I had barely sat down again at my desk when there was a tap at the door.

'Primrose? What can I do for you? No, no need to cry. Just sit down and take a deep breath.'

Her sobs turned to hiccups. What was she trying to say? I passed her my handkerchief. That seemed to make her sob all the harder. If only there was a maid to hand, or better still Harriet.

'Oh, Mr Rowsley, sir, I'm so sorry. I know I should have said this before. I know I should. You see, I didn't know—'

'Didn't know what, Primrose? Another deep breath, now.'

'I didn't know . . . It's my ma, you see. She . . . she said you were the man who interfered with her when she was my age – she said it was the agent, you see. And when she fell pregnant, her sweetheart left her. And she lost her post. That's why she moved to Bridgnorth, but when I was born, they put her in a lunatic asylum.'

There but for the grace of God could have gone my Harriet, when she was raped. But this moment wasn't about her. Yet. 'So who brought you up, you poor child?'

'My grandmother in Ironbridge. And when she died, my great aunt in the village, but she's lost her mind now. And then I got a post here and I resolved to kill you for what you did to my mother. So when I tried, I didn't mean to hurt *you*. That man! And I see you being kind to Billy and now to me and Mrs Rowsley says you've only worked here a year and so I know you couldn't be the man and I'd tried to kill you!' She howled like an injured animal.

'Gently,' I said. 'Gently. That's better. When was this, Primrose? No, I'm not going to bite you. Just tell me when.'

'I saw all those picture cords being cut – they weren't me, sir – and I thought when I saw you coming out of the chapel, I could just . . .' Another huge sob. 'And then one night, I tried to smother you in your bed, too. With my pillow.'

'Only someone stabbed you in the foot! That must have hurt.'

'Oh, I told everyone my new boots pinched. I'm sorry. I wish I was dead.'

'Am I dead, Primrose? No, I'm not, am I? But I am going to ask you to do something very hard. I'm going to take you to talk to one of the police officers and tell him what you've just told me. And I want you to hear what I shall tell him. That you are not to be arrested, provided Mr Pounceman forgives you, which I am sure he will. I forgive you. Absolutely. Here, you need this handkerchief, too. Come on!'

And to my enormous relief, she got up and walked along to the room where I knew we could find Burrows. A man with a brand-new daughter. He might be fierce with her – but I knew he would understand.

He did not welcome the interruption, but he heard her out. And me. And told her kindly and firmly she could go back to the kitchen. Could she carry on working here? That was more Harriet's province than mine. Harriet, with her own dreadful history. I must talk to her before Primrose did.

But there was no sign of her where I expected her to be, at the site; Mrs Briggs was officiating at the archaeologist's luncheon.

Billy slipped me two notes: one from Burrows saying he had vacated the sewing room, the second from Harriet saying she wanted to arrive at the lunch late. She gave no reason. Billy didn't know where she was. I tried our bedchamber – I needed to change from my riding gear anyway. There was no sign of her. Knowing she could be anywhere in the House, I gave up, simply rejoining the archaeologists outside. Mrs Briggs, looking notably smart – elegant, indeed – served me lemonade. In her housekeeping days – those when she had nothing else to do but be unobtrusively efficient – Harriet had always favoured sober-coloured dresses like the black one with its contrasting cuffs and collar that Mrs Briggs sported today. She was a veritable white admiral butterfly flitting amongst the cabbage whites of us linen-clad men. Puzzled, I joined Palmer in the shade.

As we talked, he pointed at the excavations as if he was

discussing his morning's work. In fact, he was asking about Harriet's health. 'She would claim, would she not, that she is as tough as her favourite boots, but today I saw a side I've not often seen before – she was so anxious, so unsure. Any one of us here could have killed that young man. Any one of us here, had we managed to get access to the library key, could have stolen that aestel – though most of us would, I suspect, also have taken the gospel, too. Any one of us here could have cut those picture cords and killed you and Pounceman – of whom there has been very little news lately,' he added.

If I talked about the cords, I might drop out Primrose's story – and Harriet had a right to hear it first.

'Anyone might think his whereabouts were being kept deliberately secret,' he prompted me.

'Anyone can think what they like, Palmer,' I said dryly. 'Meanwhile, do you see whom I see?'

Her back to the tables of food, Mrs Briggs hadn't noticed Harriet's arrival – a holly blue butterfly, perhaps, in her pale blue uniform.

'She wants to see rather than be seen, doesn't she? So let's look at what she might be looking at – and apparently talk about the hypocaust.'

'She's watching la Briggs, isn't she? We should, too.'

So my eyes followed Mrs Briggs. Slowly but steadily, she moved towards Wells, not greeting him face to face but standing beside him. Did one pass something to another? If so, the movement was so swift, so deft, I could not be sure. Whatever it was, it must be small, small enough to conceal in a hand. I could see neither transfer anything to a pocket.

'If he's smuggling out an artefact, I'll kill him,' Palmer said, with a beatific smile on his face. 'But we can't use citizen's arrest and search them both! I beg your pardon' – now she had moved to Head's side – 'arrest all three, and not even the redoubtable Burrows could search Mrs Briggs. We need lady policemen, do we not? Heavens, what am I saying? Policewomen. Women in the mould of Harriet and Bea.'

'Don't frighten the horses, Palmer! People like Farmer Twiss are anxious about village boys being educated and loathe the very idea of girls going to school.'

'So the Billys and the Primroses of this world should continue to waste their God-given talent. Look at the boy: alert and standing as straight as he can. Could they operate on that foot?'

'Think of the torture inflicted on Byron in an attempt to cure him.'

'No wonder he turned out bad, mad and dangerous to know. Who wouldn't? Ah! Mrs B's making her way back inside. No, she's loading trays. Both hands. She must have something in that apron of hers.'

'Or a side pocket – those skirts can conceal a multitude of sins. We are powerless, damn it.'

'Not entirely. I will drift after Head – no, he's engaging Harriet in conversation now. There's no reason why you shouldn't join them. Unless you would prefer me to?' he added impishly. 'No, if you will excuse me, I might carry a tray to the nether regions.'

She greeted me brightly. 'I've sewn that button back on, Matthew,' she said, totally confusing me. 'Tell me, Professor Head, how do men on their own manage basic tasks like that? My dear husband simply stares in disbelief at the button in his hand and the shirt it should be attached to as if reuniting them is a labour of Hercules.' Her smile showed her dimples. Heavens, she was flirting with a man I suspected of – well, I was not quite sure what it was I suspected him of.

He frowned as if she had asked him to explain the riddle of the Sphinx. 'My late wife . . . And I suppose the laundry-woman . . .'

I suspected his frown became one of irritation. 'You see, my love,' I said quickly, 'I am not the only man to find needles puzzling.'

'So I see. I suppose I must forgive you both. But when the new village school is finished, one of the subjects on the curriculum should be basic repairs. I will speak to the head teacher about it myself. Tell me, Professor, what are your views on universal elementary education? Even for people like Billy?'

*   *   *

'That was interesting,' I observed, when she finally let him escape, heading indoors. 'What on earth made you engage him in such a conversation?'

'To see if I can get the measure of him. He's always been charming to me, but a man "may smile, and smile, and be a villain". And there's below-stairs gossip that he is flirting with Mrs Briggs. Even if he isn't, there's something afoot. You saw how smart she is. Not a workaday outfit at all.'

I smiled. 'That chimes in with what Palmer and I saw,' I explained. 'Mind you, she was equally close to Wells for a while.'

She nodded. 'It would be hard for one person to have wreaked all the havoc with the pictures and committed the murder without leaving more trace than a handkerchief – I suspect she picked up mine when I was trying to comfort Jemima – and pair of spectacles.'

'Which might have been planted. Harriet – we need to talk in private. About Primrose.' I took her hand and led her away.

She listened intently, gasping in horror and anger – yes, she was reliving my illness but also her past, the rape that left her barren. 'What shall we do?' she whispered at last.

'Burrows knows. He knows I won't press charges. It all depends on Pounceman.'

'Whom I took back to the rectory two hours ago. Oh, Matthew – he must forgive her. But then – what then? Damn, here's Wells. We must talk later.'

'Let him wait. Let's just walk back together.'

'And I'll tell you something you ought to know. I've asked Dick and Luke to search the chapel. The floor must have been cleaned so anyone going in or out would leave no footprints. So they are seeing if anything has been hidden there.'

'My God. That's risky.'

'Or a waste of time. In any case, Elias has sent Nathaniel to keep a discreet watch.'

I sighed with relief. 'Have you any idea where Elias has gone now? Burrows? And Wilson?'

'Billy tells me that Wilson and the police officers have all gone to talk to Mrs Marchbanks, whom Ellis moved back up to be under Nurse Webb's eye. He gave me this note from Mr

Wilson, which I've not had a chance to open yet. In return, I asked him to deliver to Mr Wilson a very fine missive – no, there is no other word! Letter is too prosaic a term for anything written on such beautiful paper.'

> Forgive the informality of this communication, which I write in haste.
>
> Sgt Burrows and I are now in possession of information which makes it seem unlikely that our friends the M's killed the young man. However, we feel that it may trigger a reaction in the guilty parties if it is known that Prof M is incarcerated, and accordingly he has agreed to be 'arrested' and conveyed to the lock-up, in fact to the comfort of the Family wing, where he is ensconced with his wife. If a communication should arrive for me, <u>its place is in your husband's safe</u> until it can be opened in Sgt Burrows' presence.

'Drat!' she said. 'But I rely on Billy to have delivered it safely. Heavens, I'll go and check!' She took to her heels.

And I would check what, if anything, was going on in the chapel.

I was cheered by the sight of Nathaniel. 'It's like this, sir. If anyone comes along this way, I tap on the door, real gentle, like, and the lads go quiet as mice. But if I get worried about anything, I blow this here whistle that young Elias gave me.' He produced one from his livery pocket.

'Not this time, Nathaniel. I want you to lurk where no one will see you. If anyone comes in, wait till he comes out before you blow your whistle. And – better still – apprehend him.'

THIRTY-TWO

S ergeant Burrows intercepted me on the stairs. 'Ah, I was coming to look for you. We have a bit of a plan, you see, and it involves you. If you care to let us into the library, I can explain there.'

'And as we walk, we can talk about Primrose.'

He smiled. 'Ah, your husband's told you. Good. He said it was his job and no one else's. Now, there might just be a solution. You don't want her here, I'd say. But we've found someone who might. But I'll say no more now.' He waited while I unlocked the door. 'This is what we're going to do.' He checked his turnip watch. 'Yes, please lock it again,' he said, the moment I had closed the library door behind us. 'We're going to wait for a visitor. Maybe two, since both the Marchbankses swore they would be happier in their own chamber.'

'So they're free to wander anywhere! I thought – didn't you arrest him?'

He smiled. 'Yes – but I put him on his honour to stay with his wife being as she was so poorly.'

'But I took Mr Pounceman back to the rectory to keep him safe if she was there!'

'Calm down, Mrs Rowsley. I've prepared this nice little trap. Here. It's my theory someone got hold of a key somehow, maybe a duplicate, even – that's how our thief got in and found the aestel.'

'But—'

'I'll explain everything later. We just need to concentrate on the next few minutes. Now, this is a nice big room, and we've got plenty of places to hide in, haven't we? So we shall be safe and sound. But if you'd rather just leave us here and lock us in, I shall understand. And to be honest, that's what you should do, only Pritchard says you'd never forgive us if we made you.'

'Is Matthew safe? Then I am more than happy to stay here.

But I need to tell you something. Two footmen are currently in the chapel,' I explained.

'Oh, dear. Well, all's well that ends well, I suppose. Elias, you've gone pink. What have you been up to?'

'I gave whistles to all the retired footmen, Sergeant, in case they saw anything . . . anywhere.'

'So you knew!'

'Only unofficially, Sergeant.'

'I'll have your guts for bloody—' He stopped. 'Mrs Rowsley, quick: where's the best place to conceal ourselves? I fancy we haven't got long.'

'That was his lordship's favourite alcove. He reckoned no one would ever know he was there but he could see any comings or goings.'

'Pritchard – there! And where else?'

'There – behind that case of extra-large volumes. I could go here—' I pointed to the corner opposite my favourite desk.

'Good, those draperies will provide some camouflage for that dress of yours. Off you go. And we maintain silence until I give the order. You too, Mrs Rowsley.'

Nodding, I took up what I was sure he would call my post, seated within reach of so much that was precious. Books, yes, some family miniatures, a tiny Japanese carved mouse his late lordship used as a paperweight. This was my home – but someone was just about to invade it. I counted to a hundred. Two hundred. Three— I heard the door handle turn. I braced myself. No, I must not think of poor Ned and his smashed skull. I must trust the policemen. They would protect me. But my hand closed around the mouse.

The intruder must be well inside the room now: the thick carpet meant I heard no footsteps, but the creak of his shoes got closer. I dared not breathe.

'Good afternoon, sir.' Sergeant Burrows spoke as placidly as if they had passed each other in a lane. 'Now, why don't you just sit down and tell us how you managed to let yourself in.'

There was other movement. That was the sound of the key in the lock. 'Thank you, Constable.'

'What are you implying? The door was unlocked!' That did not sound like Professor Marchbanks; it certainly wasn't his wife. Dr Wells? After all, he was the academic whom Francis trusted least, afraid that finds would make their way into his private collection. And surely he was one of the men that Mrs Briggs had been near at luncheon. As was – surely it could not be Professor Head, one of the few experts who had gone out of his way to be pleasant to me!

'Just take a seat, sir; this needn't take a minute. But before you do, just hand over the key, if you please. I said, the key, sir.'

'Don't you give me orders! Unlock this door now!'

'No need for that, sir. Just throw it down, if you please.' There was an edge of anxiety in his voice, as if the intruder was flourishing more than just a key.

I found myself on my feet. Unlike Elias and his sergeant, I had a weapon to hand.

'Don't be foolish, sir: just throw it down.'

The knife was at Elias's throat. My throw would have to be accurate or it would hit his head, not my target's. The netsuke – odd that I should recall the name now when I should be thinking about more important things – in my hand, I threw.

There was a lot of blood. But it wasn't Elias's or Sergeant Burrows's. And I would not let myself faint.

'Come along, Mrs Rowsley. Not like you to swoon. Will you be all right or shall I get Elias to summon Doctor Page?'

For the first time in my life, I had to apply my vinaigrette to my own nose. There. 'Don't you need Doctor Page to attend to – him?'

'Oh, he's got a broken nose, that's all. And he'll have a lovely black eye by supper time. And that little mouse is still in one piece. Nothing to worry your pretty head about.' He snorted. 'This here *Professor Head*' – he paused to relish his grim pun – 'will have far more than a broken nose to worry about when he gets sent down. And there I thought it was the Marchbankses. What a good job Mr Wilson talked about his shopping expedition. Here, is that offer of a gig still open?'

'Gig?'

'Yes, the gig. With that lad Dan to drive it. I'd rather this gentleman was in the lock-up than bleeding all over your carpet.'

He gave me the sort of smile he probably gave his children when they desperately wanted a treat. 'I'll be back later to explain everything, Mrs Rowsley, don't you worry. I just hope,' he said, looking ruefully at the carpet, 'that that blood won't stain.'

I pulled myself straight. 'I'll see to it the moment you get him out of here.' The ammonia I would use would be nothing if not therapeutic. 'Here, take this so he doesn't drip blood anywhere else.' I whipped off my apron and folded it into a pad. But, of course, he needed a hand to hold it there and he was already handcuffed to Elias. Dear, kind, reliable Elias, whom he would have killed. 'Oh, use his tie to keep it in place, for goodness' sake! And please hurry and get him out of here, or the damage could be permanent. To the carpet. That matters more than a murderer's nose. I don't want a reminder of you, you vile animal, every time I step into this precious place!'

THIRTY-THREE

'The trouble is that we don't quite know what we're looking for,' Luke said, his face dappled by the light of the great stained-glass window. 'And whatever it is, we've not found it yet.'

I looked at the rolled-up dust sheets. 'Shall we finish checking this side of the aisle and replace all these before we start on the next? Just in case,' I added, with the young men joining in. Still laughing, they started again. At least they were still dressed as labourers; my linen suit would not be so forgiving. Down to shirtsleeves at least, I joined in with a will.

It was all too clear that only the aisle had been swept and that Pounceman's fear that rodents were about was justified – only mice, I suspected.

'We'll have to borrow a farmyard cat for a night,' I said. 'I know her ladyship didn't like dogs – did she dislike cats, too?'

Thatcher shook his head. 'The sad thing was that she loved her animals. All of them. But when she was with them, she would start to weep and sneeze, and then it seemed she couldn't get her breath. But I'm sure Farmer Twiss would oblige. Very well, I think we've finished this side. It's probably easier to put these back if we work together, gaffer. Sorry.'

'Actually, I quite like *gaffer*.' It made me think of smocks and clay pipes. 'Yes, let's work together.'

We repeated the process on the other side of the aisle, with no result. It was Luke who spurred us on. 'If I was going to steal something grand, I'd put it in the grandest part of the church. And since the altar is made of solid stone – it made me shiver, furtling around something as important as that – you can't hide anything there. So I'd try the pulpit or one of the family tombs.'

'Or,' Dick said slowly, 'in one of the vaults. And you'd have to be dead brave to do that. Sorry,' he added as we groaned.

We split up – the youngsters peering into and under the

monuments and me venturing into the pulpit. Despite spending much of my life in and around churches and, yes, cathedrals, I felt the same sense of being caught trespassing that Luke felt. However, into that pulpit I must go.

Nothing.

'Gaffer. That joke about the vaults. The steps down into this one have been swept, too. Shall I try the door?' Was it a trick of the light that he looked green?

'Would you prefer me to?'

He set his shoulders, saying, as he descended to the forbidding door at the foot, 'The dead . . . the remains . . . can't hurt us, can they? They are dead; their souls are—'

'What's that?' Luke asked.

'Nathaniel. Tapping the door. Under the dustsheets, quick.'

We dived, Dick landing next to me. We braced ourselves for the sound of the chapel door opening. But there was silence. Then – yes! – open it swung. There was no ghastly creak, of course – George was far too punctilious with his oil can to allow hinges to make a sound. The footsteps approached us and walked past. Where were they going? The altar? The pulpit? Did I hear the swish of fabric? Surely not. Not Mrs Marchbanks, so recently on her sickbed. Or could it be—?

'Mrs Briggs! Get those whistles blowing, Luke!'

Dick and I grappled. Not fiercely enough. Our fingers slipped on the silk of her dress. Nathaniel grabbed her, dragging her arms up behind her back.

'Take her to the servants' hall; lock her in a storeroom,' I said.

Joined by a couple of other former footmen, he obeyed.

Dick thrust something at me. A sealed envelope. Without hesitation, I opened it, Dick peering over my shoulder.

THE MS ARE UNDER ARREST. THIS IS THE TIME TO GO. THE STATION, AS SOON AS YOU HAVE READ THIS.

'Who's this meant for? How are we going to find Elias and the sergeant?' Dick asked.

'God knows!' Dick and I stared at each other. Where was

Harriet's cool head when it was needed? And – my heart lurched – where was Harriet?

She might have smelt strongly of ammonia and been carrying out to the yard a bucket of water, but she was safe. Abandoning the bucket, she ran to me. My God – there was blood all over her apron!

'My darling! Where are you hurt?'

'It's not my blood,' she said trying to sound calm but not entirely succeeding. 'It's Professor Head's. He's gone off with Elias and the sergeant to the lock-up. But he left a lot of blood on the library carpet so I had to clean it up.' Her flat delivery told me more than words could that she was omitting a very great deal. 'Let me just get rid of this and—'

Dick took it and disappeared, with very obvious tact.

We did not hold each other long. In fact, she pushed me away. 'Ugh. You smell of damp and mouse droppings. Where have you been?'

'Finding this.' I held up the letter. She moved it further from her eyes and squinted. 'The poor woman would be disappointed, wouldn't she, when she got there and found Sergeant Burrows' colleagues waiting for her – yes, he telegraphed and asked for reinforcements. What a shame she won't get there. Nathaniel has tied her up in the linen room.'

Dick, now bucketless, asked, 'How do we get her down to the lock-up?'

'In the state coach if necessary!'

Sergeant Burrows looked like a cat that had visited the dairy when he returned at about four o'clock – just in time for a nice cup of tea, as he pointed out. Without the unfortunate Pritchard, detailed to accompany his colleagues escorting the reprobates to Shrewsbury Prison, from which he would have Harry Tyler freed, we drank it in the garden. Harriet's hands still shook so much that she let Billy pour the tea. She had also invited Bea, Thatcher, Luke and any of the staff not still in the hayfields to join us, since, as she said, what had been planned and what had actually happened, indeed, involved them, too. Naturally, most of the experts also gathered, the exception being the Marchbankses.

'First of all,' he said, putting down his teacup so that he could stand and hook his thumbs under the flaps of his tunic pockets, 'I would like to thank Mr Montgomery Wilson for all he has done to solve a most wicked crime – and, indeed, prevent another one. Do any of you recall him saying he'd suggested to Professor Head that they had met before in Shrewsbury, and the professor denied it? Now, a witness like Mr Wilson is a policeman's dream. So I detailed some of my colleagues to visit the many shops there. Guess what: yes, a Panama hat was purchased of exactly the make and size of a hat worn, we think, by the man – my apologies, the *gentleman* – searching for Matthew's jacket in the hayfield.'

'Why should anyone want his jacket?' Bea asked.

'Because I dropped a letter he wanted to make sure never reached its intended recipient.'

'We'll deal with that in a few minutes, if you don't mind, Matthew,' Burrows said. 'Now, to return to Professor Head's shopping trip in Shrewsbury. He visited several other establishments. One was' – he paused dramatically – 'a lock-smith's! Yes, claiming that his elderly aunt was in the habit of losing keys, he had several copied – all those, in fact, in your key cupboard. I have no doubt that neither you, Mr Thatcher, nor Mrs Rowsley was involved in his obtaining them. The finger clearly points elsewhere. To be fair, I don't think he wanted any of your personal belongings, though he might have wanted to visit your office, Mr Rowsley, if he'd known that the aestel was lodged there, not in the House safe.'

There was a gasp from the servants. 'I'm sorry we had to mislead you all,' I said. 'But Mrs Briggs had already shown an interest in the contents of the safe and . . .' I shrugged.

Burrows nodded, continuing, 'What Head wanted was access to the library – unsupervised access. When everyone was gathering to drink sherry or simply retiring to bed, he would be exploring. How did he happen upon the book with the jewel? Ah, that's not clear yet. I need to have further conversations, as Mr Wilson puts it, with the Marchbankses. Now, they're a rum pair, aren't they? It does indeed seem that Mrs M can't read or write, but she can do some strange thing I've never heard of before – she can use a system of symbols invented by a Mr Pitman. It's all beyond me, but she can read back her notes as sweetly as a child can say its catechism.'

'You said "further conversations". Does this mean you aren't happy with what she – what her husband too, of course – told you?' I asked.

'Doctor Page would only let me speak to her for five minutes: seems she really is unwell. But he's not convinced, any more than I think Mrs Rowsley is, that all her swoons are genuine. Heavens, you went out like a light when you thought you might have killed the professor. Or was it the blood?'

'Blood doesn't bother me. Killing someone – yes, I thought I had,' Harriet admitted.

'Takes a lot more than a little mouse – though goodness knows how you learned to throw like that – to kill such a hard-hearted man. Now, there's another piece of information Mr Wilson gave me only this afternoon; I doubt if anyone's heard it yet. Why don't you tell them why I wet my whistle?'

Billy obliged with more tea while Wilson stood. Then Billy and Primrose slipped away, inasmuch as the little tea cart could do anything silently. I would ask George to put together a new one.

'Your hosts and I had doubts about their housekeeper – not about her honesty, but about her general demeanour, shall I say. I took it upon myself to write to the lady who had provided the testimonial Mrs Briggs offered. Lady Bibury. It was this letter that Matthew offered to post and then dropped. It was Professor Head who picked it up and returned it to him. He must have recognized the address and realized what we were doing. And he was determined to prevent us. But he was too late! The letter was in the post! Lady Bibury graciously responded – yes, writing in her own hand! – that she had no knowledge of any Mrs Briggs. However, she had asked various of her acquaintances, three of whom identified her as a Miss Briggs who had, according to one employer, very recently married a widower, an academic from Oxford. Did he marry her for love or because he needed to cajole a useful employee into enabling him to commit a crime?'

Harriet raised a finger. 'Mr Wilson, how did the professor know there was an aestel here?'

'May I answer that, Wilson?' Palmer asked. 'In short, he didn't. But he had enough experience working in the field to know that wonderful objects are sometimes uncovered. Perhaps he meant to steal what he found – but our custom of recording and photographing every find must have frustrated him. The fact that he took all those keys to Shrewsbury before the dig started argues that he wanted – how shall I put it? – an insurance policy. Even if he found nothing valuable in the dig, he could root around indoors and appropriate what he found there: there's so much lying around he might well have done without anyone except George, with that marvellous memory of his, noticing. I suspect that even if the Marchbankses were not his accomplices, they might have let slip something about the treasures in the library – or he might have overheard a conversation.'

'Which brings us back to the Marchbankses,' Harriet said grimly. 'Mrs M fainted when she first saw the aestel and when she saw the gospel in which it had lain. Did she know what it was? If so, how?'

'As I told you, they have worked in many great libraries,' Palmer said. 'Perhaps she had seen one in an ancient tome and recognized it. Perhaps it was indeed she who stole it, and hid it in that trench to be recovered later. Yes, we saw her wandering around over there, didn't we, Wells? But did she have the strength to kill young Ned when he saw it? If she had, surely she would have shifted his body in an attempt to retrieve it.'

'Hitting is one thing,' Burrows pointed out. 'Shifting a dead body, especially in a tight space like that trench, would take muscle. And why should she be out there in the first place? At night?'

'Ask her,' Wells said, beard aflame with righteous anger, it seemed.

'Yes, when can they be properly questioned?' Fielding chimed in.

'You can't interrogate a woman who might be at death's door, can you, sir?' Burrows sounded very shocked. 'I hope Marchbanks himself will confess or at least let information drop when he is questioned.'

'And when will that be?' Wells asked.

'When his wife is well enough to be left.'

'Sergeant,' Palmer said, 'I would give much to attend that interview – I could tell you which questions to ask! I could, at the risk of sounding arrogant, pursue details only a very few archaeologists know. I urge you, I plead with you, to let me loose on him.'

How would Burrows react to all the educated, aristocratic voices? He bit his lip. Anger? Indecision?

A rattle and squeak announced Billy and Primrose and the return of the kettle and teapot. Perhaps some delicate sandwiches and dainty cakes would ease the tension.

At last, the sergeant spoke. 'I'll go and speak to him now – you might write down a few questions for me to ask, but that's all, Sir Francis. All this talk, it's making more heat than light. I can't tell you anything until I've updated Constable Pritchard, any more than he can tell you till he's spoken to me. Then we will discuss what to tell you. And this is my last word, ladies and gentlemen. Maybe till after supper. Maybe till tomorrow morning. You can't hurry justice, you know.'

THIRTY-FOUR

'So neither Professor nor Mrs Marchbanks did anything wrong?' Matthew asked in some disbelief as we all gathered after breakfast the following morning. Sergeant Burrows stood at the head of the table, Elias with Luke and Dick by the doors; they might almost have been expecting someone to escape.

'I didn't say that, Mr Rowsley,' Sergeant Burrows said firmly. 'I said neither did anything *illegal*. Mrs Marchbanks, a lonely, miserable soul if ever there was one, thought Mrs Briggs – who had helped her on occasion when she had swooned – was not just trustworthy but a friend. So when she found the jewel, late one afternoon as she arranged the books her husband wanted to take to some library in Oxford, she told her about it. Mrs Briggs was quite amused that she had – let's be frank – deceived her. She had the key to the library, you'll recall, so she could easily let herself in and take it. Nice big pockets in your ladies' aprons, of course. Then she had to give it to her husband, of course. How? It was part of his plan that their paths should never cross. She conceived this stupid idea – and you'll be surprised how many criminals are stupid, even clever ones, if you get my meaning – that she would bury it in a ditch so that her husband would have the honour of finding it. She could communicate all this via notes left in the nice clean chapel. Yes, he'd be famous! The toast of the academic world!'

'How little did she know of us,' Francis muttered, even Wells joining in the laughter.

'Into the ditch it went – and young Ned saw it all. His widow told Constable Pritchard and Mrs Rowsley he went off late in the evening to dig it up with a view to claiming a reward. Possibly – but I won't speak ill of the dead.' He took a sip of water. 'Head turns up and doesn't like what he sees – which is this amazing jewel slipping into someone else's hands. So he hits him. He says he just pushed him, but Mrs Briggs – Mrs

Head – says he asked her to burn a shirt he'd got blood on. So if he did just push, then he hopped down and killed him as he lay. Hence the blood.'

'I thought she'd burned gloves,' I said.

'Oh, she did that as well. Gloves with reddle on them. Her own. She tells me her husband forced her to make the pictures unsafe to stop people wandering around when he might be looking for items worth stealing.'

'Why should she wear gloves in the first place? She wouldn't know about the reddle till she got it on her hands, surely.'

'Come, Mrs Rowsley, one of the estate workers does a job around the House you're now in charge of – what's more likely than she'd sit him down for a cup of tea and a gossip? So she knows what to worry about and takes precautions. And disposes of the evidence.'

Bea shook her head. 'But why should she tell you all this? Damning herself with her own mouth?'

'Because she tells me her husband made her. He's going to hang anyway. But she wants to make sure she's seen as a victim, like Ned. She doesn't want to lose her house and everything, does she?'

Mr Wilson's face was sombre. 'It will be interesting to see if a court sees her as a victim or as an accomplice. I would favour the latter, I must say. She wanted the money his success would bring even if she did not expect him to kill for it. Of course, whatever he or she did, the law states that she cannot testify against him, frustrating though that may be for us.' He nodded the point home.

Primrose raised a timid hand. She had already packed her meagre belongings ready to go back to Sergeant Burrows' household as an extra maid, a move we all felt was for the best. 'Please, Sergeant, sir: she was unkind to all of us. Milly – she was supposed to work after she had that bang on the head. Billy – she was vicious bad to him. And how Mr Thatcher put up with her I shall never know.'

'You didn't like her, did you, Harriet?' Bea said. 'But I thought Professor Head was charming. He went out of his way to be pleasant, especially to you.'

'He did.' On the other hand, there was that time he almost

literally dragged me from the dining room. 'But being an unpleasant person doesn't make her a killer. Let's wait and see.'

After a moment, Francis said, 'So Marchbanks himself is as pure as the driven snow. What a shame. I had come to wish he was a villain and that I could unmask him – a peace offering to Harriet for bringing him here in the first place.' His smile vanished. 'He will be searched before he leaves, I trust? And his wife? True, he put some material for the Bodleian on a shelf – but apart from an aestel, did anything else find its way into a Marchbanks pocket, male or female? Not just from the library, where there was supervision apart from when she swooned, but from the muniment room? You allowed them free rein there, didn't you, Harriet? Not, I hasten to say, that you could have done anything else, except chain them to a bench in the corridor when your duties lay elsewhere.'

'My own feelings, Palmer, and those of Sergeant Burrows,' Mr Wilson said. 'We trustees need to recruit someone utterly trustworthy and discreet to put all the family records in order. Dear me, a retired clergyman, someone like that.'

'And two more of the same for the library,' Mr Burford said. 'You might consider Hurley and me, actually. We're polite, we act well and we'd love you to teach us to play cricket and how to throw as well as you do.'

Although the archaeologists would stay for the rest of the summer, Ellis Page tactfully and perhaps truthfully suggested that Mrs Marchbanks ought to be in the care of her own physician. Accordingly, after their luggage and even their persons were searched, Nurse Webb having been pressed into service, they prepared to get into the best Croft coach, specially cleaned for the occasion. Naturally, Matthew and I were there to see them off. She made a point of speaking to me as she settled in her seat, apologizing for being so silly as to be unwell and thanking me for our patience and care. I deflected any praise to the staff, especially Nurse Webb and her team.

'It must be terrifying to own a house this size!' she whispered, rolling her eyes.

'I merely run it, Mrs Marchbanks – and many people help me.'

'No, no, Mrs Rowsley,' she whispered even more quietly but with force. 'You own it. My husband told me. But he has hidden the documents – no, not stolen them; don't think that for a moment. He says you'll never find them – you must know how he hates and fears you – but you must, Mrs Rowsley, you must. You must. Oh!' She clutched her chest, and I think she fell back against the squab.

Surely she was too ill to travel! But the coach was already moving, and I was left to pray that she was not as ill as I feared.

As I walked solemnly through the doors of the place I loved so much, I knew – to my shame – that I could not rest until I had tested her theory.

Yes, to be mistress of Thorncroft would be something!